THE MASK BEHIND THE MAN

Vic smoothed the plastic over his face. He went to a mirror and looked and—

It's the real me . . .

He was a blank. Just a pale oval. Suddenly, he felt as though he were recognizing himself for the first time. The face beneath the plastic—that was the mask. The plastic did not conceal, it revealed.

Thirty minutes later, Vic was driving into Hub City. He parked two blocks from City Hall. There was no sign of life, not even a street lamp. He got the mask from where it had been folded into a shirt pocket, smoothed it into place. A moment later, his clothing had changed color, and he had no features . . .

Also by DC Comics

DC Universe: Last Sons

DC Universe: Inheritance

DC UNIVERSE
Helltown

Dennis O'Neil

WARNER BOOKS

NEW YORK   BOSTON

Cover illustration by James Jean
Book design and text composition by Stratford Publishing Services

Warner Books
Hachette Book Group USA
1271 Avenue of the Americas
New York, NY 10020
Visit our Web site at www.HachetteBookGroupUSA.com

Printed in the United States of America

First Printing: November 2006

10   9   8   7   6   5   4   3   2   1

For Mari, Meg, Beth & Larry . . .
and the excellent Ruth E. O'Neil

Today I shall be meeting with interference,
ingratitude, insolence, disloyalty, ill-will,
and selfishness—all of them due to the
offenders' ignorance of what is good
and evil.

Marcus Aurelius
Translated by Maxwell Stanisforth

DC UNIVERSE
Helltown

People still sometimes talk about what happened that cold, cold winter in Hub City—the explosions, the lives saved, the lives lost, the mysterious woman and the masked man. Or was it two masked men? Nobody seems certain, not even the parents whose children were victimized and nearly killed.

At the time, the events merited some reporting in local media and got briefly mentioned by a couple of cable news nets. A few reporters even speculated that the Hub City violence might be connected to what happened to a certain steamboat way upriver, but none of them ever firmly established cause and effect.

Most bizarrely, there was even a comic book series based on the story, which got a lot of it wrong.

What you're about to read is the truth, at least as much of it as I know. But I warn you, not every question will be answered, and that seems appropriate because this tale is really all about questions more than answers.

Who am I? Well, that's one of the questions I don't intend to answer. But feel free to speculate.

CHAPTER **ONE**

Charles Victor Szasz, who was not yet either Vic Sage or The Question, couldn't find his way back home.

He felt like an idiot.

True, he hadn't seen Hub City in almost ten years—in fact, he hadn't even been to this part of the country for that long—and hadn't bothered to stock up on maps or discuss his trip with someone who might know the local geography, but what the hell? . . . he knew the place was somewhere southeast of St. Louis, somewhere north of Cairo, on a river called the Ohatchapee, and there had to be road signs and such, no? How hard could it be to find a town of over forty thousand people in a limited area?

He hoped to be settled in a motel room by dinnertime, but felt no need to hurry. From St. Louis, how long would he have to drive? Couple-three hours? Something like that. So he decided to play tourist for just a little while. St. Louis was the first real city he'd ever seen and he had an urge to revisit it after all these years.

A little preliminary to the main event . . .

He parked his battered 1988 Ford station wagon at a lot near the riverfront, at the edge of Laclede's Landing, and walked south, with the cityscape to his right and the Mississippi to his left. It was the first Saturday in September, and hot, and small groups of families and tourists were wandering around downtown St. Louis. Some were just sauntering beneath the trees of the riverfront park, enjoying the day, while others moved quickly, obviously bound for a destination.

Charles Victor Szasz paused and looked up at the arch, gleaming in the noonday sun.

World's largest croquet wicket . . .

But impressive, he had to give it that. Hundreds of feet tall, completely sheathed in stainless steel—worth whatever it cost, which was probably plenty. He wondered if small-plane pilots still flew through it. He remembered reading a story in the *St. Louis Post-Dispatch* that someone left at the orphanage about one flyer who had dared the deed when he was . . . what? Eleven, maybe. The local authorities, according to the story, had been quite perturbed. Young Charles Victor Szasz had rooted for the pilot then, and he would now, too.

He bought a hot dog and a can of orange soda from a guy with a cart and sat on a bench while he ate, watching people pass, paying particular attention to females in shorts. A tall woman, slender, mid-twenties, long chestnut hair, glanced at him and immediately turned way. He didn't blame her. He knew what she saw: hair that needed cutting, an unshaven face, sweat-stained flannel shirt with the sleeves rolled up, twill work pants, shabby cowboy boots he'd found abandoned on the Galveston docks. A homeless guy, the woman probably thought. She wasn't far wrong: Charles Victor Szasz had seventy-eight bucks in small bills stuffed into his hip pockets, the Ford, a duffel bag stuffed with dirty clothes, and not another thing in the world.

To hell with the snooty bitch . . .

He stood, started toward where he'd stashed the Ford. A block from the parking lot, at the top of a narrow street that ended at the cobblestoned embankment, he paused and gazed across the Mississippi, which glistened in the sun and looked like molten metal, to St. Louis's smaller, grittier twin, East St. Louis. It had acquired a gambling boat since he'd last seen it.

Couldn't hurt, he thought, resuming his walk.

Forty minutes later, he had left St. Louis and was driving toward where he thought Hub City had to be. Two hours later, he was peering through the windshield, trying desperately to recognize a landmark, any landmark, and failing.

Could it all have changed in just ten years? Or have I taken one punch to the head too many?

Four hours later, on a dirt road between corn fields, he saw a man sitting on a fence, playing a guitar. A very old man, Charles Victor Szasz saw as he got out of his Ford: tufts of white hair sprouting at odd intervals from a shiny brown scalp, the face below a maze of wrinkles, shirtless, dressed in faded farmer's overalls. Playing and singing what the musically undereducated Charles Victor Szasz was pretty sure was the blues.

I had me two women, one short and one tall;

Yeah, I had me two women, one short and one tall;
Now they both found another and I got no one at all . . .

" 'S'cuse me," Charles Victor Szasz called.

The bony fingers stilled on the guitar strings and the old man looked up from under bushy white eyebrows.

"He'p yeh?" he said in a voice that was hoarser than his singing voice. He had an accent, but Charles Victor Szasz couldn't identify it. Deep South, surely. But where, exactly? Alabama? New Orleans?

"I wonder if you can point me toward Hub City."

The old man shook his head, slowly and mournfully. "Don't think yeh want to go there."

"I'm afraid I do."

"Ever been there?"

"I think I was born there."

Now the old man nodded. "That's all right, then. Yeh only *think* yeh know where yeh was born, yeh got to find out. I can understand that."

The old man pointed, spoke some highway numbers, and described a barn with silo attached that marked a necessary left turn.

"Get that far," he concluded, "just follow your nose. It'll take you straight to Hub City."

Charles Victor Szasz said a thank you and the old man returned to his music.

Sheer misery, sheer misery, come walkin' with me . . .

As Charles Victor Szasz was turning onto a narrow, winding strip of blacktop, something beneath the hood of the Ford began to *thunk*.

This cannot be good . . .

But maybe the engine would remain functional until he

reached Hub City and maybe his seventy-eight dollars
would pay for repairs and maybe he would win the lottery
and move to Hollywood and marry Jessica Alba.

He switched on the radio. Neither the air conditioner
nor the heater worked, the windshield wipers were unreli-
able, and two of the windows would not roll down, but the
radio worked perfectly. That was good. He enjoyed sam-
pling local disc jockeys as he went from job to job. But
there didn't seem to be any local disc jockeys to sample.
He got several St. Louis stations clearly, and one from
Columbia, but nothing from Hub City or any of the surrounding towns. Finally, at the extreme left side of the
dial, he located what he was searching for.

". . . station KWLM," a midwestern voice was blurt-
ing, "serving the greater Hub City area. That's what it
says, folks. 'Greater Hub City.' What they call an 'oxy-
moron.' Like jumbo shrimp. Anyway, we've got a record
cued up so we might as well play it . . ." The music
started: A woman was singing, pleasantly, about how she
doesn't know why she didn't come.

The sun was low in the western sky. Ahead, to his left,
he saw a silo and the blackened remains of a barn that had
obviously recently burned. As the old man had instructed,
he turned left. "Just follow your nose," the old man had
said, and suddenly Charles Victor Szasz understood what
he meant. He sniffed, and fought the urge to gag. The air
was foul and was getting fouler with every turn of his vehicle's wheels. He passed the remains of the barn and,
rounding a curve, saw the gleam of water and knew it
must be the Ohatchapee, a Mississippi tributary that was
more creek than river except during the spring floods,

when it could wash over its banks and inundate the surrounding area, causing a lot of problems for residents. *Ohatchapee,* Charles Victor Szasz remembered, was an American Indian word. He didn't know which tribe originated it, but he recalled that it meant "beautiful waters."

The stink was rising from the beautiful waters.

The air was full of haze and the sun's last rays, filtered through it, were a pale yellow, and the foliage of the trees that lined the road was stunted and sickly. Charles Victor Szasz felt as though he'd wandered into some kind of science fiction existence, another planet or dimension. Then the sun vanished below the treeline and suddenly the road was dark. He switched on the Ford's headlights and discovered that only one of them worked, dimly. The engine continued to *thunk.*

So the big question is, will this crate last till I get to where I'm going?

Well, if not, no big loss. The wagon had been driven hard for nearly 170,000 miles and was obviously close to that big used-car lot in the sky. If necessary, Charles Victor Szasz could throw his duffel bag over his shoulder and hoof it the rest of the way to Hub City. And then what?

The smell had gotten worse. It made his eyes water and seemed to clog his nostrils. For a moment he thought that, somehow, it had affected his vision, too, because he saw a red haze ahead and that had to be an illusion, didn't it?

But it wasn't. White pinpoints of light twinkled in the redness, which glared from the open roofs of the buildings, and, as he came closer, he saw funnels spewing gouts of black smoke into the sky. The road ran between two industrial sites, great dark blocks silhouetted against the even darker horizon, surrounded by high chain-link fences topped with rolls of barbed wire. Heavy machinery filled the night with screeches and muted explosions that became deafening as the Ford approached.

If this isn't the gate to Hell, it's a damn fine facsimile . . .

There was an asphalt parking lot on the far side of the buildings, beyond the fence, lit only by a single mercury vapor lamp high on a pole. It was crammed with cars and small trucks, hundreds of them. As Charles Victor Szasz drove past it, a large, dark pickup pulled from the lot and began to follow him, keeping about fifty yards to his rear.

The road took a few turns and then opened out into Hub City's main thoroughfare. The stench in the air was less here, barely noticeable. The city government obviously didn't waste much money on nonessentials like lighting; there were only two lampposts per block, and about half of them were broken. But there were other sources of illumination in the form of fires licking from the tops of barrels, which cast garish, dancing shadows on the nearby buildings. Many of those buildings seemed to be deserted, their windows and doors boarded or bricked over.

It's a lot grimmer than I remembered . . .

There seemed to be no motels or hotels or even rooming houses on this main drag. Maybe on the other end?

The dark pickup kept its distance as Charles Victor Szasz drove out of Hub City and onto a narrow country road. Finally, in the distance, he saw neon letters: OTE. Almost certainly an abbreviated version of MOTEL.

The structure behind the damaged sign was small, as

motels go, with fewer than a dozen doors in the long strip of building behind a square office with a large, cracked picture window. Inside, a stout man in a Hawaiian print shirt was hunched in a chair, peering at a tiny black-and-white television screen propped on the desk in front of him.

Charles Victor Szasz parked and went into the office. The stout man looked up, smiled, stood, and went to a counter that was just inside the door.

His voice brimmed with joviality: "Can I welcome you to one of our fine accommodations, sir?"

"I'd like a room for the night, yes," Charles Victor Szasz said. "A cheap one."

"One price fits all here. We like to think we treat every one of the Lord's creatures the same."

"That's a good policy."

"We like to b'lieve it is," the stout man replied, pushing a white registration card and a ballpoint pen across the counter. "Yessir, we do. If you'll just fill this out—"

"Okay."

"Will you be with us long?"

"Just tonight."

"Passing through, hey?"

"Something like that."

"Well now, I welcome you and wish you a happy and blessed good evening."

"Thanks. Back at you."

The stout man lifted the now-completed registration card to within an inch of his eyes. "I don't b'lieve I can make out your last name. Smith?"

"Szasz. S-Z-A-S-Z."

The stout man's smile drooped. He dropped the card onto the countertop and peered at his customer. "And what kinda name would that be, exactly?"

"I'm not sure."

The nuns never told me and I never bothered to find out . . .

"Wouldn't be Jewish, would it?"

"I don't think so."

"And just how is it that you don't know if you're Jewish or not?"

"You'll have to take my word for it, I guess."

"How do I know you're not lying?"

Charles Victor Szasz felt his muscles tighten and the familiar, happy surge of adrenaline. It would be a source of deep satisfaction to knock this blimp onto his flaccid ass. But accommodations seemed to be few and far between around Hub City, and fatigue was beginning to be a factor. A man, even a very tough man, can only go so long without sleep, and sleeping in the car gets old fast. He quelled the surge.

"I was raised Catholic. At St. Prisca's Orphanage."

The stout man was not mollified. "St. Prisca's burned down eight years ago. Closed about a year before that."

"I left ten years ago. Went to college and then took a construction job out west." A pause, and then: "The sisters named me after a priest who said Mass there. A Father Damien Szasz."

The stout man peered at the ceiling. "I do seem to remember a Cat'lic preacher called something foreign like that. Dead now."

"Do I get a room or not?"

"Cost you eighteen dollars."

"I guess that's not for the presidential suite."

The stout man looked blank. He accepted the money he was offered and counted it carefully—three fives and three ones—and said, "Guess you're not Jewish, anyway. We got a policy against Jews."

"They're not the Lord's creatures?"

"They *killed* the Lord!"

Again, the adrenaline surge and, again, he quelled it.

He accepted a numbered key from the stout man and went outside. No need to move his station wagon; the room he'd been assigned was next to the office.

The light spilling from the cracked window shone dully on a black SUV, parked across the road, lights out, engine running.

Probably not the welcome wagon . . .

Charles Victor Szasz got his duffel bag from the station wagon. He found the door to his room unlocked. Inside was pretty much what he expected, a tiny chamber with a narrow bed, a rickety nightstand, a bathroom with a commode and curtainless stand-up shower, and nothing else. Compared to this, the Bates Motel was the Waldorf.

CHAPTER TWO

Vic quickly rinsed himself under the shower head—there was no soap and the water was cold—and padded to where he'd dropped his duffel bag. He had no clean clothes, so he got out his least dirty shorts, put them on, and pawed through the bag until he found the book he'd bought from a street vendor in Chicago for a dime. It had neither cover nor title page, but he'd never been a stickler for niceties. It seemed to be a novel about eccentric cops by someone named Janwillem van de Wetering, and it would do.

He fell asleep and dreamed the Dream—the burst of light, the white oval where a face should be . . .

Ten hours later, remembering an old Kristofferson song, he put on his cleanest dirty shirt and checked his bankroll, hoping that the twenty-dollar-bill fairy had visited him while he slept. No such luck. He had exactly sixty American dollars left. A few meals, another night here at the luxurious OTE, and maybe a tank of gas, assuming the station wagon could still operate and then ... zip, nada, zero.

Okay, no panic. He'd been broke before.

Where to start? With breakfast. He'd eaten nothing since the St. Louis hot dog and, sixteen hours before that, a greasy burger and what were advertised as hash browns at a truck stop. Time to eat.

He went outside, stretched, and spotted a CAFÉ sign in front of a square frame building a bit up the road. During the short walk, he got an idea.

The café was empty at nine-thirty in the morning. Folks hereabouts would be early risers. He ordered coffee, bacon, and eggs—when in the heartland, do as the heartlanders do—and asked the frizzy-haired waitress if she knew where radio station KWLM might be. Obviously happy to do something other than pour coffee and plunk down plates, the woman drew him a map on a napkin and refilled his cup on the house. He thanked her and added a 20 percent tip to his bill, which left him with fifty-five and change.

Outside, there was no sign of the black SUV and the air was only faintly scented with industrial stink. The sky was blue, the clouds fluffy, and there was an autumnal hint of chill in the breeze ... in all, a fine day.

At the motel, the stout man poked his head out of the office door and asked, "You checkin' out?"

"I'll let you know in an hour or two."

"'Cause I got to charge you another day if you don't check out by noon."

"I'll get back to you."

The waitress's map was clear enough, mostly because

the route to radio KWLM was extremely simple—follow
the river until the first left and up the hill—and because the
station's tower was visible for several miles. The tower
dwarfed the station, which was one story's worth of white
cinder blocks standing alone on the hilltop. There were two
cars and a motorcycle parked on a strip of asphalt. Charles
Victor Szasz guided his station wagon into the area next to
the bike, got out, and went into the station.

There was a woman standing behind the reception
desk, bent over, scribbbling on a notepad. She was tall,
slender: green eyes, chestnut hair. She could have been
the woman in the park's nicer, older sister. She glanced up
and raised her brows questioningly.

Charles Victor Szasz grinned as widely as he could,
hoping his smile was so dazzling that the woman
wouldn't notice his shabby clothing, and said, "I'm not
sure what I should ask for, ma'am. I guess I want to see
the boss. Station manager? Is that what the boss of a radio
station is called?"

"I'm not the receptionist," the woman said. "She's on a
bathroom break, I guess. But I know the station manager.
He likes to be called Mr. Horace. May I ask why you're
looking for him?"

*She probably thinks I'm digging his swimming pool.
Or asking for a handout.*

"Again, I'm not sure. I have questions that maybe he
can answer."

"And maybe he can't." This from a newcomer who was
standing in the door to an inner office. He was a bony man
whose olive skin was stretched tight over his skeleton,
with a lot of jet-black hair that hung in a cowlick over his

forehead. He was wearing a white shirt and tie and dark trousers.

"You are?" he asked.

"My name won't mean anything to you, but for the record, it's Charles Victor Szasz."

"Okay, Mr. Charles Victor Szasz, you want to sell me something . . . no, not dressed like that. So maybe you got a story you want to tell?"

"Something like that."

The bony man crossed to Charles Victor Szasz and thrust out his right hand. "I'm Mr. Horace."

"No first name?"

"Not on the first date."

They shook, then Horace looked at his watch. "I've got fifteen minutes."

"That should be enough."

"It'll have to be."

The woman moved next to Horace, who turned to her and asked, "You got something for me, Myra?"

"The phone number you wanted. It's on the desk. Now you owe me."

"Consider yourself owed."

The woman nodded to both men. "Mr. Szasz, nice almost meeting you."

The men watched her go out into the sunshine. "Myra Connelly," Horace said.

"You say that like you expect me to react."

"She's on television. Next town over, and sometimes she freelances for CNN. You haven't seen her?"

"Never had the pleasure."

"You have now."

They went through the inner door to an office so barren it could have been mistaken for a cell except for a couple of chairs, a battered oak desk, and a big-screen television on a metal stand tuned to a news station with the sound muted. Horace went behind the desk and gestured to the visitor's chair on the other side of it.

"Okay," Horace said. "Shoot."

Where to begin . . . ?

At the beginning? How would the beginning be? Beginnings can be good.

Well (Charles Victor Szasz began) it was a dark and stormy night. That's not an homage to Bulwer-Lytton, or even Snoopy. It's fact, as reported by the state meteorological office in the capital. It was a dark and stormy night and some person or persons left a one-month-old baby wrapped in a worn Navaho blanket on the front steps of St. Prisca's Catholic Church in downtown Hub City. Father Damien Szasz, being on his way to his weekly poker game and having left his reading glasses in the sacristy, was about to unlock the church's front door when he noticed the soggy blanket and found the infant inside. He put his raincoat around baby and blanket and ran behind the church to the orphanage, also named for St. Prisca . . .

"How long did you stay there?" Horace interrupted. "With the nuns?"

"Years. Till high school."

"Then?"

"Foster homes until I left for college."

"*Bad* foster homes?"

"I guess not. No. They were okay."

"Good. I was afraid we were getting into Charles Dickens territory. So you went to college—"

—to a small liberal arts school upstate. No idea, really, why he was there or what he was expected to do. So he watched other kids and learned to go through the motions. Told his adviser that he planned to major in English or journalism, and why not? He *did* like to read. He was doing all right for a year and a half until he punched out a professor . . .

"You did *what*?"

"I hit him. In the face. With my fist."

"Can I ask why, or will that get *me* punched, too?"

"I guess because . . . he was patronizing me. I don't remember everything, but . . . he said he couldn't blame me for being ignorant because with my background I never had anyone to teach me how to behave. Or something like that."

"They expel you?"

"By nightfall."

"You came back here?"

"For what? Hub City had nothing for me. I rambled around for a while. Dishwasher. Busboy. When I got lucky, construction crews. Loading trucks. None of it was union, so the pay was lousy, but I had to eat."

"Now, the big question. What brings you back to the armpit of the Midwest, also known as Hub City?"

"I might say I couldn't get reservations at the black hole of Calcutta."

"And, Mr. Szasz, I might laugh if you did. But don't count on it."

"First, Mr. Horace, a question for you. You said you

could give me fifteen minutes. You've already given me nineteen."

"How do you know? You're not wearing a watch."

"But you are."

"And you bothered to look at it from over there."

"It *is* on public display."

"If I decide to laugh at your wisecrack, I might also decide to be impressed. So how about answering my question."

"Why am I back here?"

"That's what I want to know."

CHAPTER THREE

And that's something that Charles Victor Szasz wanted to know, too . . .

A month earlier, he'd been in Chicago just a week out of his last job and in the process of ending a relationship. There had been a visit from a protective brother and some shouting and finally some punches. The brother left, bloodied, vowing to return with friends, and then the woman screamed, "Who are you? Who the hell *are* you?"

He'd flung his duffel bag over his shoulder and got in his car and began driving. No particular direction, no destination, just . . . just leaving where he was, as he had done so often before. Just getting out.

He stopped for gas outside a Missouri River town called Alton and as he was paying for it, the weary, bored clerk asked, "Where you headed?"

"Uh . . . no place in particular."

"Well, hope you have fun when you get there."

He didn't return to the interstate. Instead, he drove

along country roads between fields of corn and under the kind of sky a man can't see in the city, full of stars, with a round, hard moon, and whitish wisps of clouds, and then, as the dashboard clock showed midnight he stopped the car and got out.

Who the hell are *you?*

Where you headed?

He couldn't answer either question and, suddenly, he felt a need to answer at least the first one. He realized that he had been needing to know who he was for years, maybe a lot of years, and there was no reason not to learn his identity except fear, and he would not let fear stop him. He would not let fear stop him from anything, especially not this.

So the decision to learn who he was dictated the answer to his second question, where he was going. All he knew about his origin was that a priest found him on church steps in a place called Hub City. That had to be where he would begin his search, Hub City.

He looked across the desk at Horace and said, "I'm here, I guess, for the same reason that people pay to have their family tree traced."

"You think you'll find out who your birth parents were?"

"Something like that."

"Well, good luck. Six, seven years ago, somebody torched the old city hall and all the birth records and such went up in smoke."

"What about the church? The orphanage?"

"You might have better luck there . . . but I wouldn't count on it. Look, Mr. Szasz, before you get too deep into this, maybe you should see what's what around here. Take a ride with me."

"I thought you had some unbreakable appointment."

"Whatever gave you that idea?"

In the parking lot, they got into the red Oldsmobile. Charles Victor Szasz noticed that the Honda was gone; that ride had probably belonged to the reporter, Myra Connelly.

"I'll show you why Hub City doesn't make anybody's list of vacation paradises," Horace said, "and why snooping around and asking questions might be a bad idea."

Hub City had looked bad the previous night. Hub City looked even worse in daylight. Most of the storefronts were boarded over with stained slabs of plywood. Those that weren't, those that still housed businesses, had bricks in the windows and thick bars on the doors. There were a few stoplights along the main street, but none of them were working. Occasionally, a man or woman slouched along the cracked sidewalks, but only occasionally; mostly, the downtown area was deserted. It reminded Charles Victor Szasz of one of those sci-fi postapocalypse flicks— the day after doomsday.

"Pretty grim," he said.

"Yeah, that it is," Horace replied. "Everybody who could get out did, years ago."

"Doesn't look like there's much business left."

"Virtually none. If you want groceries or clothing, you've got to drive to the mall in the next town."

"What about the big plant I drove past?"

"McFeeley's Works," Horace said. "According to one

survey, the biggest polluter in the Midwest, maybe in the country. Also the biggest supporter of local politicians."

"I'd think it would bring some money into the area—"

"It does provide jobs, but most of the workers don't live in Hub City."

"Why do you stick around?"

"That, Mr. Szasz, is a long and convoluted story that I seldom feel like telling."

"I won't push it."

"Push away. Won't do you any good."

Horace turned and slowed as they passed a concrete-block structure with a cracked sidewalk and boarded windows.

"Police station," Horace said.

"Looks like it's out of business."

"Not officially. Nobody ever announced that Hub City no longer has a police department. But I can't remember when I last saw a cop."

"What do you do for law and order?"

"Mostly, we do without."

They drove on in silence until they heard a whine that became a roar and two tattooed men wearing sleeveless denim jackets and Nazi helmets riding motorcycles passed the Oldsmobile.

"Local biker club," Horace said. "Rumor is that they stage death fights on weekends. One of many rumors I haven't been able to check out."

"Why not?"

"Because no reporter wants to risk his life for what I pay, and I can't blame 'em."

The car lurched and shook. Horace cursed and said, "Feels like a blown tire."

It was. The left rear tire had fallen apart and scattered scraps of rubber on the street.

"Tires are a problem here," Horace said, "because so many of the streets are so bad."

"You have a spare?"

"Always."

Horace popped open the trunk and leaned in to get the spare tire. He stopped and looked past the car at the bikers, who had turned around and were skidding to a stop.

"Now we got trouble," he muttered.

The bikers were dismounting. Horace wiped his palms and approached them.

"You guys want to give us a hand?" he asked. "Be happy to pay you for your time."

"You gonna pay, all right," one of the bikers said, grinning. He was red-faced and sported a bushy beard. His companion, clean-shaven but equally red-faced, was pulling a length of chain from his motorcycle's saddlebag.

"Lemme hold your wallet for a minute," the beard said.

"Why don't you guys just be on your way," Charles Victor Szasz said, moving first beside and then in front of Horace.

Beard looked back at his silent companion, who was folding the chain in half, and said, "Ask me nice and maybe I will. Say 'please.' Say 'pretty please.' Get down on your knees and say it real loud."

Later, Horace tried to describe the fight to Myra Connelly and didn't do a very good job of it. They were standing in a portico outside a hospital emergency room, where Myra had come to interview a woman who had given birth to triplets.

"It happened in a hurry," Horace said. "I guess not ten seconds passed from start to finish. All I'm sure of is, Szasz got hit with the chain and a bunch of punches— must've been eight or nine. Then he started hitting back and pretty soon, both of the punks were stretched out on the road and Szasz was standing over them, rubbing his knuckles and spitting blood. I asked him why he did it, the fight, and he told me he just hates bullies. The punks got up and rode away and we changed the tire and drove here."

Charles Victor Szasz came out of the waiting room and approached them. There were dabs of iodine on his various cuts and scrapes and he moved stiffly.

Myra Connelly smiled at him and said, "I hear you're a tough guy."

"I'm an idiot. Only an idiot takes on two guys at once."

"You want to do a story on him?" Horace asked Myra.

"Well . . . I wouldn't rule it out." To Charles Victor Szasz: "Where are you staying?"

"I'm not sure. Where's cheap?"

"I might be able to help you with that," Horace said.

Myra moved away, toward where her Honda was parked in a driveway. "Maybe I'll be in touch."

And maybe I'll win the lottery and marry Jessica Alba . . .

The trip back to the radio station passed in silence until, as he was guiding the Oldsmobile into a parking slot, Horace said, "You looking for a job?"

"Sure."

"Okay, but before I go any further . . . you determined to stay in Hub City? You'll do that no matter what? Because if you get killed, I don't want it on my conscience."

"For a while anyway."

"Right. You said you studied journalism in college?"

"For a couple of semesters."

"Can you write an English sentence?"

"Provided it isn't too complicated."

"Can you read it after you've written it?"

"I guess so."

Horace turned off the engine and leaned back in his seat. "Okay, here's the deal. I need a reporter to cover Hub City. As you know by now, it's dangerous, and as I told you earlier, the money's lousy. But the job's yours if you want it."

"And I try to answer my own questions while I'm asking yours?"

Horace nodded. "Exactly. You have anything you want to ask *me*?"

"For openers . . . why bother reporting on Hub City? Does anything interesting really happen there?"

Horace chuckled. "A lot. It might be the most interesting place in America because it kind of encapsulates everything that's wrong with this country. Any kind of violence, hatred, corruption you can think of, Hub City's got it."

"What about your other reporters?"

"There are only two. One's in his late sixties, retired from the St. Louis paper. He's part-time, won't do anything rough. The other's Myra. She's *damn* good, but I won't ask her to go to the bad areas."

"That's chivalrous of you."

"No it's not. If she got killed, I'd have to replace her, and good reporters aren't exactly lining up to work for me."

"But you don't mind if *I* get killed?"

"I might, if you turn out to be a good reporter. But how likely is that?"

"You sure know how to flatter a guy, Mr. Horace."

"I don't lie any more than I absolutely have to. Maybe that's why I'm not rich."

"One final question before I give you my answer. Why do you stay here? I mean, couldn't you get a job in St. Louis, Chicago, maybe some place like Springfield?"

"Two reasons. One, they don't need me in those places. Two, my old man was a sixties antiwar protestor, a real tie-dyed idealist. I inherited some of his DNA."

"Just some?"

"I look lousy in tie-dye. You want the job?"

"Yes."

Horace opened his door. "Let's get you started."

Charles Victor Szasz was shown his workspace, a cubicle the size of a pantry, and spent the next hour doing paperwork. At one point, he looked up at Horace and said, "This wants to know what my previous jobs were. But there's only eight lines. I've had eighteen, twenty jobs in the last year alone."

"Just put down your greatest hits."

When the forms were all filled out, Horace said, "Okay, next item. You have any other clothes?"

"Yeah, some rags I wear around the house. These're my church-going threads."

"You're not exactly dressed for success."

"Depends on what you want to succeed at."

"For cesspool cleaning, you're fine," Horace said, taking his wallet from a hip pocket. "For journalism, no. Tomorrow, you go to the mall on the interstate and buy something that Goodwill wouldn't refuse."

"They have the *damndest* habit of asking for money, those mall shops."

Horace took bills from his wallet, counted off ten of them, and handed them to Charles Victor Szasz. "Your first week's salary."

"Thanks."

"Next item. Your name. It's tricky, foreign-sounding, and people around here don't like tricky and foreign."

"I've noticed."

"You got any objections to changing it?"

"Hell, it's not even my real name."

"How about . . . Charlie Sassoon? No, forget that. Sage? Charlie Sage? Chuck Sage?"

"Maybe *Vic* Sage?"

"Yeah, that's good. Sounds both rugged and reportorial. Okay, I now pronounce you Vic Sage."

"Amen."

"Last item. Living quarters. You stayed at the motel last night?"

"My own, special evening in paradise."

"Lucky you. You get another dose of paradise tonight. Tomorrow, I'll introduce you to a man who has a cottage for rent. It's pretty far out, maybe twenty miles, but it'll be clean and cheap."

"Two of my favorite things."

Horace stuck out a hand, and Vic Sage shook it.

"I hope this works out for both of us. See you in the morning. Nine sharp."

"See you then."

As Vic Sage was getting out of the Ford, the motel clerk bustled from the office. "You said you'd be right back!"

"No, that's not exactly what I said."

"Well, I'm charging you for another night, mister."

The clerk reminded Vic of someone, but he couldn't say who, not at that moment. He gave the clerk another eighteen dollars and got back into his station wagon and began cruising. He was aware that he wanted to go somewhere, see something, but where and what?

The town was not the place he remembered. It was a bit bigger—had it grown in the last decade?—and, as he'd seen earlier, incredibly shabby. He turned onto a barren street without knowing way, and drove two blocks, and stopped. There it was, his boyhood home. The church and the orphanage behind it had both burned. Only concrete foundations, fragments of walls, and the occasional charred beam were left. Vic walked across a weed-covered lawn, past the remains of the church, and into the St. Prisca's Home for Children. Broken glass crunched under his feet and the air was laden with a scent far more foul than that of burned wood. There were bottles and fast-food wrappers and some heaps of dried excrement in the corners.

*Local homeless folks using St. Prisca's as a toilet . . .
wonder what Sister Hectora would think of that?*

He walked on, through what had been the room where
prospective adopters met children, and through the remains of the chapel where Father said Mass on Sundays
and sometimes on other days, and to the kitchen, where
kindly Sister Francesca cooked meals, and on to the tiny
closet behind the walk-in pantry where Sister Hectora
locked him when he had been bad.

Charles Victor Szasz, she would say, shaking her finger
at him. It was never just Charles, much less Charlie or
Chuck. No, to Sister Hectora he was always *Charles Victor Szasz Charles Victor Szasz Charles Victor Szasz.* She
made it sound like she was saying *Beelzebub.* She would
say the name, shake a finger, then lock him in the closet,
telling him to "think about your behavior."

Once, after he had been hunkering in the darkness for
over two hours, Sister Hectora flung open the door and
asked, "Are you ready to apologize?"

"Go to Hell," he had said, and Sister Hectora crossed
her hands over the front of her habit and stumbled backward.

A lot of recrimination followed that incident, harsh
from Sister Hectora, hesitant from Sister Francesca, and
almost kindly from his namesake, Father Szasz.

It was about then, when he was eight or nine, that the
Dream began; at least, that's when he thought it began. He
could have been having the Dream for a while without realizing it. He had the Dream several times a week, that he
was aware of, and it was always the same: a tall man in a

raincoat and a hat was carrying a baby. He, Charles Victor Szasz, was the baby; somehow he knew that. But who was carrying him? The priest? No: The priest did wear a hat and a raincoat, sometimes, but he was short and chubby and the man carrying the baby was neither. In the Dream, there was always a sudden burst of light—from what source?—and the baby could see what was between the hat and the raincoat collar and it wasn't a face, it was just an oval of pure white.

The Dream was about all that was left from his childhood. Shortly after he told her to go to Hell, Sister Hectora took away his privileges. Soon, the good sister fobbed him off on county officials who put him into foster care. As soon as he could he ran away. He had never returned until now.

The sun was low in the sky as he returned to his station wagon. After another diner meal, he retired to his room and read the coverless book until he felt like sleeping.

The next day, he checked in with Horace, got directions to the mall, and went shopping. The store Horace had recommended was supposed to be a repository of bargains, but to Vic Sage, everything seemed insanely expensive. He bought some clothes and a pair of shoes, and lunch at a counter in the rear of the store, and returned to the radio station.

He put on a new shirt and twill trousers in the men's room and went to Horace's office.

"You'll do," Horace said, glancing up from a sheaf of yellow papers he'd been reading.

"What's next?"

"Living quarters. I talked to a guy I once did a story on. Name's Aristotle Rodor—"

"*Aristotle?* Really?"

"A guy who was Charles Victor Szasz until yesterday's got no business hocking on an 'Aristotle.' Anyway, he's still got the cottage I told you about for rent and he's willing to talk with you."

"When?"

"Sooner's better than later."

Horace scrawled directions on the back of one of the yellow sheets and told Vic Sage to report back at nine the next morning.

CHAPTER FOUR

Aristotle Rodor lived out in the country—*way* out in the country. But his place wasn't hard to find. From a mile away, looking past flat, open fields, he could see windmills and flat sheets of glass on metal frames gleaming in the sun. Sage turned off a stretch of blacktop onto a rutted dirt road, stopped, and got out of his station wagon.

"Back here!" someone called from behind a rambling, white Victorian that must have been at least a century old and looked nothing like the neighboring farmhouses.

The caller was a small, compact man wearing coveralls, a straw boater, and horn-rimmed glasses. He was holding a hoe and standing in a garden filled with growing vegetables. Sage had never been good at judging age, but he guessed the gardener to be in his seventies.

"I'm Vic Sage."

"Well, who *else* would you be? And I, of course, am the lord of this particular manor, Aristotle Rodor. Come come come." Rodor turned and began walking toward the

Victorian. Sage followed, looking around, seeing a small cottage near the big house and a red barn maybe a thousand yards down a small slope.

Fifteen minutes later, they were seated at a huge wooden table in the kitchen sipping lemonade. At first, Sage couldn't believe he was being offered *lemonade,* but that's exactly what Rodor poured from a crystal pitcher.

"Horace tells me you have quite a story," Rodor said after a sip.

"Pretty *boring* story. You don't want to hear it."

"I'll be the judge of that after you tell it to me, sonny."

Sage found it surprisingly easy to share his autobiography with this small, somewhat crabby man and so he did, omitting almost all the fights, a few dozen jobs, and an unfortunate incident involving a police cruiser in Kalamazoo.

"I expect I've just heard a highly edited version of your life, but that is neither unexpected nor particularly problematical," Rodor said. "You seem like a decent sort—rough, but decent. I guess I can stand you if you can stand me. Do you want to see the cottage?"

Shiva crossed the border from Mexico and spent a month sightseeing around Texas. Then someone offered her something that sounded interesting in Kansas City and she went there, but the situation was more tedious than interesting and she left after a couple of days. Next, she visited for a week with Richard in the mountains. They agreed that the first one to acquire a broken bone would be the loser. After five days of sparring for eight hours a day, no bones were broken so they called it a tie; that was

on Friday. They sat meditating outside the cabin, eyes
wide open, until the moon was overhead Sunday night
and then Richard fixed an enormous meal. They ate and
slept and ate again and then Shiva asked Richard what he
knew about a place called "Hub City." Richard answered
that Hub City was the worst, the absolute pits, absolutely
no doubt about it. Shiva shouldered her backpack, smiled,
and walked down the mountain to a town where she could
get a bus ticket to Hub City.

The man who sold her the ticket asked, "You sure
you want to go there, missy? I hear it's bad. I hear it's
real bad."

Shiva smiled, leaned across the counter, and kissed
him on the cheek.

The bus driver refused to go past the city limits. "Sorry,
lady," he said to Shiva, "but last time I was in Hub City I
was lucky to get out alive."

"But I have a ticket."

"And I have a wife and kids."

Shiva dug her thumb into a spot behind the driver's left
elbow. He screeched and his arm went limp.

"The pain will be gone by tomorrow," Shiva said, "and
you will regain full use of the limb shortly thereafter.
If you ever refuse to do your duty again, I will not be so
generous."

She went down the three steps and out the door of the
bus, and looked back at the driver. "Give my regards to
your family."

She walked onto Hub City's main street. She stopped
and spoke to a man clad in rags who was leaning against a
graffiti-covered wall. She asked him where the worst

place in the area was, a bar or a club or an arena no sane, decent person would go near.

"Sie hall," he answered.

"Pardon?"

"Sit. E. Hall," the raggedy man said, enunciating every syllable.

"City Hall?"

The man gestured toward the street. "Follow the river and turn left."

Shiva handed the man a bill. "If you joke with me, I shall return and cause you much pain."

The man squinted at the bill and rubbed his eyes and squinted again. The woman had handed him a hundred dollars.

Shiva continued walking. There were occasional whistles and yells and a few lewd suggestions, but no one approached her. It was dark when she reached the place the raggedy man had told her about. It was, indeed, City Hall—or it had been. In the light from a truck parked at the curb, engine idling, she could see a shallow flight of concrete steps, three columns, and, on an archway above a door, the words, graven in stone: *City Hall.*

There were dozens of cars and pickups parked haphazardly on the barren front lawn. Shiva had to step over a man wearing a baseball uniform who was sprawled at the bottom of the steps, his eyes open and staring, white powder smeared across his lower face and, just outside the entrance, a young woman who was apparently wearing only a long, black cape, who sat with her back against the door-frame, endlessly chanting, "Hotcha hotcha hotcha . . ."

Inside, a party was in full, noisy progress. Men, some

accompanied by women, stood in groups either gulping from bottles, smoking thin cigarettes, or both. Others sat on a marble staircase that led to a balcony, and still others were grouped around a pool table on which a game of eight-ball was being played.

Shiva stood, surveying the scene and smiling. Two men chugging from bottles approached. The taller of the two, clad in jeans and a bowling shirt, lurched over to her, winked, and asked, "You're wearin' real loose clothes and all, but I bet underneath you're somethin'. Buy you a drink?"

"No."

"Why not?"

"I could perhaps cite many reasons. You are beyond ugly—you are repulsive and sickening. You stink. You are almost certainly stupid and inept. If you do not leave my vicinity immediately I shall cause you great grief."

She smiled, showing teeth that were white and perfectly formed.

The man stared at her. "Say that again."

"You are repulsive, smelly, and inept."

"You can't talk to me like that."

"Did I mention stupid?"

The man brought his arm up and Shiva seemed to shrug. The man collapsed onto the floor, clutching his stomach and gasping for air. His companion grabbed for Shiva and was immediately stumbling backward into a group of three men playing cards at an oaken table. The table overturned, spilling cards, money, and liquid and causing two of the three card players to fall onto their backs. The third reached into his hip pocket and had a small revolver half-drawn when Shiva was suddenly standing beside him and he was pitching forward, falling onto his face.

Shiva turned and raised her voice. "Good evening. I am called Lady Shiva. Perhaps I should be called Lady Kali, but the misnomer need not concern you. I have heard that this city, this Hub City, is wicked and dangerous. I am fond of wicked and dangerous places. But I fear this Hub City will be a disappointment to me. The wickedness I have seen is childish and the danger negligible. But perhaps I am mistaken. If any of you are able to convince me that I have erred, I should be happy to confer with you."

A small, balding man in a seersucker suit stepped away from the wall and said, "Miss? Maybe I can help you."

CHAPTER FIVE

Vic Sage was ten minutes early. He hung around the reception desk drinking bad coffee from a vending machine until Horace entered and immediately dispatched Vic to the hospital.

"Heard something on the police scanner about a car crash," Horace said. "Get names and particulars. See if you can talk to a survivor."

Myra Connelly was entering the station as Vic was leaving. "How're the injuries?" she asked.

"What injuries?"

"From the fight . . . oh. You're being macho. Well, I'll let you go chew horseshoes, or whatever you macho guys do."

Before Vic could reply, Myra hurried past him.

She wouldn't know macho if it bit her in the ass . . .

At the hospital, Vic found the emergency room empty. He introduced himself to the nurse at the desk.

"Anybody know exactly what happened?" he asked.

"The victims told the paramedics that a deer jumped out in front of them and the car turned over when the driver tried to avoid it."

"These people have a name?"

"Stabelhausen. The husband works for the McFeeley plant. Don't know what the wife does."

"Thanks. Mind if I talk to them?"

"I guess it's okay. They could go home, but the doctor wants to observe them for a day or so. They're in adjoining rooms on the second floor, just left of the stairs."

Vic decided to talk to the husband first.

The door to the man's room was ajar. Vic tapped it lightly and entered. The patient, a portly man in his forties, was sitting up in bed, his back propped against the mattress, watching a television that was on a frame hung from the ceiling.

"Excuse me," Vic said. "I'm a reporter from KWLM and I—"

"I'm not interested," the man said without looking at Vic.

"I just want to ask a few—"

"Get out of here."

The man's tone was more frightened than belligerent. Vic nodded and left.

The wife was also watching television. Vic knocked, entered her room, and tried a slightly different approach. "What's on?" he asked, nodding to the television.

"Tony Danza."

"What's he doing today?"

"Cooking something."

"Something Italian, I bet."

The woman smiled. She was about the same age as her husband, but thin, almost emaciated-looking.

Vic pulled the visitor's chair close to the bed and sat. "Mind talking for a few minutes?"

"Well . . ."

"Won't take long. Just some red tape."

And if she wants to believe that I'm a cop or maybe a doctor, it's all right with me . . .

"Okay, then. First, how did it happen? The crash?"

"We were run off the road, like I told the other doctor."

"And who ran you off?"

"Big black SUV."

Like the one that followed me a couple of nights ago . . .

"Any reason?"

"We were leaving on a vacation."

"Did you see who was driving the SUV?"

The woman leaned forward and squinted at Vic. "Who did you say you are?"

"My name is Vic Sage."

"And what is your job, Mr. Sage?"

"I . . . I work for a radio station—"

The woman crossed her hands in front of her face, as though shielding herself from an attack, and said, "You better just get out of here right now."

"I just want to—"

"Get out!"

"Ma'am, I don't want to—"

"Nurse!" the woman screamed.

Vic stood and retreated to the door. "Sorry to have bothered you."

As he was getting into his station wagon, he saw the black SUV, engine idling, waiting at the far end of the parking lot.

Time to have a talk . . .

He broke into a run. But as he approached the SUV, it jolted forward, tires screeching, and turned toward the access road.

No way I'll ever catch it in my heap . . .

It was not yet eleven, and Horace had given him only one assignment. Vic decided to cruise the area a bit. During his years at the orphanage, he had really seen very little of the countryside; there was neither budget nor tolerance for things like field trips. The region, Vic saw, was actually pleasant, once he got away from Hub City and the smelly river: fields and farms and gentle hills and the kind of small, midwestern towns that consist of a gas station, a convenience store, and a few wooden houses.

Coming over the crest of a small hill, he was suddenly seeing a panorama of ugliness: several acres of wrecked and rusting cars, trucks with heaps of bald tires and twisted metal scattered among them, the whole surrounded by a cyclone fence topped with rolls of barbed wire.

Could this be where they took the Stabelhausen car . . . ?

He parked the station wagon near the only gate in the fence and went to where a man wearing overalls and a straw hat who must have lived eighty very hard years was leaning on a wooden shack.

"He'p yeh?" the man asked.

"I'm looking for a car that might have been brought in this morning."

"White Chevy over there," the man said, pointing. "You wanna buy her?"

"No, just look her over."

"Go right ahead."

The car's top was partially caved in and there was a dent on the left rear door, with a streak of black in it. But the front fenders were undamaged. Vic peered through the windows and saw that the backseat area was filled with suitcases and a few household items—not what you'd bring with you on a quick shopping trip. Nothing coincided with what he'd been told about the accident. What it *did* look like was that something painted black had struck the Chevrolet's left rear door, hard, and that, whatever it was, had knocked the car out of control and turned it over.

Vic waved to the old man in the straw hat and returned to his station wagon.

CHAPTER SIX

It was one in the afternoon when he knocked on Horace's door and entered the office. Horace looked up and asked, "Get lost?"

"Decided to sightsee a little. Orient myself."

"That's not always a good idea around here, sightseeing."

"Something I'd like to ask you about." Vic told Horace about the frightened couple and the SUV.

"And you want to know what I think about all that, Mr. Sage?"

"Yeah."

"I think it's natural for people who have just survived a bad car crash to be scared and a little out of their wits."

"And the SUV?"

"My advice is, ignore it. You don't get in its way, it won't get in yours."

"You sound like you know who owns it."

"Mr. Sage, I did not hire you to get you killed and I'm through with the subject."

"I'd like to use a computer."

"For what reason?"

"Get some background on the people at the hospital."

"What you need to know about them is, they survived the crash. We'll inform the world of that on our five o'clock newscast and we won't mention it again. This is not the sinking of the *Lusitania*—"

"The what?"

"The *Lusitania.* It was a big boat. It sank. Look, take the rest of the day off and be back at nine tomorrow morning."

Vic was a mile from Aristotle Rodor's property when the *clank* in his engine became a hiss and the car rolled to a stop. He got out and saw, behind the station wagon, a trail of oil and grease and a few nuts and bolts.

He was wondering what to do next when he heard the roar of a motorcycle engine and turned to see one of the men he had fought with speeding up the road.

A little midday exercise, coming right up . . .

The biker stopped, dismounted, and said, "Trouble, huh. She just stop on you?"

"Something like that."

"Lemme have a look."

The biker got a wrench from his saddlebag and lifted the hood of the Ford. He poked and prodded and then looked underneath the vehicle, then wiped his brow on his arm. "Transmission's shot. Prolly cheaper to get a new ride than replace it."

"What I figured."

Okay, now he's going to drop the nice guy act and attack . . .

But the biker only said, "Sorry, man. Bitch when that happens. You need a ride?"

"I guess."

"Hop on."

This is too weird not to see where it goes . . .

Vic mounted the Harley behind the biker and, feeling silly and profoundly uneasy, put his arms around the man's barrel chest.

For the next five minutes, he bumped and swayed and inhaled the odors of sweat and grease. Then they were at Rodor's gate and Vic dismounted, and tensed.

Okay, now it happens . . .

But the biker merely nodded and sped away.

Rodor was tinkering with a flat sheet of glass on a metal frame, one of a dozen placed on and near the houses.

Vic hiked up and path until he stood beside his landlord. "Can I ask what you're doing?"

"Making an adjustment."

"On what?"

"I haven't explained these to you? They're solar panels."

"And what does a solar panel do?"

"Converts sunlight to electricity. What the hell *else* would it do?"

"That really works?"

"Did you turn on a light last night?"

Vic nodded.

"In that case, it works. I get additional power from the windmills, but I don't usually need it."

"What about cloudy days, storms—"

"Whatever I don't use immediately is stored in batteries. I am, you might say, off the grid. The bastards who run the power companies can get rich off someone else."

"Did you invent this stuff?"

"The technology has existed for years. I *did* tweak it a bit."

"Cost much?"

"It paid for itself years ago."

"Mister Rodor, I have a problem."

"Probably more than one. I say that because you're not wearing a halo. Anyway, solving problems used to be my specialty. What's yours?"

"My car died."

"Gone to that great junkyard in the sky, eh? Any hope of resurrection?"

"I doubt it."

"And a reporter needs wheels."

"Exactly. So my question is, do you know of any cars for sale cheap? And I mean *very* cheap."

"Come with me."

Rodor led Vic down the slope to the barn. They went inside and Rodor stopped by a large object covered with a paint-spattered tarp. He pulled away the tarp, revealing an old-fashioned Volkswagen Beetle—circa 1968, Vic estimated. The right front fender was dented, and the paint job on the left front fender was a different green than the rest of the car.

"Does it run?"

"You'd be surprised," Rodor said. "In fact, you will be. Get in."

Vic moved to open the right-side door.

"No no no," Rodor protested. "You drive."

Vic got behind the wheel and waited until Rodor was seated. He saw a key sticking from the steering column, twisted it and—

There was a deep, throaty roar.

"Put it in gear," Rodor said. "Carefully."

Vic depressed the clutch, moved the gearshift, and the car lurched forward, out the barn door, and partly up the slope before Vic could apply the brake.

Rodor was grinning. "Which are you more—startled or impressed?"

"Call that one a toss-up."

"I got the idea from a movie star," Rodor said. "Reverse snobbery. Put a high-performance engine in a low-tech vehicle. It's kind of dumb, but I like it."

Vic moved the gearshift and slowly released the clutch. The car topped the slope. Vic steered to the road, switched to a higher gear, and stepped on the gas. About four seconds later, the speedometer read seventy and Vic stomped the brake to avoid sluing into a curve.

"Wow," he whispered. "I'm impressed."

"Well, you damn well oughtta be. Shall we go back?"

Later, in the kitchen, over glasses of the root beer that Rodor favored, he told Vic that the Volkswagen was an experiment, an attempt to design a high-performance engine that runs on chicken poo.

"Did you say 'chicken poo'?" Vic asked.

"I did. To be precise, the methane byproduct of chicken poo, of which there is an abundance in the area."

"Chicken poo."

"Yes, chicken poo. That's what my daddy called it and that's what I call it."

"Obviously, the experiment was successful."

"Yes and no. Like several other of my efforts, it cannot be made cost-efficient. It *could* be, if some major industrialist supplied resources, but I have been assured that the nation is not ready to replace what comes out of an oil well with what comes out of a chicken's rear end. Maybe someday."

"I wish you luck with it. Meanwhile, I still have my problem—"

"You're kind of dense," Rodor said. "The Volkswagen is yours."

"I can't begin to pay what it must be worth—"

"Then call it a loan. When your ship comes in, you can pay me."

"I can't accept—"

"You can and you will because you are not stupid, and any man who isn't dumb as a post can see the benefit of something being used as opposed to rusting away in a barn. If it will ease your mind, you can consider yourself my research assistant assigned to test the engine. In fact, that's what you *will* be. You'll make note of performance and report to me . . . oh, once a month?"

"Okay, if you're sure . . ."

"Anything else on your mind?"

"You know anything about computers?"

"A bit."

"I see this stuff on TV . . . finding out about people. There's a couple of accident victims I'd like some background on."

"I'm afraid that's a bit beyond my expertise. I'm not much of an online person. Surely one of your collegues can assist you?"

"The only colleagues I've met are my boss, who for some reason doesn't want to help, and a woman, Myra Connelly."

"And is there any reason why a woman might not have the skills you require?"

"Uh . . . no."

"I believe I detect some male chauvinism in you, Mr. Sage."

"Could be. I've never had any reason to think about it."

"When you have a moment, you might."

"Okay. When I have a moment. Use your phone?"

"Go ahead."

Vic got Myra Connelly's number from four-one-one, made the call, and when Myra answered told her what he wanted.

"I might be able to help," she said. "Can you come here?"

"Sure, I guess. Right now a good time?"

"It'll take you about an hour."

"An hour it is."

"I'd better give you directions."

Twenty minutes later, Vic was guiding the VW off the Rodor property. He stopped where his Ford had died. The asphalt was stained, but the vehicle itself was gone.

Efficient. Wonder if they'll make me pay for the towing . . .

Myra Connelly lived even farther from Hub City than Rodor did. Vic drove for seventy-five minutes, until night had fallen, he'd missed a turnoff twice and finally, an hour and a half after he'd started, braked in front of her house, an old-fashioned bungalow with a wide front porch. The property was shallow, longer than it was wide, with the house situated at one end. In the side yard, there were swings, a seesaw, and a sandbox.

Vic was angry with himself for getting lost and wondered, knowing his temper, if he shouldn't beg off tonight's meeting. If Myra annoyed him, for any reason at all, his response might be ugly; there was about a platoon of ex-girlfriends who could testify to that.

There was a black SUV parked in the Connelly driveway, he realized with a start.

There's either a hell of a lot of black SUVs in these parts or that guy gets around . . .

The porch light was on and by its glow Vic walked up a short sidewalk. The passenger door of the SUV opened and a tall man sporting a black suit and a blond buzz-cut got out and said, pleasantly, "I don't think you're in the right place, sport."

"Is this the Connelly house?"

"I can't say."

"Well, then, I'll just knock on the door and ask."

"Not a good idea." The man stood in front of Vic, blocking his way. "Real *bad* idea. I were you, I'd get back into my faggoty little car and go somewhere else."

"You're not me." Vic stepped to the side and continued

up the walk. The man grabbed his shoulder and Vic stumbled backward a few steps.

"Take off," the man said.

"Huh-uh." Vic started around the man.

He didn't see the punch that caught him flat on the left side of his face and sent him staggering onto the grass.

Then the familiar, happy surge of adrenaline. Vic put the buzz-cut down with two punches. The driver's-side door of the SUV opened and another dark-suited man was halfway out. Vic kicked the door into his midsection, took two steps forward, grabbed a handful of shirt and swung, and then *two* men lay sprawled on Myra Connelly's front lawn.

"What's going on here?"

The voice—thin, almost a squeak—had come from the porch. A man stood silhouetted against the light. Vic couldn't see him clearly, but he could tell, from his shape and posture, that the newcomer was no threat.

Vic gestured to the sprawled attackers. "These yours?"

"They are in my employ—"

"I hope you have good health benefits."

Vic elbowed past the man, who, he now saw, was pasty and wearing a ludicrously bad toupee.

Myra Connelly was standing in the doorway, behind the mesh of a screen.

"Hi," Vic said.

He heard the SUV's door open and close—

I won't give them the satisfaction of looking . . .

—and the engine start and move away.

"What happened?" Myra asked.

"Little disagreement. Nothing to get excited about."

Myra stood aside and said, "Come in."

The Connelly living room was about what Vic expected: clean, well-furnished, heavy on figurines and framed photographs. No fewer than eight of the pictures were of a little girl who had a lighter version of Myra's chestnut hair and a mole on her left cheek.

"Your daughter?" Vic asked.

"Jackie. She's visiting her grandma in Wichita."

"How old?"

"Seven in November."

"And her father?"

"Funny . . . Benny Fermin asked the same question not fifteen minutes ago. I'll tell you what I told him. Jackie's father hasn't been a factor for years and that closes the subject."

Touchy . . .

"I'm sorry I can't offer you a drink," Myra said. "I just used up my last two bottles of beer."

"No problem. Alcohol makes me stupid."

Vic and Myra sat at either end of the couch and Vic asked, "Who was your visitor, anyway?"

"Benedict Fermin."

"You say that like you expect me to recognize the name."

"He's the mayor. Of Hub City. Next to the Reverend Hatch, the biggest noise we yokels have."

"So the guys with him were . . ."

"A chauffeur and a bodyguard. Did you do something to them?"

"Does knocking them on their asses count?"

"You did that?"

"Afraid so."

"Ouch."

"That's about what they said. Only it was more like *ungf.*"

Myra laughed.

"Do you always entertain big shots?" Vic asked.

"I don't know if I'd consider Benny Fermin a big shot. 'Pipsqueak' might be a better word. And no, I don't always entertain him. In fact, this was the first time."

"What was the occasion."

"He was just in the neighborhood. So he said."

"The real reason?"

"At the risk of sounding like I lack girlish humility . . . I think he admires me. A lot. And not for my mind. In fact, I think he has designs on me."

"You don't reciprocate?"

"Wellll . . . if we were stranded on a desert island and he were the only man around . . ."

"Yes?"

"I'd probably butcher him and eat him."

Good sense of humor for a woman . . .

"You said there was something I can help you with, Vic?"

"Yeah. A fifty-something couple wrecked their car today. Some things don't make sense and I'm curious."

"Not a bad quality for a reporter. This couple have names?"

"Stabelhausen S-T-A-B-E-L-H-A-U-S-E-N."

"I know them. At least, I've met them a couple of times. He's some kind of scientist at the McFeeley plant."

"What kind of scientist?"

"I don't think I ever knew."

"The wife?"

"She was a stay-at-home mom till their last kid moved away. Now, I don't know what she does."

"Anything else of interest?"

"No, but . . . do you know how to Google?"

"What?"

"Google."

"No, but I'll bet you can teach me."

"That I can. I am, if I may say so myself, one hell of a Googler. Come with me."

CHAPTER SEVEN

A block away, Mayor Benedict Fermin was in the back seat of his SUV, hunched over a small radio receiver, twisting a dial. Lanny, his chauffeur, was in the driver's seat and Willie, his bodyguard, was in the shotgun seat, and both were swiveled around watching Fermin.

"Damn thing ain't working," Fermin muttered.

"Where'd you hide the microphone," Lanny asked.

"It's not a microphone, it's a *bug,* and I stuck it under the coffee table."

Suddenly, Myra's voice, distorted and tinny, erupted from the receiver: "*Do you know how to Google?*"

Vic Sage's voice: "*No, but I'll bet you can teach me.*"

"It's him," Lanny gasped. "That sunnabitch what sucker-punched me."

"Me, too," Willie said.

"Quiet!" Fermin shouted.

Myra's voice: "*. . . one hell of a Googler. Come with me.*"

"What's she mean, Google?" Fermin asked.

"Sounds dirty to me," Lanny said, winking at Willie.

"*Gotta* be dirty," Willie added, winking back.

"You think he's gonna . . . *meddle* with her?" Fermin asked.

"Sounds worse'n that." Willie said.

"Way worse," Lanny said. "We gonna wait for 'im, that sucker-punching sunnabitch? 'Cause I want another crack at 'im."

"No," Fermin said. "Take me back to the office."

Myra looked up from the computer keyboard at Vic, who was standing behind her, peering at the screen.

"You saw it," Myra said. "The mighty Google never lies. The Stabelhausens are as close to nonentities as you can get and still qualify as human. He's a chemist who got a Ph.D. and has spent the rest of his life underachieving and she's his wife."

"They don't *seem* like the kind of people who get intentionally run off the road," Vic said.

"Anybody else you want Googled?"

"No. Yes, come to think of it . . . my landlord. Aristotle Rodor."

"Quite a character, if what I've heard is true. Spell the last name."

Vic did and Myra tapped keys. A few seconds later, information began scrolling down the screen:

Aristotle Rodor was born on the campus of a small liberal arts college where his mother taught music and his father was a professor of classics and philosophy.

"Which explains the 'Aristotle,'" Myra said.

"I thought maybe his parents just hated him," Vic said.

The young Rodor was, by any reasonable criteria, a genius. He was playing Mozart on the piano by the time he reached his seventh birthday, but his passion lay in science. He was accepted at MIT at age fifteen and was awarded his doctorate in physics at age twenty-three. He taught at various institutions in the Midwest, including St. Louis University, until he was in his thirties, when he abandoned academia for the private sector. With a partner, a Wilson Steigler, who had an MBA from Harvard, Rodor created a research and development firm and for a while he did very well indeed. But the dot.com bust of the nineties sank the company and Steigler managed to get possession of most of its patents.

"Reading between the lines," Myra said. "your landlord probably salvaged just enough to live on. Funny that he's never tried to begin again. Broken spirit?"

"He doesn't *seem* broken," Vic said. "He's a cheerful old dude. A bit cranky, but underneath that, cheerful."

"And underneath the cheeriness . . . tears, maybe."

"Or just content with what he's got."

"If that's the case," Myra said, "he is a lucky man."

"Amen."

"Now, Mr. Sage, I want to Google *you.*"

"Go ahead. But you'll be wasting your time. Compared to me, the Stabelhausens are major celebrities."

"Maybe I'll do it later."

"Knock yourself out."

Myra stood, and they moved into her living room.

"You mentioned a Reverend Hatch. Does *he* have a story?"

"Big, fat one with sugar sprinkles. We can Google him if you want, but I can give you the broad outline. He runs the Tabernacle of the Highest Holiness, which is probably the biggest church in the state. Draws a lot of water around here. Big shot. Quite respected. They have a service tomorrow night, if you want to see Hatch first-hand."

"Would you come with me?"

"Some other time, maybe. My daughter's coming back tomorrow. But you won't have any trouble finding it. Take the East Bridge over the river, take the first left on the other side and you can't miss it. I mean that literally—you really can't miss it."

For a moment, Vic and Myra stood facing each other. Vic shifted his weight and said, "I'd better be getting back."

"It is getting late."

"Thanks for the Googling."

"We'll have to do it again sometime."

Is she asking to be asked . . . ?

Vic nodded to Myra and let himself out. Once, he glanced back and saw Myra standing silhouetted in the doorway.

By the time Mayor Fermin, Lanny, and Willie arrived at City Hall, the party was at its height, which meant that men were sprawled on the lawn, fighting in the streets, and vomiting in the gutters. They went up the mayor's pri-vate staircase in the rear of the building and entered his office.

There they found the mayor's aide, Les Kielty, wearing

his usual seersucker suit and standing next to a breath-taking woman. She was six feet tall, dressed in a loose, green garment that resembled an old-fashioned duster and, beneath it, green trousers. She wore what looked like black slippers on her feet—no socks, no stockings. Her hair was black and long, her eyes almond-shaped, her skin pale.

"Mayor Fermin, this's somebody I want you to meet. Her name's—"

"Shiva," the woman said. "I might be more properly called 'Kali' and perhaps one day I shall be, but that need not concern us now."

"You ain't from around here?" Fermin asked.

"I am not."

"So what brings you to these parts?"

Shiva smiled, dazzlingly. "I have heard that this Hub City is a place where I might exercise my art."

"And what art is that, little lady? You a painter? One'a them potters?"

"I hurt people. Occasionally, I kill them."

"That's a pretty good one," Fermin said. He began to laugh and then, abruptly, stopped.

"She kicked the crap outta some fellas downstairs," Kielty volunteered.

"Were they drunk?" Lanny asked.

"Not too much," Kielty said.

Lanny stepped close to Shiva. "You wanna kick the crap outta me, doll? Maybe I'll letcha if I can have a kiss fir—"

Shiva's hand went to the center of Lanny's chest and he dropped, his eyes wide, his mouth open and gasping.

Shiva looked down at him. "He is in extreme pain, which will last another minute. If he speaks of kissing me again, I will put him in pain that will only end with his death."

Shiva went to Willie, patted his cheek and then kicked the place she had patted. Willie joined Lanny on the floor, unconscious.

Shiva turned to Fermin. "Do you require further demonstration?"

"No, littl—no, miss, I do not. I gotta say I'm impressed."

Lanny got to his feet and leaned against the wall. "It stopped hurting," he whispered. "Just like that."

"It's just, I don't have no job for you right now," Fermin said to Shiva.

"Boss, what about the guy at the Connelly house?" Lanny asked. "That'd be a job for her."

Fermin rubbed his chin with his knuckles. "It might be at that."

CHAPTER EIGHT

Vic arrived at the station at eight-forty-five the next morning and looked for Myra's car. It was not in the lot. He went inside and amused himself by drinking rancid vending-machine coffee until Horace entered at nine.

"Heard about a fire on the police scanner," Horace said. "Farmer's hen house burned down. Go talk to him. Not the biggest story I've ever heard of but maybe you can find something to make it interesting."

Horace wrote directions on the back of a napkin and Vic went to see the farmer, who showed him around the charred and smoking remains of the hen house. Inside, a lot of poultry had burned to death and there was a nasty smell in the air. The farmer had no idea how the blaze started, but everything was insured so he wasn't too worried. If there was anything interesting here, Vic wasn't finding it. He realized that he should be taking notes, or maybe recording the interview, but he had neither paper nor tape machine, so he'd have to remember what was said. That was okay; his memory had always been good.

He returned to the station, parked, and asked the receptionist if Myra was around. She wasn't.

Vic tapped on Horace's door and went into the office.

The station manager looked up from behind his desk. "How'd it go?"

"Okay, I guess."

"Good. You'll be going on the air with it at about five-fifteen, which means you should be in the studio no later than ten after. You'll have a minute."

"Going on the air?"

"That *is* what we do around here. Go on the radio and tell people things. It's called 'broadcast journalism.'"

"I've never—"

Horace held up a flat palm. "Nothing to it. You talk. The microphone does the rest. You don't even have to yell."

"Should I write a script?"

"Do you *want* to write a script?"

"Well, I don't know . . ."

"Look, just be in the studio at ten after."

Horace turned his chair around and began reading something on a yellow legal pad. Vic left and got a cup of bad coffee and went into the parking lot. Myra's car still wasn't there. He went back into the station and considered writing his hen house story. But he had no idea what a radio script even looked like—his brief sojourn as a journalism major had not included any instruction on broadcasting—and he had not yet been assigned either a computer or a typewriter. Finally, he got a stack of the newspapers the station subscribed to and for the next couple of hours amused himself by learning what had happening in Springfield, St. Louis, Kansas City, Chicago, New York, Washington, Cape Girardeau, and Los Angeles, not to mention China, Israel, Lebanon, Australia, and a few other foreign locales.

At five-five, he went to a door marked *Studio*. A red sign above it read: *Keep Out. On the Air.*

Vic opened the door noiselessly and entered a room the size of a large, suburban garage. There was a large window at one end, behind which he could see a freckle-faced kid sitting behind a control board. Horace, wearing headphones, sat at a table facing the kid, reading from his legal pad and speaking into a thing that looked like a large, silver cigar. He motioned Vic to a chair beside him and, when Vic sat, handed him headphones. Vic put them on and heard Horace in stereo:

". . . weatherman says tomorrow will be cloudy, high in the eighties, low in the sixties, with rain likely. Now, let's hear from KWLM's newest star reporter, Vic Sage. Something get burned, Vic?"

Vic glanced at a big white-and-black clock above the window.

He said I'd have a minute . . .

For the next fifty seconds, he told the story of the hen house, not omitting details such as the exact number of hens that perished and the square footage of the house itself. The freckle-faced kid held up ten fingers and Vic said, "And that's it from me. Back to KWLM central."

Exactly one minute had passed.

Vic left the studio and sat on a sofa in the waiting

room. At five-thirty-one, Horace came out and Vic asked, "How'd I do?"

"You're sure you never did this kind of work before?"

"Positive."

"In that case, I'm almost impressed. *Almost.* I don't think the ghost of Edward R. Murrow is worrying, but you didn't stink up the airwaves."

"Edward R. Murrow?"

"Radio and TV guy. Before your time. As almost everything was."

"What would you have done if I *had* stunk up the airwaves?"

"I called the hen house guy and got the story over the phone. I'd've covered for you."

"You didn't trust me?"

"I hope the questions you ask during interviews aren't that dumb. Okay, as you've guessed, today was a kind of audition. Tomorrow you get some real reporting to do. Now get out of here."

CHAPTER NINE

Myra was waiting for Vic, standing next to the VW.

"Heard you were looking for me."

"With both eyes."

"You still planning to attend the Reverend Hatch's shindig tonight?"

"Yep."

"My evening's opened up. It turns out that my daughter is spending an extra day with my mother. They're going to see a circus, or something. Anyway, that leaves me free to go with you to Hatch's tabernacle tonight, if you still want me to."

"Yes, ma'am."

"We can grab what passes for dinner on the way. There are a couple of places that don't poison the food."

"Sounds good. Your wheels or mine?"

"Yours are cuter. So let's have you follow me home so I can drop mine off and then we'll go in yours."

. . .

Ninety minutes later, Vic joined a parade. There were at least a hundred vehicles of all kinds, from ancient, battered farm trucks to stretch limousines, lined up on a newly paved road leading to a concrete parking lot. Men in Day-Glo vests, waving red flashlights, were directing traffic. Following orders, Vic put the VW between two pickups and he and Myra joined the procession of men and women shuffling toward a long, low building with a high, pointed spire topped with a crucifix that shone in the last rays of the sun. Everyone was speaking in whispers, as though they were in a funeral home. There were three black Humvees parked near the entrance: not the modified, stateside Hummers sold to suburban families with a taste for motorized muscle, but the old-fashioned military monsters intended for use in combat zones. Vic noticed that the front fender of one was slightly dented and discolored with a scraping of white paint.

Vic and Myra and the others passed through an arched doorway flanked by two tall, ramrod-straight men standing at attention.

"Good evening and may the Lord bless you," they said over and over again, as though the words were recorded on a tape loop.

Vic and Myra sat on the end of a pew at the back of what looked like the most luxurious school auditorium in history. There was nothing austere about the Tabernacle of the Highest Holiness. Although the pews reminded Vic of those in the St. Prisca's of his youth, they were upholstered in thick pillows of scarlet fabric. The walls were also covered with scarlet cloth and the windows were of stained glass, pictures of Bible scenes that glowed in the sunlight behind them. Vic hadn't been inside a church for years, but he was pretty sure that this one wasn't typical.

Suddenly, organ music, just a bit less than deafening, swelled from hidden speakers. The lights dimmed and a single white spotlight illuminated a silver pulpit. A tall, cadaverously thin man dressed in a gray business suit stood behind it. He raised his arms and shouted, "Good evening and may the Lord bless you," and the congregation roared, "May the Lord bless you."

"That's Hatch," Myra whispered.

Hatch stepped from behind the pulpit and the auditorium lights brightened. He began to speak, pacing back and forth, occasionally waving a hand or fist, his voice, a resonant baritone, rising and falling. Vic found himself becoming spellbound. Hatch's presence, his charisma, were almost palpable. Vic knew that the preacher must have a microphone concealed somewhere on him, that the rich tones he was hearing were amplified and possibly enhanced, but that did not matter. He could not stop paying attention. It was as though he were listening to, not words, but music—the most entrancing music he'd ever heard.

". . . they talk of this eee-volution," Hatch was saying. "They tell us that our ancestors were animals living in the treetops and in the mud and—*listen to me now!*—slobbering over raw meat and picking bugs out of their fur and wallowing in their own filth. Without humanity. Without souls. Without any shred of decency. And do we believe them, those who speak of eee-volution? Do we think they speak the truth? Yes. Yes, we do. But they are not telling the whole truth! *Who* are descended from the beasts of the field and the jungle? Are the Chinese? Are the blacks? Are the Indians and the Eskimos and the Mexicans? *Yes and yes and yes.* Are we? Did your forefathers drag their knuckles around the ground and suck on their own tails? Well, I say no. I say no they did not. I say—*listen to me now*—that the Lord Himself brought us down from heaven and preserved us until it was time to do His bidding and subdue and conquer and triumph in His almighty name. Do you hear me now? Do you hear my words? Do you know I speak for him?"

The congregation roared *yes!*

A platoon of men who looked like the two at the front door passed among the crowd accepting donations. Myra put a five-dollar bill in the basket one of them extended to her; Vic dropped in a quarter.

There was some singing then, hymns that sounded like Broadway show tunes, done by a group Vic judged to be professional, and the service ended.

As Vic steered the VW onto the highway, forty minutes later, Myra asked, "What did you think?"

"He's impressive."

"Surely you don't *believe* that nonsense."

"Not one single word of it." Vic said. "Not now. But while he was talking . . . well, I can see how he's gained a following."

"So can I. He plays on people's fears of whatever's not familiar to them and then he assures them that they're so special they'll be okay. Did you recognize the source of his evolutionary theory?"

"He wasn't just making it up?"

"He may have been. But it's very close to something Heinrich Himmler said."

"Himmler was a Nazi, right?"

"One of Hitler's main men."

"Great minds run in the same direction and all that."

They rode for a few minutes in silence.

Then Vic asked, "You a churchgoer?"

"Sometimes. I guess I'm a believer, but I'm not always sure in what. I'm solid with the Sermon on the Mount. Also the First Amendment. Anything else is negotiable."

"You'll be at work tomorrow?"

"Huh-uh. I'm taking a personal day."

"Your daughter's return?"

"Yeah. I haven't seen her in two weeks."

"That's a long time for you?"

"An eternity, feels like." Myra looked down at her lap and chuckled. "I know, I know . . . I'm singing the song of the single mom."

"Not a *bad* song."

"But getting just a tad clichéd."

Vic let Myra out in front of her house, said he'd see her soon, and went home.

CHAPTER TEN

The phone was ringing when Myra let herself into her house. She picked it up and heard her mother, complaining that she had been calling "all dern evening" and then delivering her news: Jackie would be arriving in Hub City an hour later than the original hour because that train had been *canceled* and she would be taking *another* train and did Myra *understand* and was Myra *sure* a little girl would be all right riding a train by herself?

"She'll be getting on at your end and I'll be waiting for her at mine," Myra said. "What could go wrong?"

A block away, in the driver's seat of a black SUV, Benedict Fermin was hunched over a radio receiver, listening. He'd seen *her* get out of *his* car and now, trembling with anger, he was overhearing her conversation with her mother.

At nine the next morning, Vic looked for Myra's car in the KWLM lot and then remembered that today Myra was picking up her daughter. Vic didn't know how he felt about Myra having a daughter . . . his experience with girlfriends' children had been pretty dismal.

But she wasn't his girlfriend. Of course she wasn't.

Horace was waiting for him inside. "Today, you get something more interesting than a hen house."

"Hard to believe there *is* such a thing."

"Trust me, there is. Rumor has it that City Hall's being rented out to partiers on weekday nights. I want you to go down there, have a look around, maybe talk to a clerk or two, assuming there are any left. Take a couple of hours and be back in time to go on the air at about five-fifteen."

"What if I don't find anything?"

"Then report the rumor and why you believe it isn't true."

"Okay, see you in a few hours."

"One more thing. What's your cell phone number, in case I need you earlier?"

"I am not absolutely sure what a cell phone is. One of those little things people walk around holding to their cheeks?"

"You *are* aware, Mr. Sage, that this is the twenty-first century?"

"No! Really? When'd *that* happen?"

Horace sighed, took a small telephone from a desk drawer, and handed it to Vic. "Take this one. It used to be Myra's, before she got one that takes pictures."

For the next few minutes, Horace tutored Vic in the care and management of cellular telephones, and then Vic went to City Hall.

•   •   •

Vic could see that the center of Hub City's municipal government had been, once, perhaps a hundred years ago, a handsome building, with six tall columns flanking the front entrance, marble steps, white stone walls. There was a half-acre of lawn in front of it, and a statue of a man on horseback holding a sword aloft, probably a Civil War hero. But there was no grass, at least no *green* grass, and the lawn was littered with bottles and cans. Graffiti was scrawled on the columns and walls, and the sidewalks were webbed with cracks.

Vic parked the VW behind one of the ubiquitous black SUVs and went up the walk, stepping over the cracks and litter. Halfway up the steps he met Mayor Benedict Fermin coming down them. Fermin stopped as though he had run into a wall and stared, wide-eyed, at Vic.

Vic stood in front of him. "You're Mayor Fermin? I'd like to ask you a few questions—"

"Go to hell!" Fermin shouted. "You son of a bitch, you just go to hell!"

Vic watched Fermin stumble down the rest of the steps and hurry in the direction of the SUV.

What's bunching his *underwear? He still pissed about the other night . . .?*

Although there was no air-conditioning, and probably had never been any, the inside of City Hall was cool. The only light came from the dirty windows, but it was enough for Vic to see that the floor and furniture were filthy.

"Hello," he called, and the word echoed.

Eleven o'clock on a Tuesday morning and nobody's working . . . what is wrong with this picture . . . ?

He walked through the building, knocking on doors, sticking his head into empty offices, asking if anyone could hear him. Apparently, there was no one to answer him. He walked outside, and around to where a flight of steps led to a second-floor door. He went to it and, when he was close to it, he could read faded lettering, stenciled on the wood years ago: *Office of the Mayor.* After knocking and waiting a full minute for someone to answer, Vic entered. The room was dusty and ill-furnished. There was a battered wooden desk, a couch with stuffing bloating from the seams, two wooden file cabinets and . . . nothing else.

His Honor doesn't believe in surrounding himself with amenities . . .

Vic left City Hall and wandered the area until he came upon a ragged man sucking something pale and yellow from a bottle.

"What's happening with City Hall? Is it always deserted?"

"Pretty much, except for party nights."

"Who attends these parties?"

"Anybody's got the twenty bucks admission."

"Who runs them?"

"Fermin, I guess. Say, you don't have an extra dollar?"

Vic gave him a five and returned to the VW, now alone in front of City Hall. He went to the diner where he had had his first Hub City meal, ate greasy meat, and drove back to the station.

In his cubicle, he heard the opening notes of "Mary

Had a Little Lamb." He looked around: no radio or music player of any kind. The melody sounded again, and again, and again. Finally, he realized that it was coming from his own pocket—specifically, from the cell phone Horace had given him.

He pulled out the gadget, remembered to press a button, put it to his face, and said, "Hello."

Myra's voice: "Vic? That you?"

"Myra! What's up?"

"Something terrible. I need your help."

"Sure, anything I can do . . ."

"Can you meet me tonight? At . . ." She hesitated, and Vic throught he heard someone else speaking. Then: "At the foot of Bronte Street, the old pier. You know where that is?"

"I'll find it."

"Make it ten o'clock."

"Okay. Ten it is. Myra, can you give me some idea of what's going on?"

"I'm sorry, Vic."

"Myra . . ." But he was talking to nobody. He put the phone back into his pocket, got coffee, read some papers, and at five went into the studio and took his place beside Horace. When the freckle-faced kid pointed to him, Vic talked for a minute about the empty City Hall and the abundant signs of rough partying. At the end of a minute, he rose, nodded to Horace and the kid, and left the station.

CHAPTER ELEVEN

Shiva entered Benedict Fermin's office without knocking and found the mayor behind his desk, hunched over an open magazine. When she got closer, she noticed that it was a catalog of spyware.

"I am bored," she said.

"Fella said he seen you in the park this morning, dancing."

"I was performing a *kata*."

"And that is?"

"Something you would not understand. I am bored."

"You said that."

"You made no reply."

"Well, you're in luck. I'll have a little job for you later, probably after dark. Lanny and Willie are out on an errand, and soon's they get back you can go to work."

"I do not need Lanny and Willie."

"'Course you don't. But they gotta do their jobs 'fore

you can do yours. If you could come back at around six, that'd be good."

Shiva pivoted on her heel and strode out.

At nine-fifty-five, Vic was wishing he'd talked Myra into meeting somewhere inside, preferably with a fire. The weather had turned nasty. A cold rain was pelting Hub City and a thin fog rose from the river. The wind had shifted, bringing with it the stench from the plant.

There had once been streetlights at the foot of Bronte Street, and shops, and homes. But the lamps had long ago been smashed by merrymakers, and the shops were empty, the homes deserted. The area was dark, and quiet except for the sound of the rain.

Wishing he had a raincoat, or at least a hat, Vic got out of the VW and peered into the gloom. He saw nothing of Myra, or any other living being, but there was a black SUV parked down the block.

"Hello!" he called. "Anybody here?"

Two of the SUV's doors opened and Vic was pretty sure three people got out. They moved toward him and he saw that he had been right; there were three of them, two men and a very tall woman. Vic recognized the men: the two losers he'd decked on the Connelly front lawn.

"Know who we are?" one of the men asked.

"I don't think I got your names, but I do recognize the bruises I left on you. Where's Myra Connelly?"

"Damn," the man said. "I knew we forgot to bring something. But we brung something else you'll like a whole lot. What she's gonna do is kick your ass."

The men stepped back, leaving Vic facing the woman.

"Lady," Vic said. "I have no idea who you are, and I really don't care. My advice is, hike on out of here."

Even in the darkness, Vic could see that her smile was exceptional. "And if I choose to stay?"

"I don't want to hurt you."

"But perhaps I *do* want to hurt *you*."

"Never happen."

"Did that hurt?" the woman asked, and suddenly Vic was aware of a sting on his right cheek and realized that she had slapped him.

"Not much," he said.

"That?" she asked, and Vic's belly was hurting.

"Try again," Vic said, and this time he saw the kick coming, but not before the woman's bare heel caught him on the jaw and dropped him.

He got to his knees, and then he managed to stand and again face the woman.

"I am called Lady Shiva," she said. "What are you called?"

"Charles Victor Szasz," he said, and wondered why.

"Well, Charles Victor Szasz, I have been asked to kill you. I think it would be amusing to do so."

"Never happen," Vic said, and knew he was already fighting for his life.

She slapped him again, hard, and he swung his left fist at her head. She kicked him in the chest and he staggered backward and charged forward and was kicked again. Time stopped and the world became a blur. He was conscious of only one imperative: survive. To do that, to do just that simple thing, he would have to defeat this person who was punching and kicking him. He could not strike her back. He flailed and swung and charged with his shoulders hunched and his head down and she was never where she should be. Then, he felt his fist connect with flesh and he was spinning and falling.

He could not get up.

But he had to, and so he did, and was knocked down, and he got up and was knocked down and got up.

"We'll take it from here," a man said.

"Yeah, we wanna finish it," another man said. "We owe the bastard."

Vic felt himself being grabbed under the arms, held upright, and then something happened, a burst of whiteness—lightning?—and he saw one of the losers grinning at him, raising a lead pipe over his head, and then darkness and more pain and the sound of bones cracking.

"You will stop now," Lady Shiva said.

"Hell," Lanny said, "we're just getting started."

"He ain't dead yet, I don't think," Willie said. "And even if he is, we can still bust him up."

Lady Shiva stepped forward and kicked and struck with the middle knuckle of her left hand.

Lanny and Willie were dead.

CHAPTER TWELVE

Vic realized that he was not dead because he was capable of realizing anything at all, and besides, there was no long tunnel with a circle of light at the end and no phantom presences whispering instructions. No pearly gates or people with wings and halos either, nor any red dudes with horns and pitchforks. He had one other reason to know he was alive: He hurt.

But *how* alive was he? Ah. Good question. Not very, he thought, during those brief intervals when he *could* think.

What else was there to be aware of? Location? He had no idea where he was, only that he wasn't lying in the rain on a filthy Hub City street. At least, he was pretty sure he wasn't because he felt warmth, and the rain had been cold. Okay, locale remained a mystery. How about companionship, then? People, in the form of shadows and distant voices, were intermittently hovering over him, but he did not know who they were. Friends or foes? Friends, probably, because they weren't harming him, hadn't killed him. Okay, companionship remained a question mark, but not a menacing one.

And what was *this*? A new sensation! Something warm and viscous being spooned into his mouth. Might we be tasting soup? Might this be some sort of wonderful *bean* soup? And what is happening with our limbs? They're tingling, and quite pleasantly so. Ah. Life is good.

Dark. Light. Dark. And soup. Vic's existence.

Until he opened his eyes and was looking at a gaping maw with long, sharp teeth. He closed them, because a gaping maw with long, sharp teeth was not pleasant to see. Not particularly alarming, but not pleasant.

Dark.

And light.

And the gaping maw with long, sharp teeth, which, he now saw, was really a window with icicles along its upper edge. He looked down at his own body. He was lying on a narrow, low bed and covered with a heavy quilt. The room around him seemed to be a cabin, with rough board walls and an unadorned wooden floor. There was a big stone fireplace at one end with a stack of logs blazing in it, and a kitchen sink and some cabinets at the other. The only other furnishings were a table, two chairs, and a floor-to-ceiling bookcase filled with hardcovers. There were two doors, one leading to the outdoors and the other opening on what was obviously another room.

Vic tried to sit up and gasped with pain that seemed to radiate from his ribs. He waited a moment and tried again, this time ready for the pain and ignoring it.

He sat with his back against the headboard, gathering his strength, and then swung his legs to the floor.

"They aren't broken," someone said. "Your legs, I mean."

Vic turned toward the voice. A man in a wheelchair was in the doorway to the other room. He was dressed in a flannel jacket, flannel pants, and work boots. His hair was gray, long, and tidy, and he sported a full beard. He was smiling.

"For some reason, they left your legs alone," he said. He wheeled himself forward. "But they did a real number on the rest of you. Ribs, both arms, sternum . . . and you don't even want to know about your skull. But you're better than you were and you'll get better still. If you want to, you can make a full recovery."

"If I *want* to?"

"Yep, if you want to. I think you do."

"You're a doctor?"

"Not officially. I didn't go to medical school. I don't have a piece of paper. But I've picked up a few things here and there." He stuck out his hand. "I'm Richard."

Vic shook the hand. "Vic Sage."

"Glad to finally hear your name. Shiva didn't know what it was, but she had the impression that the one on your driver's license wasn't accurate."

"Shiva's the woman I fought?"

"And who saved your life."

"She beat me senseless and she didn't know my name?"

"Shiva's not big on things she considers unimportant. Including names."

"You said she saved my life?"

"That's my guess. Shiva's also not big on telling stories. But extrapolating from what she *did* say . . . a couple of guys were beating you to death with pipes. So she killed them."

"*Killed* them?"

"I can't be sure, but . . . knowing Shiva, yeah, she killed them."

"Why? Weren't they her . . . I don't know the word—*colleagues*?"

"*No*body is Shiva's colleague."

"But she killed them to save me. Why?"

"That she *did* tell me. She said she liked the way you kept getting up after you couldn't get up."

"Is that supposed to make sense?"

"To Shiva, it probably does."

"She brought me here?"

"In that cute little car. Which, by the way, is outside getting snowed on. Sorry about that. I don't have a garage."

"And you doctored me?"

"Not much. Shiva did most of the doctoring. If there's anything she's better at than killing people, it's mending them. She would have taken you to the nearest hospital, but she figured you might not survive there. Seems you made the local authorities a bit irate."

Richard wheeled himself to the fire and stirred it with a poker.

"Is this Shiva here?" Vic asked.

"Took off yesterday," Richard said. "As soon as she was sure you'd be okay."

"*Will* I be okay?"

"According to Shiva, you will. If you want to."

"There's that 'want to' again."

"You'll likely be hearing it a lot in the coming months." Richard wheeled himself back to Vic's bedside. "My advice is, learn to love it."

"What's happening in the coming months?"

"Here comes another 'want to.' If you *want* me to, I'll teach you how to fight. Shiva seems to think it's a good idea."

"I already know how to fight."

"No kidding. Want me to tell you how badly Shiva beat you before the guys with the lead pipes went to work?"

Vic stared at the icy window for a long moment and said, "Okay, point taken. But—no offense—how can *you* teach fighting?"

"Oh, the wheelchair, you mean. Well, trust me, I'll manage. We'll get started in . . . oh, three days. After you're used to being out of bed and awake."

"What do you teach? Some kind of Jackie Chan stuff? Karate, Kung Fu, something like that?"

"First," Richard replied, "I'll teach you to breathe. Then to stand up. Then to bend over. Then to eat. Then to walk. Then to relax. Then how to enter a state beyond thought. Then we may get to the Jackie Chan stuff."

CHAPTER **THIRTEEN**

Vic left the cabin a day later, moving shakily on legs he could not trust. Outside, he leaned against the cabin wall and gasped; the air was cold enough to sting his skin and make his lungs ache. He looked around: The cabin was in a valley surrounded by mountain peaks. Snow covered everything, including the Volkswagen, which was a white mound Vic could barely identify. The world was bleak and beautiful.

"Where are we?" Vic asked. "What country?"

From the open doorway, Richard said, "The United States. Pennsylvania. Mountains, as you can see."

Vic took three steps forward, the snow crunching under his shoes, and swayed.

"Go ahead," Richard said. "You won't fall. Unless you want to."

Vic walked to the VW, paused, and returned to the cabin.

"How do you feel? Richard asked.

"Woozy."

"No, how do you *really* feel? Think before you answer."

"I guess . . . glad to be alive."

"That's a start."

Vic thought that Richard had been kidding when he'd said the first lessons would be how to breathe. But he hadn't. Breathing *was* the first thing Richard taught, for eight hours a day, for an entire week.

"Okay, you've got the basics," Richard said. "The rest is practice. Let's do some more."

"Let's not," Vic said, his patience exhausted. "What's this deep breathing got to do with combat?"

"Everything," Richard said, with no trace of his usual affability. His voice was quiet and gravely commanding. "The punching and kicking—that's easy, and only of limited use. The good stuff comes with learning to control your body's systems, how to control your emotions. Now—let's do some more."

The next six weeks were devoted to what Vic guessed was some form of yoga. At Richard's prompting, he placed himself near the fireplace and twisted his body into shapes that, at first, hurt like hell and were eventually deeply comforting.

Outside, the wind howled and snow and sleet pelted the Earth as Richard's calm, relentless instruction continued. At first, Richard began each day with an announcement: "Today is our fifth day together . . ." And sixth day, and fortieth and on and on, until, during one yoga session, Vic suddenly realized that Richard had been omitting the announcements—for how long?—and questioned Richard about them.

"You don't need it anymore," Richard said.

But why had he ever needed it, whatever "it" was?

Some of Richard's teachings were given in front of the fire and dealt with Vic's physiology, his sympathetic and parasympathetic nervous systems and the interactions between his mind and body. He learned to slow his respiration and heart rate, how to create mental images that would warm him.

There were only two meals most days, the first shortly after Vic arose, the second when the winter sun was overhead. Vic could not always identify what he was eating: grains, he guessed, and some kind of dried vegetable and bean concoction that Richard cooked in a small cauldron hung over the fire. Whatever it was, it was a long way from Vic's previous diet of fast food and grease, and it tasted okay. Some days, they ate a third meal at sundown, and others, they did not eat at all.

"It's a good idea to put some regularity in life," Richard explained, "and a good idea not to put in too much."

Vic bathed daily in a tub of water, which was filled from an outdoor pump and was, necessarily, cold. He got used to it.

There was an outhouse. He got used to that, too.

They went to bed each night shortly after the world outside had darkened. Although he seldom left the cabin, and did nothing he would identify as hard labor, Vic was always exhausted.

His beard grew long and straggly, as did his hair. There was no mirror in the cabin, nor any need for one, but Vic imagined that he looked like some wild and feral aborigine.

He had become so absorbed in what Richard was teaching that he all but forgot that he was supposed to be learning martial arts; each new posture, each new technique, seemed to be its own very adequate reason for being, not a means to another end. Then, one day when the snow was partially melted, leaving splotches of brown around the cabin, Richard said that they'd be moving the class outside.

"Time you got some training wheels for asskicking."

The air was cold, but the bright sun tempered it a bit. Vic found himself glad to be outdoors.

"Okay," Richard said, "power stance."

Vic assumed the posture Richard had taught him the first week, upright, limber, almost totally relaxed—"the way everybody ought to stand all the time," Richard said.

Then Richard guided Vic through a series of dancelike movements that seemed distantly related to blocking and punching and kicking.

"This is stuff you have to learn so you can forget it," Richard said.

"That's enigmatic enough," Vic said.

"Eventually, it won't be. If you progress."

"You sound doubtful."

"Only because nothing is certain."

That night, they had one of their rare third meals, a fresh green salad with bits of some whitish-brown stuff scattered throughout it, topped with a pungent dressing, and a thick vegetable curry loaded with spices.

"By now," Richard said after they were done eating, "something's nagging at you. Bothering you. But maybe you can't identify what it is. Don't say anything yet. Look within."

Vic stared into the fire and waited until he felt like speaking. "Yes. Something is nagging at me. 'Nagging' is exactly the right word."

"But you don't know what."

"No, I don't."

"Learn to heed that nagging. Mostly, you won't notice it unless you train yourself to. That's something that's yours to do, that training. I can only make you aware of the need for it, though what I taught earlier about meditation might help."

"Are we talking about some kind of intuition?"

"You can call it that and I won't complain. But what it really is is your subconscious processing information that doesn't necessarily reach your awareness. *Listen* to the nagging. Listen to what it's telling you."

"You don't need the wheelchair," Vic said suddenly.

"Right," Richard said, standing and stretching. "How'd you get to that?"

"It just came to me."

"From where?"

"The meal. Where did the food come from, the spices, the fresh greens? Where has the food been coming from the whole time I've been here? Where has the chopped wood been coming from? Why are there no wheel tracks leading to and from the outhouse? Dammit, I've known all along that you didn't need the chair—I must have!"

"But you chose to believe the most superficial impressions because that's your habit and that's what's easiest."

"I guess."

"Guess?"

"Okay, I know. Can I ask why?"

"Sure," Richard said, "but you know that, too. Think about your state of mind when you came out of the coma. Think about the way the world has taught you to protect yourself."

"I don't get it."

"Sleep on it. We'll talk more in the morning."

As they were finishing a breakfast of oatmeal, which Vic had once despised and now found tasty enough, and which had never before been breakfast in the cabin, Vic said, "It was my ego."

"Yes," Richard said. "Go on."

"If I'd thought you weren't handicapped . . ."

"That a man uses a wheelchair doesn't mean he's handicapped—"

"Okay, granted, but let me get through this. You in a wheelchair weren't a threat to me. I didn't have to prove myself by beating you. So I could hear what you had to say without putting up all kinds of psychological barriers."

Richard clapped his hands. "Bravo. You pretty much got it."

"I'm assuming you can do the stuff Shiva does."

"Yes. Some of it not as well, some of it better."

"Will you show me?"

Richard grinned. "Want me to break some boards with my hand?"

"Sure, yes, I'd like to see that."

"Okay, let's go outside."

The morning was a copy of the previous one, except that the sun was a bit warmer and the ground a bit more bare. Richard led Vic around to the back of the cabin where a pile of sawed logs and a few old boards were stacked against the wall beneath a canopy.

Richard picked up one of the boards. "I haven't done this in years. Hope I still remember how."

He threw the board up and as it descended broke it in two with his fist. "Like riding a bicycle, only riding a bicycle is more useful."

He threw another board up and splintered it with a kick. Then he threw four boards high overhead and when they were about seven feet from the ground leaped high and shattered them all with punches and kicks.

Vic whistled appreciatively. "Can I learn to do that?"

"I guess you could, if you put your mind to it," Richard said. "But you have to understand that what I just did wasn't martial arts or much of anything else except showing off. Why devote months, maybe years, to learning how to show off? You're a little old to be impressing girls on the playground."

"Then how come you're so good at it?"

"I once liked to show off. Sue me."

"Can Shiva do that stuff?"

"With her eyes closed, probably. Okay, enough Q and A. More later, if you want. For now, let's train."

The work Vic did that day was different, more overtly

physical, more about using his body as a weapon. But Vic was less tired when he sat down to the noon meal than he had been when he had trained inside the cabin and moved very little.

"More questions?" Richard asked.

"Okay, here's one. Why haven't I heard of you? Or Shiva? Why aren't you famous, like Jackie Chan and Bruce Lee?"

"Not our trip. Fame takes time and effort. We'd rather devote ourselves to other things."

"Such as?"

"Getting better at what we do. Understanding it better. In my case, just being. Just appreciating breathing."

"You're saying that the guys in the movies aren't as good as Shiva and you?"

"Not at all. Depends on how you define 'good.' But it's apples and oranges . . . we don't do what they do."

"What you do is . . . what? More pure?"

"I don't judge. You ought to work on that, too."

"Not judging?"

"In my judgment," Richard intoned, "you are overly judgemental." And in a normal voice: "That was a joke, Vic."

"Thanks for the bulletin. One more question."

"You are *big* on the question. Okay, just one."

"From what I've read and seen in movies, guys like you want to be called 'master' and there's a lot of bowing and scraping . . ."

"You do not yet realize that I have earned the right to be called 'master.' That time will come."

"When it does?"

"You'll say whatever's appropriate."

CHAPTER FOURTEEN

They went outside, and Richard suggested that Vic might want to try running. He could probably run a mile without much difficulty.

"I expected this kind of thing to come first—running, calisthenics."

"What would be the point in you huffing and puffing when you did not yet know how to breathe?"

Vic ran. The path was muddy and his boot soles sucked at the ground, but he was able to maintain a brisk pace until he came to the end of the path and saw, down a steep flight of steps carved into the mountainside, a small village—just a single paved street bordered by a dozen stores and houses.

Civilization . . .!

Vic considered going down and looking, maybe speaking to someone other than Richard for the first time in . . . how many months? He really did not know. But then he remembered that he hadn't shaved or cut his hair in . . .

how many months? And he hadn't worn machine-washed clothes in . . . how many months? Looking like he did, he might scare small children and send grandpas scurrying for their shotguns.

Maybe next time . . .

The run back was harder because now the path had a slight upward slant. But no problem. Vic had often seen men jogging in parks and city streets, and despised them—silly sissies trying to be something they were not. Like some of the bullies at St. Prisca's, their masculinity was a brittle shell filled with mush. He had needed neither running shoes nor gymnasiums. His body was hard and powerful because he did honest, brutal, physical labor. But here, on a muddy slope, under a clear blue sky, he understood why at least some of the joggers did what they did: It was enjoyable. Richard was standing in the cabin door when Vic returned. "You go into town?"

"Didn't seem like a good idea."

"Probably wouldn't be. How'd the run go?"

"Great. I had fun."

"Glad to hear it."

The training resumed, and now included a daily run. Once, Vic saw a man and a woman, young, teenagers maybe, hiking up the steps from the town. He grinned and waved and they waved back.

Maybe I don't look so bad . . .

The earth changed. Trees sprouted leaves, grass thickened and greened. Birds flew and small animals appeared from behind logs and along the path, and occasionally Vic saw a deer.

Then, in the distance, Vic began to hear shots.

"Hunters," Richard explained.

"What do you think of them?"

"I don't have an opinion. As long as they don't shoot at *me,* I don't care what they do."

"What if they *do* shoot at you. Accidentally, say."

"I deal with it as the situation dictates."

Vic belatedly realized that Richard almost never issued a direct order; rather, he suggested. One day, he *suggested* that perhaps it was time to establish a routine for Vic.

"I'm doing something I don't like to do and maybe I shouldn't," Richard said. "I'm assuming that eventually you'll want to return to Hub City and you won't really be ready to."

"Why not?"

"If you reach your full potential, you won't have the need for this quest of yours and you'll certainly not need to fight."

"Quest?" Vic asked.

"Your real identity. Your parents."

"How do you know about that?"

"You talked while you were in the coma. At length. About your childhood and your curiosity and all the fights you've been in . . . You sure had a lot to prove. Oh, and a woman, Myra."

"I talked about Myra?"

"Admiringly. None of it should be important to you. But I suspect you have to live a bit more or a lot more before you understand what I'm talking about. And to do that . . . I guess I should teach you what Shiva wants you to learn."

The routine was established: up at dawn. Ten-mile

run—mostly away from the road, up the mountain trails. Breakfast. Yoga. Strength training. Lunch. Yoga. Sitting quietly and attending to breathing. And finally, for two hours just before sunset, martial arts. Then a small meal, sometimes only an apple, and bed.

"What exactly are we doing?" Vic once asked. "Karate, Tai Kwan Do, Judo, what?"

"It doesn't have a name because we've never bothered to give it one," Richard answered. "It's mostly based in Tai Chi. There's a tiny bit of Jeet Kune Do. Shiva's contribution. She's a closet Bruce Lee fan."

"Who's this 'we'? You and Shiva. Anyone else?"

"A man named Bruce."

"This Bruce have a last name?"

"I'm sure he does."

"It's not 'Lee,' is it?"

"Let's get back to work," Richard said, and that ended the conversation.

Vic met "Bruce" a week later. He was returning from his morning run and saw a car parked next to the VW. Vic couldn't identify the make of the new vehicle, but it looked both expensive and odd. It was a small, sleek coupe, sporty, with huge, truck-size tires, which, Vic realized, would be necessary to negotiate the bad road up here from the town. And there was a surfboard strapped to its roof. How far was the nearest ocean? A couple of hundred miles? Did people surf in rivers?

In the clearing behind the cabin, Vic saw Richard and a stranger, a tall, powerfully built man with dark hair. He was dressed in what looked like resort clothing until Vic noticed how the shirt and trousers left him totally unencumbered, with total freedom of movement. This was not resort wear; it was combat clothing.

"This is my friend," Richard said to Vic. "We're sparring."

The stranger nodded to Vic and turned to Richard. They began . . . what? Sparring, Richard had said. But what kind of sparring *was* this? For minutes at a time, neither man seemed to move. Then there would be a flurry of motion, lasting less than a second, and the stranger would fall. Gradually, Vic realized that he was witnessing a demonstration few men were ever privileged to see: two absolute masters performing subtly and with such enormous skill that it wasn't even visible.

That both were masters was obvious; that Richard's mastery was greater was also obvious. He never fell.

Finally, Richard told the stranger, "You've improved."

"Thank you," the stranger said, bowing slightly. "Now, do you mind if we spend a few minutes doing the other stuff?"

"The theatrics? All right. For a few minutes."

What came next reminded Vic of the times he had snuck into a movie late at night, usually in a marginal neighborhood, and watched what he called Kung Fu flicks. These, he considered to be his secret vice. Lots of leaping and spinning and high-kicking and the occasional "*yawp*" or "*heee-yah!*" But Richard and the stranger weren't play-acting. The blows and kicks were real and when they stopped, an hour later, the stranger was leaking real blood.

The stranger used the pump and basin to clean himself,

got an unbloodied shirt from his car, and joined Vic and Richard in the cabin.

"You surf?" Vic asked the stranger.

"You noticed the board. Well, yeah, I can surf and I have. But not recently. I've been letting people assume that I'm lost. Very, very lost."

"It doesn't hurt my reputation in the area to have a somewhat daffy city boy visit," Richard said. "Confirms local suspicion that I'm eccentric, but harmless."

"*Are* you harmless?" the stranger asked, smiling.

"Absolutely," Richard replied. "Wasn't always, but am now. Why don't you guys go do something manly. Beat each other senseless and thus establish a male bond like they do in the movies. Or something else. I'm gonna be busy for an hour or two."

"Want to run?" the stranger asked Vic.

"I guess I could."

"Want to take the north trail?"

"You've been here before?"

"Often."

"North is fine," Vic said and began to run.

They ran side by side except where the path was too narrow to accommodate two bodies abreast; in those places, the stranger slowed to let Vic pass him.

They came to the top of the trail and began to jog along a flat ridge.

"Known Richard long?" Vic asked.

"Long enough."

"And how long is that?"

"He said you'd have questions."

"So he set up this little meeting?"

"He suggested that I might have advice for you."

"He never does anything other than suggest, does he?"

"No. I think that's because he's never a hundred percent certain that he's right. But I don't know anyone who's right more often than he is."

They left the ridge and began to descend toward a valley on the far side. The trail was steep and Vic often found himself sliding on loose dirt. Somehow, the stranger kept his footing.

"So what's this advice?" Vic asked.

The stranger's tone was jovial; he was bantering. "Richard didn't say. He just indicated that there might be some."

Vic chuckled. "Okay, want to take a shot at guessing what it might be?"

"I can't say too much without revealing what I don't want you to know," the stranger said, and there was no joviality in his voice. "Richard says he doesn't think there's any danger, but I have to go with my own instincts here, even though I'm probably wrong."

"Look," Vic began, "I don't want you t—"

The stranger continued as though Vic had not spoken. "Richard thinks you may be about to embark on my path. He thinks it's a bad idea, for both of us. It has to do with quests, and refusing to relinquish the past. With trying to symbolically avenge an atrocity that can't really be avenged. It's lonely and maybe it's ultimately futile. But it's my life. Maybe it doesn't have to be yours."

The stranger sped up and passed Vic.

"I'm not sure what the hell you're talking about." Vic

yelled, and increased his pace until he was again next to the stranger.

"Me?" the stranger said, reverting to joviality. "I'm not talking about anything. I'm just blathering."

"Did Richard teach you how to fight?"

"No. That I learned on another mountain, in another country, from someone very different from Richard. But I wish he'd been my teacher. He's the best in the world, and I don't mean just as a martial artist."

"Who's second best."

"Probably either Shiva or me. I hope I never have to find out."

They turned and began to run back toward the cabin. During the whole of the hour it took them to arrive there, the stranger told Vic a long, absolutely hilarious story about a wool-eating contest and a moth from St. Louis. He delivered the punch line just as they reached the door of the cabin and Vic leaned against the wall, laughing.

It was late afternoon, not too early for the evening meal. Richard served them the same bean soup that Vic had ingested when he first awoke from the coma. After they'd eaten, the stranger announced that it was time for him to get lost again and the three of them walked to his weird automobile. As the stranger was lowering himself into the driver's seat, he looked at Vic and said, "You might want to get in touch with me. Especially if Richard is right about your embarking on my path, and I think he might be."

"I have no idea what your 'path' is," Vic protested. "I have no idea what you're talking about."

"If it happens, you'll know it. That's when you'll want

my input. You can reach me by computer. Go to a website devoted to the Japanese game Go. The site's called 'Girls on the Go Go.'"

"You're kidding."

"No. It's somebody's idea of cute. Then type in 'Busda kanel tra home tra home.'" The stranger spelled out the words.

"What language is that?" Vic asked.

"None."

"What's it mean?"

The stranger shrugged and said, "From now on, I'll be looking over your shoulder. You won't know it, but I will."

"Was that a threat?" Vic asked Richard as they watched the stranger drive away.

"No. Just a statement. Or maybe a promise of help."

That night, Vic did something he hadn't done in months, not since he'd awakened in the cabin. He dreamed the Dream. It began as it always had: a tall man in a raincoat and a hat was carrying a baby. He was the baby. Then—in a sudden burst of light the baby could see that the man's face wasn't a face, just an oval of pure white. Now, though, the Dream changed: He became the man, looking down at the baby, and the baby had no face, just an oval of pure white . . .

He awoke. He was lying on the cot looking through the window at distant peaks just beginning to be edged with pink. It would be . . . what?—maybe five in the morning, maybe earlier. He dressed and went outside, expecting to be alone in the clearing. But Richard was sitting cross-legged on the ground, staring at the mountains.

"Gonna be beautiful," Richard said. "I guess this is a day of decision for you."

"How so?" Vic asked.

"Well, I've done as Shiva asked. I've taught you all I can unless you're willing to commit to a life I don't think you're prepared to lead, at least not yet. I have a sense that you know that and you also know you have to decide— stay here or go back to Hub City."

"There have to be more choices."

"Of course there are. But are you willing to consider them? Think before answering."

Vic spent several minutes watching the sun emerge from the mountain, feeling the chilly air warm on his skin. "Okay," he said finally. "I guess you're right."

"So what's it gonna be? Here or Hub City?"

"Hub City."

"Doesn't surprise me. How soon you wanna get going?"

"Is today a possibility?"

Richard stood. "I don't see why not."

CHAPTER FIFTEEN

The first problem was the VW. It had only a few drops of fuel left in the tank, and since it did not operate on petroleum products and there was no methane supply in the immediate area, Vic had to choose between abandoning it and trying to figure out a way to run it.

The problem was solved at midmorning when a big-wheeled monster pickup truck lumbered up the road and the driver dropped two large, stainless-steel tanks next to the VW.

"Methane," the driver told Vic and Richard. "Fella driving a funny car said you might be able to use it."

"I can't pay you—" Vic began.

"All taken care of," the driver said, climbing into his cab. "You have a nice day, hear?"

Vic followed Richard back to the cabin. Richard handed him a bundle of neatly folded clothing—the stuff he had been wearing when Shiva and the thugs attacked him. It was clean and a couple of rips had been neatly sewn.

"You did this?" Vic asked.

"Shiva, while you were snoozing."

"*Shiva* washed and mended my clothing? *Shiva?*"

"Well, she *is* female."

"Richard—you're joking?"

"Yes, I am."

The day's final surprise came when Vic put on his old clothes and found a thousand dollars in fifty-dollar bills folded into one of the pockets.

"Shiva again," Richard explained. "It's what she got paid for kicking the crap out of you. She thought you ought to have it. I don't think she liked her employers very much."

"Thank her for me if you see her."

"I will."

Richard served Vic a final meal at noon—the old, reliable bean soup—and went with him to the VW, which they had fueled earlier. The engine turned over on the first try, which surprised Vic—the thing had been outside during a brutal winter, after all—and did not seem to surprise Richard.

Vic rolled down the window and looked up at Richard. "I can't thank you . . ."

"No, you can't. And you shouldn't. I do what I do."

"If I can ever do anything for you . . ."

"Gotcha. Have a good trip. Remember everything that's important."

Richard smiled and walked toward the cabin.

CHAPTER SIXTEEN

The first few miles of the journey back were rough; the small car was never meant to negotiate deeply rutted, unpaved country roads. But Vic managed the drive and once he reached the town, he had no more problems. He stopped at a gas station and bought a can of cola, his first in over a year. He took one deep swallow and almost gagged. The drink was cloying, nauseatingly sweet; he dropped the can into a waste bin and went to find someone who could give him directions.

A few minutes later, he was on an eight-lane interstate, heading west.

14 months earlier:

Benny Fermin got into his office at noon, a bit earlier than usual. He was expecting good news—the news that Vic Sage was lying "dead as a doornail." But the deputy who was waiting for him told him something quite different—that, in fact, Lanny and Willie were the ones who were dead as doornails.

"What about the woman?" Fermin demanded. "That Sheeve-yah? She dead as a doornail, too?"

"Ain't no sign of her, Mayor," the deputy said.

"Well, dammit, *get* me a sign of her!"

By nightfall, the mayor, the sheriff, and Reverend Hatch, who had been brought in to provide spiritual counsel, all concluded that Vic Sage had killed Willie, Lanny, and the woman, and for some reason had hidden the woman's body, or maybe dumped it into the river. By then, the sheriff and his deputies had been swilling beer for several hours—the sight of dead bodies disconcerted them—and Mayor Fermin was obviously too agitated to assume any kind of leadership position.

"I'll send some of my ostiaries to search for this Sage," Hatch said.

"That'd be good," Fermin said. "I guess."

Neither the law enforcement personnel nor the reverend's ostiaries ever found Vic Sage, but finding Shiva proved to be no problem, because she found them. She appeared at Fermin's office the following day and told him that she wanted to confer with the entire sheriff's department and such local policemen as could be found. She suggested they meet in the rotunda of the City Hall at seven, and Fermin said he'd see what he could do.

Only one policeman showed up, and the sheriff, and three deputies, and Mayor Fermin.

Shiva suggested that they stand in a circle around her. They did, and she said to the sheriff, "Which of your deputies is your favorite? Or which do you think has the baddest ass?"

A tall, sunburned man whose uniform shirt was wrinkled and open to his sternum, revealing a tangle of dense, black hair, stepped forward. "That'd be me," he said. "The baddest ass inna county."

Shiva struck him once and he fell at her feet. "I have just slain him," she said. "You saw how easily it was done. It was just as easy the other night by the river. I demonstrate this to show you how the men at the river died. I would not want another to get credit for my deeds."

Shiva smiled, dazzlingly, and strode from the rotunda. A minute later, the sheriff blinked and pulled an automatic from his holster. He didn't pursue Shiva, just stood holding his gun.

Fermin scurried upstairs to his office, to a phone, and dialed eleven digits. "Lissen, ma'am, things is heating up real bad here. Could you maybe get some of your friends in the capital to send some help? You got some National Guard up there in the capital? Maybe you could send me some National Guard."

Fermin stopped talking and listened, drumming his fingertips on the desk.

"Okay, I'll talk to the reverend," he said finally. "But I still think the National Guard would be good. And maybe a tank."

The countryside looked both familiar and alien, like someplace he'd seen in a dream. It was dusk when Vic reached the crossroad where an old man had given him directions and sung the blues. If he turned right, he would be on the road to Hub City. If he continued in a straight line, he could go to Illinois, or Kentucky; he remembered Paducah as a nice town. And he had a thousand dollars in his pocket, more cash than he'd ever had at one time in his life. He could go someplace warm, maybe Florida, and then, in the spring, look for work.

He turned right and drove past the stinking river, the stunted vegetation, the monstrous plant, the parking lot. Nobody followed him.

Hub City's main thoroughfare looked marginally better. Nobody would mistake it for Rodeo Drive, but there were fewer boarded-up storefronts, fewer clots of men gathered around blazing trash cans.

Where to go? Revisit good ol' OTE? Maybe, but only if necessary. The logical answer was Aristotle Rodor's homestead.

Vic had no trouble remembering the route. The countryside was bathed in a pale half-light as Vic turned from the blacktop onto the lane leading to the Rodor house. He looked for his cottage, looked where it had been, where it had to be, and saw nothing but open ground. He parked at the house and knocked on the door. It opened, and he was looking at an Aristotle Rodor who, like the town, had changed, but not for the better.

The man who stood in front of Vic had hair that had turned completely white and greatly lessened; it was only some wisps sprouting from a papery white scalp. The face, too, was papery and heavily creased, and the body beneath it frail. Rodor leaned heavily on an aluminum cane and blinked behind horn-rimmed glasses.

"Vic?" he asked, and when Vic nodded yes, "come in, come in. You're not dead?"

Vic followed Rodor into the house. "What was it that Mark Twain said . . .?"

"Something about the reports of his death being greatly exaggerated."

"Well," Vic said. "That's me. Only I don't know that there *were* reports of my death."

"Not reports, exactly," Rodor said, lowering himself onto a big, overstuffed sofa. "More like speculation. Reports were few and far between, and I don't know that any of them were reliable. So where have you been? And more important, what the hell brings you back?"

Vic sat in a chair across from Rodor. "One thing at a time . . . Where have I been? East of here. I'd like to leave it at that."

"Wherever it was, it changed you. You're . . . leaner. And you don't look so pissed off."

"I'll take that as a compliment. As to why I came back . . . same reason as before. Search for my roots. And maybe something more . . . a feeling of incompleteness. Of having left something undone."

"You're not being precise, but you're not a mathematical equation—you don't have to be. Before we go any further, sonny, I'm going to give you a bit of advice."

"Which is?"

"Go. Flee. Run like the dickens. Put as many miles between here and someplace else as you can."

"Okay, I'm listening, Mr. Rodor."

"Call me 'Tot.' You shouldn't be formal with a man who's had the bejesus kicked out of him on your behalf."

"Run that by me again?"

"It happened the night after you vanished. Five men arrived at sundown—"

—They were riding in a black SUV (Rodor continued) and first they went to the cottage. After a few minutes, they came up here to the big house and demanded to see you. When I told them I had no idea where you were, they knocked me down and while one of them held a gun on me, the others searched. When they didn't find you, they returned to me and asked again where you were. I really didn't know—I hadn't seen you for about forty-eight hours at that point, and that's what I told them. But they didn't believe me. One of them dragged me to my feet and two of them began to hit me. After a while, they did some other things, all painful, and when they finally left, I guess I was unconscious. When I came to, I was lying in a pool of my own blood. I managed to crawl to a telephone and I must have phoned a hospital. I passed out again and when I awoke I was in traction in County General. I stayed there a month. Then I got myself transferred to a fancy place in Chicago and the medical men there did a fair job of patching me together. Now, I have to report to the outpatient clinic once a month and eat a lot of pills every day.

CHAPTER SEVENTEEN

When Rodor had finished his story, Vic leaned forward and said, "Mr. Rodor . . . Tot—I'm sorry, man."

"Not your fault. Their fault. The bastards."

"Do you have any idea who they were?"

"A pretty damn good one. I heard one of 'em mention the Reverend Hatch. They were what he calls his 'crusaders.'"

"Did you tell the police?"

"I filled out a report at the hospital. Nobody ever came to talk to me about it. Nobody ever will. I've lived here long enough to know that."

"What happened to the cottage I used to live in?"

"When I got back from County General, there was nothing left of it but charred ruins. I guess they set it afire, hoping you were hiding inside. That's not all. A lot of stuff was missing from here. Silverware, china, my wife's jewelry . . ."

"Your wife?"

"Matilda. Mattie. She died a long time ago. Disease. Don't bother to express your sympathy. I know you're sorry, but we don't have to talk about it."

"Any way you want it."

"Now—we have to get you settled in."

"I couldn't stay here—"

"You can't stay anywhere else. It's a big house, eleven rooms, and I only occupy one of them. Subtract two bathrooms and the kitchen, that leaves seven rooms empty. I suggest you take the one at the top of the steps. It's got some stuff in it, but there's a bed and a big window. Lots of closet space, too."

Vic followed Rodor to the staircase. "You can go on up alone," Rodor said. "I don't climb steps unless I have to."

"Okay."

"Breakfast at seven, like always. We'll talk more then."

Vic entered the room at the top of the steps. It had obviously been someone's bedroom, some time in the past. There was a bed, covered with a heavy quilt, and a chest, two closets, and an old-fashioned wardrobe. The walls were paneled in knotty pine. A large window looked out over the Rodor property. The whole room was very spare, very masculine. Could it have been Rodor's own room once? Vic didn't think so. Did Rodor have a son? That was a possibility. The old man had never mentioned offspring, but until a few minutes ago, he'd never mentioned his dead wife, either.

Vic got under the quilt and was immediately asleep.

He arose just before sunup; the habits he'd acquired with Richard were still with him. What to do? He performed the stretching and calisthenics and yoga routine Richard had taught him, and then he sat in the classic lotus posture, also part of Richard's teaching, and did what Richard called "going inside" for an hour. By then, he heard Rodor moving about the floor below. Vic dressed and went downstairs.

Rodor, dressed in a bulky blue robe, was frying eggs in the kitchen. Vic said hello and sat at the table.

They shared a breakfast, a lavish one compared to what Vic was used to, and parted. Vic had only the clothes on his back and a few pieces of underwear in the trunk of the VW; he needed to shop.

He remembered the route to the mall and by nine was entering the store Horace had recommended to him when he had first come back to the area. Exactly as he had on the earlier visit, he bought some clothes and a pair of shoes. But he skipped lunch this time. It was too early to eat and besides, he had no idea what he was going to do next.

He drove, revisiting every place he had gone to in Hub City and the surrounding area: the stinking river, the desolate main street, the ruins of the orphanage, City Hall, Hatch's tabernacle. Finally, he went to the KWLM parking lot and looked for Myra's car. It wasn't there. Should he go inside the station? No, not unless or until he knew what he planned to do.

Maybe Myra could help. If she wasn't at the station, maybe she was at home. He drove past her house: There was a fresh FOR SALE sign on a lawn that needed mowing.

He had lunch at the diner in town; he didn't recognize the waitress.

Then, he drove again, past the city and everything that surrounded it, past Rodor's and the farmland beyond, until he came to a narrow dirt road leading into dense woods. He stopped, and got out, and for a while, did nothing but breathe in the clean air and listen to the rustle of the wind in the trees and the distant chirp of birds. Then he walked, into the forest, under the canopy of leaves, sunlight flashing between the limbs onto his face, trying to arrange his thoughts.

Okay, by the numbers:

One: He had decided not to abandon his original reason for returning to Hub City. Maybe that reason was irrational—hadn't Richard said as much?—and maybe he'd come to regret it, but for now, it was a given.

Two: He had acquired new reasons for remaining in the area. Retribution for what had happened to Rodor and—yes, he had to admit it—his feelings for Myra Connelly.

Three: Someone had tried to have him killed, and that someone—probably Mayor Fermin—might still want him dead.

Four: His stint as a local journalist, brief though it had been, had given him an unwelcome visibility. He would be noticed.

And last: He needed a job. The money Shiva had given him would get him through the next few months, sure, but eventually he'd have to earn his room and board.

He sat with his back to the trunk of a huge, old oak, closed his eyes and . . .

The Dream. The white oval face framed by a hat and raincoat, the lightning, the rain . . .

He opened his eyes and knew now that he had a plan, though he could not have explained, rationally and linearly, exactly what it was. But Rodor would be able to help, of that he was certain, though he had no idea why.

CHAPTER **EIGHTEEN**

Vic stopped for dinner at the restaurant Myra had shown him and continued to the Rodor property. Aristotle—"Tot," Vic reminded himself—was in an easy chair in the living room reading a week-old copy of the *New York Times Sunday Magazine*. He looked at Vic over the top of his glasses and asked, "Have a productive day?"

"Yeah, kinda, and there's a lot I have to discuss with you. But first, I need to use your computer."

"You know where it is."

Vic went to the extra bedroom Tot used as an office and started the computer. He remembered the chat room address the stranger at Richard's had given him and accessed it. Then he typed in the code message: *Busda kanel tra home tra home.*

What the hell *did* that mean?

Vic returned to the living room. Tot was now working the crossword puzzle in the *Sunday Times Magazine* with a ballpoint pen. "Ready to talk?" he asked.

"Yeah." Vic settled into the chair across from the sofa and began a rambling, stream-of-consciousness description of his recent life, including his thoughts.

He finished an hour later and asked, "Any comments?"

Tot exhaled a long sigh and said, "I'm a man of logic and science, and what you need here is some kind of wise man. A sage, you could say. I'm not one of those. I think I can help you with some practical matters, but not with your decision-making. And before we go any further, I have a confession."

"That is?"

"I want you to go after the bastards and bring them down into the dust. They destroyed my property, they stole things of enormous value to me, they broke my bones and put me in the hospital. I want revenge and I can't get it for myself. You should know all that. I'll help any way I can, but I am not a disinterested party. I'm not speaking from the sane, evolved part of myself. What you're hearing is pure, savage hatred. I dislike myself for having it but I'd be a fool to pretend I didn't."

"Okay," Vic said. "I'll try to keep all of that in mind."

"Now . . . my value to you will probably be as a provider of tools. I know a lot of practical science and I'm pretty good on theory, too. I also have a fair amount of money—old patents, a few smart investments, a bit of luck. You tell me what you need and I'll try to provide it."

"Deal. There's something else you might be able to do for me."

"Yes?"

"Tell me what's been going on around here while I was gone."

"I'm afraid I'm no good to you there. Remember, for a month I was flat on my back and for another six months, I was in Chicago. I've been absent almost as much as you have."

"Okay." Vic stood. "Maybe time to hit the sack. To be continued, all right?"

As Vic began to climb the stairs, Tot looked up from his puzzle and called, "Do you know two words of two letters each referring to a kind of dancer?"

Vic thought for a second and said, "No. Sorry."

Vic again awoke before dawn. He put on sweatpants and a hooded sweatshirt, booty from the mall, and went to an open area behind the Rodor barn. Until the sun was well up in the sky, he did his yoga and martial arts exercises, finishing with a session of *going inside.*

He found Tot in the kitchen cooking hot cereal. They ate a companionable breakfast, and as they were washing the dishes, Tot asked, "What's today's program?"

"I have no idea," Vic said.

"Going to see your Mr. Horace?"

"Not until I'm sure what I want to say to him."

"Ms. Connelly?"

"If I can find her, maybe."

"Do me a favor. Take my car. There are some modifications I want to make on the VW. Keys are hanging next to the kitchen door."

Vic got the keys and, although he was pretty sure it was pointless, drove to Myra Connelly's house in Tot's four-door Toyota. The FOR SALE sign was still on the front lawn. Just how far had she gone? She'd mentioned relatives in

Wichita. Had she gone to live with them? Or just relo-
cated locally? He got out his cell phone and called information. There was no listing for a "Myra Connelly" or an
"M. Connelly."

*Okay, she's gone ... Not the first time a woman you
liked took a hike ...*

In the end, the day was wasted. Vic drove around aim-
lessly, hoping something he might see would cue an action. But nothing did.

Tot was working on the VW when Vic pulled onto the
Rodor property. He had just finished modifying the en-
gine; it now ran on ordinary gasoline as well as methane.
He had also installed a fuzz buster and a global position-
ing unit. The car was now, probably, the best-equipped
Beetle in history.

Tot fixed a quick dinner. They ate, did the dishes, and
then Vic taught Tot how to play Omaha. They played for
pennies, and at the end of the evening Vic was down over
two bucks.

In a casino, I'd be going home without my shirt ...

Vic said good night and mounted the stairs to his room.
He flicked the light switch: nothing. He tried again: still
nothing.

Must be burned out ...

"I unscrewed the bulb," someone said from somewhere
in the room.

Vic tensed, then almost immediately relaxed. The re-
laxation reflex Richard had taught him hadn't quite become automatic, as Richard said it eventually would, but
it was quick. Vic touched his back to the wall; nobody
would get him from behind. Then he scanned the dark-

ness. A tiny bit of light came from the stars outside the window, but it only deepened the shadows in the room. Vic did not move.

"You're waiting for me to reveal myself," the voice said, and at that moment, Vic knew that his unseen companion was not one of Fermin's thugs, maybe because Fermin's men wouldn't say something like "waiting for me to reveal myself."

"That's good," the voice continued. "You're not a fool. A fool would blunder into the darkness hoping to connect with someone."

Exactly what I would have done a year ago . . .

"Busda kanel," the voice said.

"You!" Vic said. "Richard's friend."

"Not exactly his friend. Not exactly yours, either. I might be your enemy. That'll be up to you to decide later. But for now, I want to make you an offer. It looks like you're about to embark on my path after all. I advise against it, but you'll probably ignore me. But know this . . . if you do it as you're now equipped, you won't last a week. You can handle yourself physically, but that's the least of it. Ideally, you've got to become two people— not one in a disguise, but two. It's a controlled version of the multiple-personality syndrome. You don't have the psyche for that, at least I don't think you do, so we'll have to settle for a disguise."

"You mean false whiskers, a wig, greasepaint?"

"Even a Fermin could see through that kind of thing—"

So he knows about Fermin . . .

"—unless it's applied by an expert and you won't want to waste time becoming an expert. I'm going to send you to someone who'll teach you a couple of tricks. You can take it from there. She lives in New York City. You'll find her name and address on the front seat of your car. She's expecting you the day after tomorrow."

"Okay."

"One more thing, the most important one. I'm taking a chance on you. I'm going way out on a moral limb. You want to learn your parents' identity, fine—I respect that. You want to fight the corruption around here, fine—somebody should. But you don't get to play God, ever. If you ever maim or kill anyone, for any reason, I will destroy you utterly. Do you understand?"

"Yes. But there's more I want to ask you. Like, for openers, who are you? Why are you bothering to . . ."

Vic realized that he was talking to an empty room. He groped until he found the light fixture and tightened the bulb. The room was suddenly visible, but except for Vic there was no one in it. He examined the window: The screen was intact and fastened from the inside. The only other way out of the room was through the door, and Vic had been standing within inches of it. Was his mysterious visitor hiding? Vic looked in the closet and under the bed and even in the drawers, though the stranger would have had to have been a leprechaun to fit into one of those. No joy. The stranger was gone. Impossible, of course, but true.

CHAPTER **NINETEEN**

After breakfast the following morning, Vic told Tot he'd be gone for a few days and then began the trip to New York. He had enough of Shiva's money left to be able to afford a decent motel just east of Columbus, and a good meal at a family restaurant. He had gotten used to doing his morning routine before eating or drinking anything, so he arose at five-thirty, intending to do his exercises by the swimming pool. But when he got there, dressed in sweats, he found five middle-school age children frolicking in and around the pool and suddenly, he felt too shy to begin his workout.

He got an early start to New York.

He arrived in New York City at noon the next day and used the global positioning gadget Tot had installed in the car to locate the address the stranger had left for him, in an area of Manhattan called Greenwich Village. Vic had heard of the place and expected to find it a hotbed of weirdness—girls with garlands of flowers in their hair dancing in the streets, guys in berets and tie-dye shirts declaiming poetry on street corners, maybe. He saw none of that. Oh, there were plenty of girls, many of them pretty, but they weren't dancing and wore no garlands, and there were no street-corner poets at all. He saw a lot of jeans and peacoats, but no more than he would have at a suburban mall, and a lot of suits and ties, too.

The locals probably say Greenwich Village ain't what it used to be . . .

The address he sought was on the top floor of an old house obviously divided into apartments two blocks from the Hudson River. He found the bell marked "O. Knauseley" and pressed it.

From a small round speaker above the bell came a tinny voice: "Come on up, dear."

The door buzzed and he pushed through it and climbed a narrow flight of steps. At the top stood a rotund woman wearing a floral print dress. Her hair, piled high atop her head, was silvery-white, and her face was a maze of wrinkles.

"I've been waiting for you," she said. "Yes I *have!*"

She led Vic into a living room cluttered with tables, statuettes, floor lamps, bookcases. The walls were covered with theatrical posters.

"I'm Olga, dear, but you know that," the woman said when Vic was seated, precariously, on the edge of a lumpy sofa. "Of course you do! Would you like some tea? Well, you *would,* wouldn't you, after a drive through Manhattan traffic?" She filled two delicate-looking cups from a teapot with a bamboo handle and handed one to Vic. "It's Earl Grey, which has been my favorite just *forever!*"

"Thank you."

"Say that again!"

Vic repeated his thanks.

Olga Knauseley beamed. "Such a *nice* voice! A baritone. I've always been partial to baritones. I *adored* Vic
Damone. But he was before your time. Well, before we
get started, let me tell you something about myself."

Once, Olga Knauseley had been called "Morag
Maine." She starred in a Broadway musical at age sixteen
and by the time she reached her twenty-first birthday, she
had starred in three movies, two musicals, and a melodrama. Then, she was subpoenaed by the House Unamer-
ican Activities Committee because she'd attended a few
meetings in New York with a boyfriend. Those meetings,
which Olga had mostly slept through, were deemed sub-
versive. The committee demanded that she name names—
who else had been there, they wanted to know.

"Well, I was *Morag Maine* and I was not *about* to let
some scruffy congressman push me around!" Olga explained. "I frankly didn't care about politics at all, but I
was Morag Maine and you did *not* speak to Morag Maine
that way."

A congressman had drinks with a couple of journalists
and three of the bigger tabloids labeled Morag Maine a
"red honey," a "pinko petunia," and, finally, a plain old
"commie." Within a week, her agents on both coasts had
fired her and a movie that she had been about to begin was
canceled. Nobody, including friends, returned her phone
calls. In less than a month, she had gone from being "the
next Deanna Durbin" to unemployed and unemployable.

"I dropped out of the Hollywood-Broadway scene and

learned my craft," Olga said. "Morag vanished and Olga traveled to wherever anyone would let me on a stage—Alaska, Europe, even Asia and Africa. I did everything from *Charlie's Aunt* to the classics . . . Shakespeare, Ibsen, Marlowe, Shaw. Then, when I was thirty five, I took a job teaching and discovered that I liked it better than performing. That is my real gift, to teach."

"When do we begin?" Vic asked.

"Oh, my dear, we already have. While I have been boring you with my life story, I have been observing you and I have seen a great deal. Now—walk for me. Go to the window, look out, turn around, walk back to your seat."

Vic obeyed.

"You are a very strong presence," Olga said. "My understanding is, you would like to appear less so, no?"

"I guess that's right."

"You're sure? Because most of my clients pay me to show them how to appear *more* than they are."

"Less is fine."

"Good good good. All right, watch me . . ."

Vic watched, and imitated, and then Olga had him lie facedown on the sofa while she manipulated the muscles in his back. Then she had him stand, and shift his weight, and walk through the apartment.

"Now we take it outside," she said.

They went to a strip of park that ran along the river and Vic walked as he'd been taught, with occasional corrections from Olga. They returned to her apartment and she asked him to remove his shirt.

"Don't worry," she said, grinning. "I won't get fresh, not at my age. Though twenty years ago . . ."

Olga measured various areas of Vic's back and then made a brief phone call.

By then, it was after nine.

"Buy a girl dinner?" Olga asked.

She led Vic through winding streets lined with old houses to a busy boulevard, and across it to a Chinese restaurant. Vic had never eaten Chinese food before; he asked Olga to order for him.

"I think you can allow yourself a few extra calories," she said, and spoke to the waiter, who obviously knew her. A few minutes later, Vic was eating something that looked like spaghetti and tasted like peanuts, and then a dish Olga called "General Tso's Chicken."

As they were leaving the restaurant, Olga asked, "Do you have a place to stay?"

"I thought I'd find a hotel."

"It's after ten and we have a long day tomorrow. Besides, a New York hotel room costs enough to feed a small country. If you don't mind being a little cramped, my sofa converts to a bed."

"I'm sure it'll be fine."

The sofa actually wasn't cramped at all, but Vic had difficulty falling asleep anyway. Street noises, ranging from the sound of a horrible metal-on-metal screech—what the hell is *that?*—to drunken shouts, to the unending howl of sirens continued deep into the night. He was used to the stillness of Richard's cabin and the Rodor farmhouse, and even in cities, he had never experienced anything quite like the Greenwich Village cacophony. Vic estimated that it was about three before he finally nodded off.

At seven, Olga shook him awake. "Breakfast's waiting."

recorder in his new voice, and gave him the tape. "Listen to this as often as you can, and practice when you're alone."

Olga took the cookies from the oven and put them in a paper bag.

"Time to see Charlie," she said.

Charlie was waiting for them at his front door. Olga gave Charlie the cookies. The three of them went to the workroom and, at Charlie's request, Vic removed his shirt. Charlie strapped a harness made of metal tubing and leather strips across Vic's back.

"Now walk," Charlie commanded.

Vic took two steps, stumbled, almost fell.

Olga clapped her hands. "Wonderful, wonderful!"

"You think so, huh?" Vic groaned.

"What we're doing is a sophisticated version of an actor playing, say, Richard the Third putting a pebble in his shoe to remind himself to limp," Olga explained. "The harness changes both your posture and your balance. You don't walk the same, you don't stand the same. Physically, you become a different person. Eventually, you won't need the harness—if you practice every day, that is."

In his new voice, Vic said, "I'll practice. Honest I will."

Both Olga and Charlie applauded.

CHAPTER TWENTY

"One more thing we must do," Olga said when she and Vic returned to her apartment.

"What's that?"

Olga gestured to a chair. "Sit!"

Vic did and Olga began to talk, suggesting that he relax and listen to nothing other than her words. Vic realized that he was being hypnotized, but that was okay, as he trusted Olga . . .

". . . five—awake!"

Vic opened his eyes and looked at Olga standing above him.

"How do you feel?" she asked.

"Great. But what'd you do to me? I'm not going to run around and squawk like a chicken, am I?"

"Not unless you want to. Do you? I thought not. But I am a bit sorry. I would enjoy seeing you behave like poul-try. As to what I did to you . . . merely reinforced my earlier suggestions about remembering to change your voice and walk awkwardly. From now on, it is up to you."

"Then I guess it's time to settle my bill. I assume you don't work for free."

"Goodness, no. You would be appalled at how much I charge per hour. Charlie, too. We do very few jobs and still live quite comfortably."

"Okay, what's the damage?"

"Your account is paid in full. In fact, I deposited the check before you arrived. The teller said it was the largest she had ever handled, but she *was* young."

"Who's my benefactor?"

"I don't know. We have done business twice before, your benefactor and I. Both times he paid with a cashier's check purchased at a bank in Baltimore. Once, he sent a young woman to me. The other time, I think it may have been he, himself, who needed coaching. But no names were ever used."

"Except mine."

"Who did you say you were?"

Vic stood, and for a moment waited awkwardly at the door, not sure how to say good-bye. Olga hugged him and wished him godspeed, then he went out into the brisk, spring evening.

He had parked on a narrow street around the corner from Olga's building. There were three parking tickets on the VW's windshield. He looked at them—it seemed that he owed the City of New York $180—and tucked them into a pocket. And there was a piece of folded notepaper lying on the driver's seat, across which was printed a brief message:

Get yourself beaten up. Pay the parking fines.

No signature, and Vic was certain that if he checked there would be no fingerprints or other evidence, either. His benefactor, whoever he was, did not leave calling cards. As to the message itself . . . Get yourself beaten up? After brief thought, Vic understood. In Hub City, he'd been a tough guy. He had to rid himself of that image. Maybe the best way to do that was to get flattened.

Something to look forward to . . .

He drove to the Holland Tunnel and began his trip back west.

CHAPTER TWENTY-ONE

It was midmorning when Vic drove past the McFeeley plant again, with its belches of heat and smoke and its stunted vegetation. Every time he did this he felt as though he were leaving the Earth and entering somebody's idea of Hell. He tuned the radio to KWLM and heard Horace giving the hourly news. But Myra wasn't on the broadcast.

First order of business, get clobbered . . .

There was a tavern he had noticed just to the north of downtown Hub City, if Hub City could be said to *have* a downtown. It was a long rectangle built of cinderblocks and there were usually motorcycles parked outside. He had never gone into such a place and left without bruises and blood and sore knuckles.

He parked the VW and strode into a filthy, smoky room with a long bar along the back end. Two men in sleeveless denim jackets and jeans sat nursing drinks at a table.

My pals, the local bikers . . .

Vic marched up to the bar and confronted the man behind it, who looked a lot like the pair at the table. "I'll have . . . an *orange soda*. With plenty of ice!"

The bartender shrugged and got a bottle of orange soda from a cooler. He uncapped it and plunked it down in front of Vic. "Buck-fifty."

"For a lousy soda? I can get it for seventy-eighty cents."

"Not here. Here it's a buck-fifty."

Vic put two dollar bills on the bar.

"You want change or you gonna be a sport?" the bartender asked.

"Damn right I want change."

That ought to do it . . .

The bartender shrugged again and put two quarters next to the soda bottle.

Vic glanced back at the pair at the table; they were ignoring him.

"Worst orange soda I ever tasted," Vic told the bartender.

"Life's tough," the bartender said.

What's happening . . . I should be fighting for my life by now . . .

"I'll tell you what else is tough. Your mama!"

"Could be. I never met the lady."

Me either . . .

Vic drank his soda and left the tavern.

That was a bust . . . Usually guys like that just look at me and start swinging . . .

Vic drove to the Rodor property. He found Tot in the kitchen, eating a sandwich.

"Welcome back," Tot said through a mouthful of food. "How was New York?"

"Crowded and noisy."

"Always is," Tot said. "Hate that town."

"Got an extra sandwich?"

"Bread's in the box, everything else is in the refrigerator. You look different. You put on weight?"

"Lost some, if anything."

"It's the hair . . . combed differently. But more than that."

"Way more."

Vic described the work he'd done with Olga and Charlie and then, after some hesitation, his interactions with his mysterious benefactor.

"So you're becoming a 'mystery man,'" Tot said.

"A *what?*"

"Mystery man. The press's label for urban vigilantes who disguise themselves and give themselves fancy names like Nightwing, the Huntress, the Sandman . . . and who's the famous one, the Gotham City one? . . . never mind—you know who I mean."

"I always thought they were urban myths. Or just plain baloney."

"Yeah, you may be right. I don't have enough data to form an opinion. But even if they are chimerical . . . well, sometimes life does imitate art. And it's clear that your mysterious benefactor wants that for you."

"I'm not sure he *wants* it. More, he doesn't want to get in my way if *I* want it."

"So—do you?"

Vic walked to the window and stared out at the farmland. "Ah, hell . . . I don't know. There are things I feel I should do, and I'm not getting them done as Vic Sage—or as Charles Victor Szasz. If I have to become a mystery man, okay."

"Have you given any thought to a costume? Or a name?"

"None."

"Well, maybe I can help. Give me a few hours."

"Okay, I'm gonna do some reconnaissance. I'll be back around five."

Vic intended his first stop to be KWLM. But en route, he saw a crew tarring a stretch of roadway off the main route: big, burly guys who made their living doing hard labor.

Have to be macho as hell . . .

Vic parked the VW and walked over to the pavers.

I probably didn't come on strong enough in the tavern . . .

"Any of you dorks not sissies?" he asked loudly. "'Cause you look like a bunch of mama's boys to me."

The workers looked at him briefly and returned to their tasks.

Strike two . . .

Vic got back in his car and drove the rest of the way to the radio station. Myra's car was not in the parking lot.

Vic found Horace in the studio.

"Hi," Vic said.

For a moment, Horace stared at him. "Sage?"

"The same."

"Where have you been? It's been what—a year?"

"A bit longer."

"We heard something about you being killed along

with a couple of City Hall hangers-on, but they never found your body."

"That may be because I wasn't dead."

"Yeah, I can see that. But *something* happened to you. You've changed . . . put on weight? I don't know, but something. Where were you?"

"Various places. I was badly hurt in the fight you mentioned. Someone thought I'd have a better chance of recovering somewhere else."

"*Where* else?"

"That's kind of privileged, at least for now."

"Who helped you?"

"Also privileged."

"Is there *anything* you can tell me?"

"Just that I'm back and ready to go to work."

"Just like that, huh? You vanish, we don't get so much as a postcard, and now you want your job. Am I getting this right or am I missing something?"

"No, you're not."

"Can you give me one good reason why I should rehire you?"

"I'm willing, I've had some experience, and I work cheap."

"That's three reasons. I don't know how good they are, but at least there are three of them. Okay, tell you what . . . you can work freelance, either on a per diem or getting paid by the job. If you don't disappear again in, say, a month, I'll give you a staff position."

"Fair enough."

"See you back here at nine tomorrow."

"One more thing . . . Is Myra around?"

Horace stared at his shoes and frowned. "She . . . doesn't work here anymore."

"Another station hire her away?"

"She . . . retired. Look, Sage, I'm busy. If I don't see you at nine, I'll know that you're as big a flake as I thought."

Vic nodded, and left the building.

CHAPTER TWENTY-TWO

Tot was waiting in the living room, sitting on the floor surrounded by wrapping paper, scrolled blueprints, swatches of cloth, and a few silvery canisters.

"Ready to go to work?" he asked as Vic entered.

"Doing what?"

"Creating your secret identity. I've been looking over some of my old ideas, stuff I haven't thought about in years . . . I think we can do the job."

"How do we begin?"

"Maybe by selecting a name. You know . . . a label to go with your secret identity. Any ideas?"

"Absolutely none."

"Well . . . one of the first mystery men was called The Scarlet Pimpernel."

"What's a pimpernel?"

"A plant with small flowers."

"So this guy was known as the little red flower?"

"Yes . . ."

"When did he live?"

"In the nineteenth century, I believe."

"Maybe in the nineteenth century they were impressed by little red flowers, but now . . ."

"I get your point."

"What else?"

"I mentioned the Sandman—"

"What was his story?"

"He wore ordinary clothes and used a gas gun."

"Shot people with gas? Knocked them out?"

"Yes. I suppose I could devise such a weapon for you."

"Pass. A guy tried to mace me outside a club in KC one night. Suddenly, the wind shifted and he maced himself. I imagine you'd have a similar problem with gas. The other thing is, if he's got a gun that shoots bullets and he sees me with a gun, he'll think mine shoots bullets, too, and he'll try to shoot me first. And he'll probably succeed, especially if he's, like, across the street. I mean, how far would the gas go, anyway?"

"All good and valid points."

"Next?"

"Well, some mystery men name themselves after creatures. There was once a Green some-kind-of-bug . . . a wasp? Anyway, it was green and an insect. There's Nightwing, which sounds like some kind of bird. I remember reading about a Wildcat . . . and a Bronze Tiger. And there's a woman who calls herself Black Canary and another who calls herself The Huntress."

"Let's try a different direction."

"How about something descriptive? 'The Justice Man.' How does that strike you?"

"Little truth-in-advertising problem. I'm not after justice for everyone, everywhere, though that'd be nice . . . but way beyond me. Besides, I'm not always sure what justice is."

"Then what *are* you after?"

"Good question. I guess mostly I'm after answers."

Tot rubbed his chin with the back of his hand. "Questions and answers . . . 'The Quizmaster'?"

"Would I have to use a lot of hair gel and talk in a voice like chocolate pudding? No thanks."

Both men stared at the carpet.

"Questions and answers," Vic said finally. "What's wrong with The Question?"

"Not terribly dramatic. But . . . well, until we think of something better . . ."

"Okay, what does The Question look like? I don't like capes . . ."

"You're definitely not the cape type," Tot said. "And to be honest with you, I'm not much of a designer. I'm more comfortable with theory and hardware. But let me show you something."

Tot lifted a small square of white cloth from the pile on the floor and sprayed it with a mist from one of the canisters. Almost immediately, the white darkened to an inky black.

"Could be useful if you need to change identities in a hurry," Tot said. "Now, to item number two . . ." Tot held up a rectangle of gray plastic with a matte finish. "Hold this up to your face."

Vic smoothed the plastic over his face and Tot sprayed it with another canister.

"Now," Tot said, "remove the plastic."

Vic curled his fingers around the edge of the square and pulled. Then he pulled harder, and harder still; the plastic remained stuck to his skin.

"Relax," Tot said, and used the canister again. The plastic immediately slid off Vic's face.

"It's an artificial skin I developed years ago," Tot explained. "Permeable so air can reach the skin; I thought it would have medical uses. But there are other, much cheaper products that do essentially the same job. But it might be perfect material for a mystery man's mask."

"I'd have to carry a couple of those containers—"

"Perhaps not. I have an idea about that. Let me fool around with this material for a few hours and see what I can devise. Can I see some of your exercises? The ones you learned in Pennsylvania."

"Sure, but why?"

"To get an idea of how this hypothetical costume of yours should work."

"A costume *works?*"

"Well, if you're going to be jumping around, you wouldn't want anything too constricting."

"Good point."

Suddenly, Vic remembered his strange dream, the one with the white faces. "The mask . . . can you make it white?"

"Sure, but gray would be better for hiding . . ."

"I'd like it to be white."

Tot shrugged. "I think you're being a damn fool, but it's your party. White it'll be."

They went outside and, for an hour, Vic performed

some of the movements Richard had taught him as Tot watched.

"Enough," Tot said. "I think I grasp the parameters of the problem. I'll get to work. Probably won't finish tonight."

"Okay, great."

Vic ate a sandwich in the kitchen, then went back outside. It was early, not yet seven, and there were still streaks of sunlight in the western sky. For the next hour, he did the yoga exercises Richard had taught him and then he sat cross-legged and "went inside" until the sky was full of stars and he felt like going to bed.

CHAPTER TWENTY-THREE

Vic arrived at the station at quarter to nine, reacquainted himself with the building and the foul coffee the vending machine spewed.

Horace appeared from his office at nine sharp carrying a small tape recorder. "Guy's a hundred years old today. See if you can get a statement. Something, I dunno, nostalgic."

He handed Vic a piece of lined paper torn from a steno pad with an address scrawled on it.

Vic found the house, a bungalow on about two acres of land near the river. The birthday boy, Mr. Froelinger, sat on his front porch, a blanket covering his lap and lower legs, surrounded by middle-aged and elderly people: his family.

"Tell the man from the radio what you think about living so long, Pop," Mr. Froelinger's sixty-something son prompted.

Vic held the recorder near Mr. Froelinger's mouth.

"Things useta be bad 'round here," Mr. Froelinger said in a surprisingly strong voice. "Now they's hell. I blame the Dimmycrats."

"Pop," the son said, "we have a Republican president."

"Looks Dimmycratic to me."

Vic got the names and addresses of all Mr. Froelinger's relatives, thanked them all, and left.

Not a very auspicious beginning to my career . . .

He delivered the tape to Horace and they listened to Mr. Froelinger's pronouncements.

"Nothing usable," Horace said.

"That's what I was afraid of. Sorry."

"Not your fault. Stick around. Maybe something else will come up."

Vic got the stack of newspapers and deposited them and himself on the couch in the reception area. He read, took a walk, read some more, had an awful tuna salad sandwich from a vending machine, continued reading. At four-forty-five, Horace sat next to him.

"Slow day?" Vic asked.

"Yeah. We got next to nothing for the five o'clock news. Tell you what—do something with your birthday story. Don't use the tape—just talk. Can you fill two minutes?"

"It's a nonstory," Vic protested.

"Welcome to modern journalism."

Vic went on the air at five-fifteen and for two minutes talked of that fine patriarch, Mr. Froelinger, surrounded by his loving family, looking back on ten decades of a life richly lived. And so forth.

Vic removed his headphones, left the studio, and

returned to his reading. While he was living in Richard's cabin, he had neither read, seen, nor heard any news. He had now spent an afternoon remedying that, but he felt as though he had accomplished nothing. Still the same conflicts, the same madness, and death, and horror . . . and preoccupation with the inconsequential perambulations of celebrities: who they saw, where they ate, where they bought clothes . . . compared to some of this stuff, Mr. Froelinger's story was a bell-ringer.

Horace came out of the studio.

"I do what you wanted?" Vic asked.

"My heart was so warm, I was afraid I was going to burn my shirt. See you tomorrow."

CHAPTER TWENTY-FOUR

Tot was waiting in the living room, smiling.

"Forgive an old man's crowing, but I may have out-done myself," he said. He lifted a belt from a pile of odds and ends on the sofa. "First, the belt. You indicated that you didn't want to be burdened with gas canisters. Here's my solution . . . Notice the buckle?"

"It's kind of big."

"*But*—" Tot thumbed a stud on the buckle's front and a fine mist shot from somewhere inside it. For a moment, a faint smell of talcum powder hung in the air. "The gases . . . one for the color change, one for the mask. I've managed to combine them. They're pressurized in the buckle. They'll have to be *re*pressurized every fourth use or so, but that shouldn't be a problem. Next—" He lifted a white trench coat and white shirt from the pile. He sprayed them with mist from the buckle and they changed color, to black. Tot picked up a final item, a light-gray hat, sprayed it, and it darkened to match the coat and shirt.

"Nifty," Vic said.

"Want to try them on?"

"Sure." Vic shed his shirt.

"And what is that?" Tot asked.

For a moment, Vic didn't know what Tot was talking about. Then he looked down at his own chest and saw the harness Charlie had made for him.

"Something I acquired in New York," he said.

"Are you doing penance? Is it like a hair shirt?"

"No. It's not even uncomfortable."

"If you say so . . ."

Vic put on the shirt Tot had treated. Then he picked up the trench coat and rubbed the lapel between his thumb and forefinger. "What kind of cloth is this? Feels strange."

"I forgot to tell you," Tot said. "That's one of the best parts. It's a bulletproof polymer. Does the same job as Kevlar, only it's another item that's too complicated for mass production. You don't want to get in the way of a howitzer shell, but it will resist most handgun ammunition."

Vic put on the belt, coat, and hat, and pressed the stud on the buckle. For a moment he was nearly enveloped in mist and then everything that was black became white. Vic pressed the stud again and what was white became black. Then Vic tried a few moves: kicks, punches, blocks. He was able to move freely.

"That's enough for now," Tot said. "How do you like your new toys?"

"I feel like it's Christmas morning and I'm the luckiest boy in town."

CHAPTER TWENTY-FIVE

The next morning, Vic could see his breath. He actually needed his new trench coat, not to shed bullets but for warmth.

He met Horace as he entered the station. Horace made a production of looking him up and down and said, "Well. You're finally beginning to look like a reporter."

"Do you have a press pass I could put in my hatband?"

"I'll see about getting you one."

"You have anything for me today?"

"Come into my office."

When they were seated facing each other across Horace's desk, Horace said, "To answer your question, no. No fires or car crashes or hundredth birthdays. Nothing that qualifies as breaking news. But for about a year now, something's been going on downtown. In some ways, the city seems a bit safer. There doesn't seem to be as much petty crime, and as far as I can tell, the police department seems as understaffed and inept as ever. But it doesn't smell right. I'm wondering if just maybe you can find out exactly what's happening."

"Maybe. I'm willing to try."

"All right. I'm putting you back on staff as of today."

"Thanks, but why?"

"To be honest, I have a guilty conscience. What I'm asking you to do is risk your life, and I feel you should be paid for it."

"Deal," Vic said. He stood and left the room.

Horace had been right. Hub City had improved. Nobody would mistake it for a vacation paradise: The downtown shops were still boarded up; most flat surfaces were covered with graffiti; the gutters were still full of trash. But there seemed to be fewer derelict men on corners and the stoplights on Main were actually working.

Vic parked in front of City Hall and walked to the back of the building, intending to ascend the steps to Fermin's office.

Two men stood in a military at-ease posture at the foot of the stairs. They were both tall, clad in black jumpsuits and black berets, and both held metal batons in front of them. Their whole aspect was that of soldiers, or Marines, or maybe Navy SEALs, but there were no insignia on their garments.

"Excuse me," Vic said, moving toward the stairs.

The nearest man stepped in front of him. "No unauthorized personnel allowed. Please move away, sir."

"I'm a reporter—" Vic protested.

"No unauthorized personnel allowed. Please move away, sir."

"I'd like a word with the mayor . . ."

"No unauthorized personnel allowed. Please move away, sir."

Vic felt the sweet surge of adrenaline—

Show time . . .

—and then became intensely aware of the harness he was wearing and how it affected his posture, and the tone of voice he had been using—high and a bit hoarse—and felt himself relaxing.

"Okay," he said, backpedaling. "Sorry to have bothered you guys. Have a nice day."

What could be in Fermin's office worth using a couple of goons to protect . . . ?

He walked back to the front of the building and was approaching the VW when a black Humvee with tinted windows—one of the military type he'd seen at Hatch's tabernacle—halted in front of him. The passenger door opened and Fermin slid his body out.

He smiled. "Well, if it ain't Vic Sage, the radio man. Somebody told me you was back in town. Where the heck you been?"

"Had a few health problems. Went east to get them taken care of."

"Them health problems, they wouldn't't'a come dressed in a green outfit? Maybe they had slanty eyes?"

"I don't remember exactly what happened."

"I hope everything's all right."

"I'm fine now."

"Good news to hear. Anybody tell you about my good luck?"

"No, I haven't gotten around much yet."

"Well, I went and got myself hitched!"

"Congratulations."

"Yeah, went and got myself a ball and chain. You wanna meet her?"

Fermin stuck his head inside the Humvee. "Honey-pie, come on out here a minnit."

A woman, wearing short-shorts, a tube top that left her midsection bare, and high-heeled sandals, emerged from the rear of the vehicle.

She's gotta be freezing, dressed like that in this weather . . .

"Hello, Vic," the woman said.

"Oh, that's right," Fermin said. "You two know each other. You was coworkers."

"Hello, Myra," Vic said.

"Yeah, we're real happy, we are," Fermin said. "Honey-pie, show your friend how much you love me."

Myra put her arms around Fermin and kissed him hard on the mouth.

"Hoo-*eee,*" Fermin said. "Yessir, that'll wake a man right up. You know what I think we're gonna do, Vic? We're gonna go up to my office and continue this little lovefest."

"Nice running into you," Vic said, and walked away.

CHAPTER TWENTY-SIX

Vic had imagined that his first real use of Richard's teaching would occur during some tense situation—a fight, probably, or grave danger. But he was wrong. He was driving toward the river, his breath coming in gasps, and remembering Richard's instruction about acknowledging emotional stress: "Don't ever try to deny it's there or push it away. If you do, somehow it'll reappear and bite you on the ass."

But, Richard, sometimes it's best not to act on your feelings and to focus, instead, on whatever task is in front of you. He had taught Vic a technique for calming himself while allowing the stress to remain. Vic used it now, and soon he was breathing nomally.

Vic concentrated on making the Volkswagen go where he wanted it to.

He stopped near a grove of oaks on the riverbank, several miles above Hub City, where the water had not yet been completely fouled. A few yards away, there was a dog, or a wolf, or a coyote—was that possible? Some kind of emaciated, mangy canine. The critter was standing still and gazing out at the water, as though it were expecting something—salvation, maybe?—to emerge from the river. It turned its head and looked at Vic for a full minute, then limped off into the underbrush.

Vic picked up a flat rock and threw it, then sat with his back to one of the oaks. *Now*—he could free his emotions.

But what were they? What was bothering him? Surely he wasn't jealous! He'd had his share of girlfriends—hell, *more* than his share—and if one went away, another always came along. And he hadn't even gotten past the *howdy ma'am* stage with Connelly. They didn't know each other well enough to qualify as friends, much less anything heavier.

It's stupid to be jealous . . .

But, okay—admit it, I am jealous . . . and my last vestige of macho pride is curling up and dying . . .

Now that he had let *that* particularly scruffy cat out of the bag, maybe he could learn something from this experience. Another of Richard's tricks: visualization. Richard had said that the wiring in Vic's brain permitted him to recall visual stimuli with unusual acuteness.

So—visualize: Myra. The clothing. Ridiculously skimpy, for this time and this climate. Until today, Vic had not really known what her figure was like. He'd known she was gorgeous, of course, but he couldn't have guessed at exact measurements until she stepped from the Humvee. She looked uncomfortable, stiff. Humiliated? And something else . . .

What? What . . .?

Her face. A discoloration on her left cheek, a bruise. And a purple blotch on her left forearm.

The bastard's beating her . . .

That led to a question, though Vic could not have said why: Where was Myra's little girl? What was her name . . . Jackie. Where was Jackie? With her mother?

Another question: Why the muscle guarding Fermin's office? Maybe that was where he should begin seeking answers, in that office.

He drove back to KWLM and sat in Horace's office until the five o'clock newscast was over. Horace entered and said, "Well?"

Vic told Horace about the goons at Fermin's City Hall headquarters and about the small improvements he had noticed in Hub City's downtown. Then he described meeting Myra.

"Why didn't you tell me she'd married Fermin?"

"I didn't know how to, mostly because I didn't know how involved you'd gotten with Myra. It was obvious there was a mutual attraction."

"*Mutual* attraction?"

"Yeah, but deflate your chest. It's called biology and it's been going on for quite a while. They find it useful in propagating the species, I hear."

"When did it happen?"

"Soon after you vanished. No more than a week later. Myra just walked in here one day and said she was quitting, and by the way, getting married to Fermin."

"Do you remember how she seemed? How she looked, sounded . . ."

"She looked like she'd just lost her best friend and she sounded like a dirge."

"Have you seen her lately?"

"Yeah, I caught a glimpse of her at the interstate mall. She looked like the kind of pinup girl you see on calendars in repair shops."

"Yeah. Cheap and phony. Not like Myra at all."

"Maybe you'll find out what's going on with her if you find out what else is going on."

"Is that an assignment?"

Horace shrugged. "Just an observation. See you tomorrow?"

"Nine o'clock."

CHAPTER TWENTY-SEVEN

At ten that night, Vic turned to Tot and said, "Guess it's time."

Tot handed him the belt then the trench coat, hat, shirt, and mask. "Better test it."

Vic touched the belt buckle and for a moment was enveloped in mist that smelled of talcum powder. Then the garments changed color.

"Now the mask," Tot said, giving it to Vic.

Vic ran his fingers over the white plastic. "Feels different."

"I made an improvement," Tot said. "I epoxied night vision lenses on the inner surface. For all practical purposes, you'll be able to see in the dark."

Vic smoothed the plastic over his face and again touched the buckle. The spray puffed upward and the mask clung to him. He went to a mirror and looked and—

It's the real me . . .

He was a blank. Just a pale oval. No features at all. And

suddenly, he felt as though he were recognizing himself
for the first time. The face beneath the plastic—*that* was
the mask. The plastic did not conceal, it *revealed.*

"I'd better recharge the spray," Tot said. "You've used
most of it up."

Thirty minutes later, Vic was driving into Hub City.
The night was cold, and leaves blew around the car. A
round, orange moon, streaked with wisps of clouds, was
directly overhead.

Suddenly, Vic realized that the date was October 31—
Halloween.

And ain't that appropriate . . .

The streets were empty except for one group of men
gathered around a trash-barrel fire. A year earlier, on a
similar night, he'd seen a dozen such groups. He parked
two blocks from City Hall. There was no sign of life in the
immediate area, not even a street lamp. He got the mask
from where it had been folded into a shirt pocket,
smoothed it into place, and touched the buckle. A moment
later, his clothing had changed color, and he had no features.

Happy Halloween . . .

He met no one on his approach to the rear of City Hall.
But when he got near the building, in the greenish field of
the night vision lenses, he saw two of the black-clad
guards, doubles of the ones he'd seen earlier, standing
with feet apart, holding batons in front of them.

*I could probably take them, especially with surprise on
my side . . . But maybe I'd better stay hidden . . .*

He looked around and saw an ancient oak, taller than
the building, about ten feet from the roof. Its lowest limb

was maybe eight feet from the ground. He ran, jumped, and grabbed the limb. He hadn't climbed a tree since childhood, but, with the aid of the night vision, it wasn't particularly difficult. At the top, swaying slightly, feeling the cold wind blowing from the river, he hesitated. Then, he took a deep breath and leaped. He landed on a tar-papered, sloping surface on his hands and knees.

"The hell was that?" one of the guards asked from below.

A flashlight beam briefly illuminated the edge of the roof as a guard directed it upward. Vic flattened himself and did not move.

"Think we should take a look?" the guard asked.

"We're due to inspect in fifteen minutes," the other guard said. "It'll keep till then, whatever it is."

Fifteen minutes . . . that's how much time I've got . . .

Vic slid himself to the side of the building opposite where the guards were posted and peered downward. There was a window with a narrow ledge just below him. He lowered himself onto the ledge, which was barely wide enough to accommodate his toes, and tested the glass pane with his fingertips. Suddenly, the pane pulled loose from its frame and began to fall inward. Vic caught it, pulled it out, and placed it on the roof.

Thing was ready to go . . . Putty's probably decades old . . .

The glassless opening was big enough to admit him. He dove through it, landed lightly on his hands, and sprang to his feet.

Where'd I learn to do that . . .?

He was where he'd hoped to be, in Fermin's office. It

had changed. Gone were the battered desk, ancient couch, and layers of dust. The desk, now, was new and gleaming metal, the couch modernistic. Everything was clean and almost antiseptic-looking. And barren. The old file cabinets were gone, and no new ones had replaced them. There seemed to be no place to look for information.

Vic moved to the desk and looked down at the phone, greenish in his lenses. It was ultramodern, with a row of buttons for instant dialing, caller ID, speakerphone capability.

Maybe here . . .

None of the instant dial buttons were marked. Vic lifted the receiver and pushed the first one. He heard the usual buzzing and then:

"Blessings and salutations on you, brother or sister, and may the Lord's face shine upon you. You have reached the Tabernacle of the Highest Holiness and the Reverend Jeremiah Hatch. Please leave a message after you are blessed by the beep."

Vic disconnected.

Okay, that worked . . . I'll try again . . .

He pressed the second button. Someone answered and said, "Plant."

Vic could hear the screech and roar of massive machinery in the background. "What plant might that be?" he asked.

"McFeeley's, you moron!"

"You have a nice night, too," Vic said, and disconnected.

Only a fool quits when he's on a roll . . .

Vic pressed the third button. A recorded message answered: "Mark Ten-Nineteen. Please leave a message."

Vic hung up.

He heard voices just outside the office door, coming closer, and glanced at the luminous dial on his wristwatch. He'd been here less than nine minutes. Apparently, the guards had moved their inspection timetable up.

He ran, flattened himself, and dove out the part of the window that was missing the pane. He dropped, and as he heard the door opening in the office, hooked his fingers onto the windowsill.

If they notice the pane missing, I'm cooked . . .

A voice from the office: "Anything?"

Another voice: "Naw."

The sound of the door closing.

Vic hoisted himself up until his arms were straight, his palms flat on the sill, and then reached higher and caught the sides of the window frame. He pulled, hoisting himself farther upward, until he could stand on the sill. Then he jumped, grabbed the edge of the roof, and hauled himself over onto the sloping tar paper.

A few long strides, then a jump, and he was on the oak and climbing to the ground.

CHAPTER **TWENTY-EIGHT**

Once in the VW, he pressed the stud on the belt buckle. His clothing changed color and he peeled off the white mask and stuck it in a pocket.

The clouds had thickened, completely hiding the moon, but its orange glow shone through them. Vic drove through patches of fog at the bottoms of hills, eerie in the dim light.

The Rodor house was dark; Tot had gone to bed. Vic held the mask up to his face and, peering through the night vision lenses, negotiated the short trip to his room.

He sat cross-legged on the floor, calmed his mind, and reviewed the night. Obviously, things had improved at City Hall. Why? And who paid for the improvements? More data needed, a lot more. He'd learned some interesting information: Mayor Benedict Fermin was somehow connected to the Reverend Hatch, which might explain the appearance and demeanor of the pair guarding Fermin's office—they could have been clones of the men he and Myra had seen at the Tabernacle of the Highest Holiness. Fermin was also connected to the McFeeley plant . . . and to Mark Ten-Nineteen, whatever that was.

And Myra . . . Vic was beginning to believe that the wedding had not been a free or joyous occasion for her. But if it had been forced, what coercion did Fermin use? Vic would have to find a way to speak with Myra alone.

He got into bed, and slept, and dreamed:

He was watching the emaciated, mangy canine by the riverbank and then he *was* the animal, watching a man who looked like Charles Victor Szasz . . .

And he was The Question looking into a mirror, seeing the face of Charles Victor Szasz framed by the black trench coat and the black hat, and he peeled away Szasz's face and underneath there was only a blank oval . . .

He awoke before dawn. It was November 1: All Saints Day. He went outside, into frigid air, and did his exercises, then joined Tot for breakfast.

Horace was waiting in his office when he got to the station.

"Can you tell me where Myra got married?" Vic asked. "City Hall, church, where?"

"Hatch's tabernacle," Horace said.

"Why am I not surprised?"

"I'll bite, Mr. Sage. Why are you not surprised?"

"Never mind, okay? You know of any connection between Hatch and Fermin . . . other than Myra's wedding."

"No, but it wouldn't surprise me if there were one. I actually attended the wedding. Fermin's invite, not Myra's. Surprised me, because Fermin knows I think he's pond scum. But I had the sense he was showing off . . . like the nerdy kid who scores a cheerleader for his prom date and has to brag about it. Myra's dress would have done for on-stage attire at a girly club. Ever see a wedding gown with a miniskirt?"

"How did something like Fermin ever get elected?"

"Vic, Hub City's been a case study in municipal corruption since the Civil War. I don't think there's been an honest election since the Grant administration, maybe even before that."

"I guess that answers my question, but I have another. Why do you stay here?"

"That's none of your business, Sage. Get out of here and find some work to do."

Vic hung around the station until six, choked down a sandwich from the vending machine, then drove to the tabernacle of the Highest Holiness. There were even more cars in the parking lot than there had been when he and Myra had visited the place, more than a year earlier. He parked nearly a quarter-mile from the big building and joined the throng moving toward the entrance.

A guard, wearing a black jumpsuit, one of four flanking the door, glanced down at a clipboard and then at Vic. He stepped forward and said, "Please leave the premises, sir."

"But I want to attend the service," Vic protested.

"That will not be possible. Please leave the premises. Sir."

This might be my chance to get beaten up in public . . .

Vic looked at the guards. All were over six feet tall, all carried metal batons, and all were powerfully built. And he would have bet that they'd all had a lot of combat training.

They make the ones at City Hall last night look like Campfire Girls . . .

He was pretty sure that his benefactor wanted him to be publicly humiliated to establish his wimphood. Getting squashed by this quartet of human tanks would not accomplish that. *Anyone* would get clobbered by these guys.

But he might get in a little wimpiness without taking a single punch. "Well, okay, fellas," he said, "but honesty compels me to tell you that I'm a little hurt. I really don't think I deserve to be treated this way."

"Please leave the premises. Sir."

Okay. But as Arnold said, I'll be back . . .

Vic turned, and saw a black SUV screech to a stop in a reserved parking slot. The doors opened and one of the black-clad guards pulled Myra out and hustled her inside. She was dressed as she had been when Vic had seen her outside City Hall, but her top was torn and she had a deep bruise on her cheek. She kept her eyes focused on the ground and allowed herself to be pushed.

Vic felt the sweet rush of adrenaline. He forced himself to take three deep breaths, slouch, and shamble toward his car.

CHAPTER **TWENTY-NINE**

Vic saw light under the door of Tot's workshop. He knocked, entered, and greeted the old man, who was standing at a workbench, applying a screwdriver to a small electrical engine of some kind.

"How did it go with The Question?"

Vic told him about the previous night's activities, and his visit to the tabernacle.

"Sounds as though Ms. Connelly needs rescuing," Tot said.

"You think she's a prisoner?"

"Don't you?"

"I guess it makes sense. No time like the present."

"I don't agree. You don't know where she is. At Hatch's place or at home with Fermin. Be better to do some reconnaissance first, before you go charging in like the cavalry."

"Right. How'd you get so smart?"

"Genes. Everything's genes. Plus, I eat a hearty breakfast and wash behind my ears."

"You have any idea what this Mark Ten-Nineteen is?"

"None. But I'll bet your Mr. Horace does."

"Probably. I'll ask him. See you in the morning."

The two men were shirtless, and although the night was chilly, sweat gleamed on their arms in the light of the propane lanterns ringing the area. Both of them were digging deep, narrow holes, and both were panting.

There were a dozen men dressed in black jumpsuits and watch caps standing at attention, watching the work. Another man, taller, wider, and straighter than the rest, but similarly dressed, stood to one side. This was obviously the commander.

"That's enough," he said to the laborers.

"Yessir, Colonel Crate, sir," they answered in unison.

"Execute the maneuver," the man they called Colonel Crate said.

The men dropped their shovels and stepped into the holes they had just dug. The holes were six feet deep; only the men's heads were not inside them.

Colonel Crate asked, "Do you know why you are being reprimanded?"

"Yessir, Colonel Crate, sir," the men in the holes answered.

"Why is that?"

"The window pane, sir," the men in the holes said.

Crate turned to the others. "These personnel were on guard duty last night at City Hall. Today, I found a window pane missing in one of the offices. Later, I located the missing pane on the roof of the building. It is apparent to me that there was an intruder whose presence was not discerned by the guards. Can we allow such negligence? No, we cannot. Complete the maneuver."

Two of the watchers stepped from the line, picked up the shovels, and began filling the holes. Twenty minutes later, the two in the holes were buried up to their necks.

CHAPTER THIRTY

A local boy almost drowned while fishing in the Ohatch-apee, apparently unaware that no living creature had been pulled from that river for nearly ten years. The boy was rescued by his grandmother, and that made it a story worth covering. So Vic covered it—got statements from Granny and the boy on tape, and returned to the station.

Horace listened to the tape and grunted, which, Vic guessed, meant that he approved.

"Do you have any idea what Mark Ten-Nineteen means?" Vic asked.

"Oh, yeah. The Reverend Mr. Hatch's latest venture. It's a school. Boarding school, out past the river. He opened it last year, right after you vanished, come to think of it."

"What's it teach?"

"Apart from Hatch's rather peculiar brand of Christianity, the basics, I guess. The three Rs."

"Okay, another question. Where does Mayor Fermin live these days?"

"He and Myra have a big, new place near Hatch's tabernacle. You can see it from the road. Looks to me like it has twenty rooms or more, plus an outdoor pool and tennis courts. Why? You planning to visit?"

"Do you think I'd be welcome?"

"Yeah, like smallpox."

Vic went on the air at five-fifteen and told the tale of the careless lad and the valiant granny. Then, he drove past the Fermin homestead. As Horace had said, the house, a big, boxy affair in no discernible style, was easily seen from the road. There was a high, chain-link fence topped with barbed wire surrounding the property, and a single gate, also of chain link and barbed wire. Vic could see two of the black Humvees parked near a big garage.

Something was missing? But what?

Vic went home and prepared for what he was sure was going to be a long night.

"What's the agenda?" Tot asked, watching Vic put on the specially treated clothing.

"Somehow, I've got to talk to Myra. I'll go out to the Fermin digs and play it by ear."

"I don't like the sound of 'playing it by ear.'"

"Tot, did you just make a pun?"

"Swell of you to notice. Do me a favor—two favors. Be sure to carry your cell phone—"

"Why?"

"In case you have to call for help, of course."

"Of course. Silly me. And the other favor?"

"Wait here."

Tot left the room and returned a minute later with a roll of duct tape. "Put this in your trench coat pocket."

"What for?"

"You'll probably be breaking and entering. I've heard tape is useful to burglars for holding locks open and such."

"Okay."

"Good luck."

"Thanks," Vic said, and went out to the car.

The night was moonless. A nasty wind was blowing from the east, carrying with it a chill that threatened rain.

Vic drove twice around the Fermin property. The big house was dark, except for a light in one of the third-floor rooms. Vic smoothed his mask into place, activated the belt buckle spray, then scanned the area through his night vision lenses. He could see nothing except the dead grass shivering in the wind.

He parked the VW behind a stand of trees a half-mile from Fermin's gate and ran up the road until he reached the fence. A burst of speed, a jump, and he was clinging to the chain links. He climbed to the rolls of barbed wire and rolled over them, protected by his coat, and dropped to the other side of the fence.

He sprinted toward the house.

And then he heard something. He stopped, and listened: a panting, a rustling . . .

And something leaping at him from the darkness. A dog. A big, quiet dog. A Doberman? Vic got his forearm up and jammed it into the animal's gaping jaws. They went down together, man and beast, and rolled. Vic wrenched his arm away—had the bulletproof material protected him from teeth?—and kicked. His boot caught the Doberman under the jaw and the dog flopped backward. Lying on his back, braced on his elbows, Vic kicked again, and again, and the dog whimpered and lay still.

He got to his feet and saw two flashlight beams moving toward him.

"Fido?" someone from behind the beams called.

Fido? That beast is named Fido . . .

Vic moved toward the house, counting on his dark clothing to prevent his being seen. He slipped around a corner and was next to a door. He tried the knob. No joy. He edged along the wall until he was under a small, second-floor balcony.

"Dog's hurt!" an alarmed voice yelled.

"Dog's *dead!*" another voice yelled.

Vic jumped, and grabbed the floor of the balcony. He hoisted himself up and vaulted over a low railing, and was facing French doors, slightly ajar. He pushed through them and entered the house. The room was empty. He left it and crept down an unlit corridor until he came to a staircase.

The light was on the third floor . . .

He went up the steps and found what he was seeking, a door with a strip of light at the bottom. He pressed his ear against it; someone inside was sobbing.

He went through it and found himself in a large, brightly decorated bedroom. Myra, wearing a robe, lay across the bed next to an open book. She looked up and took a deep breath. Vic moved to her and put a hand over her mouth.

Doesn't she recognize me . . . ? No, not with the mask . . .

"I'm not here to hurt you," he whispered. "I just want to talk. Understand?"

Myra nodded.

Vic took his hand from her face. "I want to know if you're here of your own free will."

Myra neither moved nor replied.

"Because if you're not," Vic continued, "I'll get you out of here."

"You're from the school!" Myra said. "This is a test."

"I don't know about any school. And I'm not testing you."

"Please don't lie to me."

"I'm not."

"Let me show you something."

"Okay."

Myra rolled to the edge of the bed and opened a drawer in a night table. When she turned back to Vic, she was holding a small, silver revolver.

Will she shoot . . . ?

"Get out of here!" she screamed.

"Myra—" Vic protested, as he got to his feet.

"Get out!"

There was a flat *krak!* and the gun twitched in Myra's hand.

Vic felt as though a sledgehammer had struck his left shoulder. He flung himself across the bed, slapped the gun from Myra's hand, and continued through the door and down the steps. The two men from outside were coming toward him. In the greenish glow of the night vision lenses, he could see that they held metal batons and flashlights.

"Somebody's there," one of them yelled.

Both aimed their flashlight beams at Vic and for a moment, he was blinded.

The night lenses . . .

He sensed, rather than saw, the baton swinging toward his head. He ducked, and drove his stiffened fingers into his attacker's midsection. The man grunted and dropped both his baton and his light.

The second attacker was already bringing his baton in a high arc toward Vic's head. Vic blocked it with his forearm and—

. . . a stab of pain in his shoulder . . .

—slammed his elbow into the attacker's chin. The man fell and Vic kicked away his baton.

Vic was still partially blinded, but he could see that he was in a corridor with a door at the far end—the door he had first tried to enter.

Vic moved. Through the door and into the cold night. Up over the fence and onto the soft ground. He heard an engine start behind him. Twin headlight beams shone through the fence and the engine roared.

Vic ran.

A black SUV pursued him, smashed through the fence and onto the tarred pavement.

Vic left the road and ran through the woods alongside it. His vision had completely cleared and he could see with no trouble.

His shoulder hurt.

He reached the VW, got in, and steered the small car onto the road.

He could see the headlights of the Humvee shining on the trees as it rounded a curve. Whoever was inside it couldn't see him yet, but another couple of seconds . . .

He jammed down the gas pedal and the car leaped forward. Vic remembered that this stretch of road was two miles or so long.

I can haul ass . . .

He parked the Volkswagen behind Tot's barn.

Just in case . . .

But he wasn't really worried. He'd left the SUV miles and miles behind.

Tot was waiting for him in the kitchen. Vic pressed the buckle and, when the mist had cleared, shed hat, trench coat, and shirt.

"Good heavens!" Tot gasped, staring at a darkening bruise that spread from Vic's inner shoulder almost to his sternum. "What caused *that*?"

"Bullet," Vic said. "Without your protective material, I'd be bleeding. As it is, I seem to be okay. It hurts, but I don't think anything's broken."

"I wish I could help you, but I have absolutely no first-aid skills. I'm quite squeamish."

"No problem."

"What happened?"

For the next ten minutes, Vic described what had happened at the Fermin homestead.

"Your second foray as a mystery man was not a success, then," Tot said.

"I sure didn't cover myself with a lot of glory," Vic said. "But I wouldn't say the night was a complete bust. At least, I learned some things."

"Such as?"

"Well, a *smart* mystery man would have done a better job of reconnaissance. The dog shouldn't have been a surprise. Next time, I'll do more looking before I leap. If there *is* a next time."

"Anything else?"

"I think maybe I know what's happening with Myra."

"You can't blame her for shooting you . . . A masked man at midnight . . ."

"Not that. The other things. Beginning with her marriage to Fermin. The only way that makes sense is if she was forced into it. And there's what she said when I entered her room . . . She asked if I was from 'the school,' and she sounded scared."

"Who could blame her. The mask, the hour . . ."

"It wasn't any of that. On the way back here, I finally figured out what was bothering me about Fermin's property. There was no kid's stuff—no swings, no seesaws. When I was at Myra's other house, the yard was a miniature playground. There's nothing conclusive there, but added to the school remark and the fact that apparently nobody's seen Myra's kid. At least, nobody's mentioned her."

"The child has been abducted."

"And is being held hostage. Myra has to be a good little slave or Jackie gets hurt."

"Nasty. Very nasty."

"Maybe this explains the third call I made from Fermin's office. The answering machine said, 'Mark Ten-Nineteen.' Maybe that's the school."

"The other call, the second one—"

"That was answered by someone at the McFeeley plant. So we're seeing a connection between Fermin, Hatch, this Mark Ten-Nineteen, and McFeeley's. And these guys in black jumpsuits I keep running into are somehow in it, and somebody named Colonel Crate. I heard one of the jumpsuit guys mention that name."

"What's your next ploy?"

"I'll start with good ol'Google, try to learn exactly what business McFeeley's is in, and who Crate might be. After that . . . I don't know. Maybe I'll visit the school."

Vic moved toward the staircase. "See you in the morning."

Vic slept soundly for the next six hours. When he awoke, the sun was already up and he remembered no dreams. His left arm and shoulder were stiff, but much of the previous night's soreness was gone. He went into the yard to perform his morning routine and when he was done, most of the stiffness was also gone.

He shared breakfast with Tot and drove the VW from behind the barn to the radio station. Horace sent him out to interview area gas station owners on how high petroleum prices were affecting their business. Vic got a few minutes' pointless response on tape and went back to KWLM. He asked Horace about Myra's daughter, whether anyone had seen or spoken to her lately.

"Come to think of it, no," Horace said. "Myra used to

go everywhere with her, but I haven't seen her . . . oh, since before the wedding. Why do you ask?"

"Idle curiosity."

"Curiosity killed the cat. But if the cat had been a reporter, curiosity might've gotten him a Pulitzer."

"I'll take that as an expression of approval."

"If that's what makes you happy . . ."

Vic asked the receptionist about Jackie Connelly and then Danny, the freckled engineer; both repeated what Horace had told him. He went into Hub City, to the diner across from the motel, and asked the friendly, frazzled waitress about Jackie.

"Never seen her," the woman said, refilling Vic's coffee cup.

"What do you know about Mark Ten-Nineteen?"

"Big place out in the country? I hear it's real expensive, like a couple hunnert thousand a year. It's all I can do to keep my grandkids in public school."

Vic thanked her and left a generous tip.

For the grandkids . . .

Back at KWLM, he used the office computer to Google Mark Ten-Nineteen and Colonel Crate. There was no information on them. He was typing an inquiry about McFeeley's when Horace summoned him to the studio.

"Family emergency," Horace said. "My son got busted for drug possession."

"I didn't know you had a son—"

"From my first marriage. Lives with his mother near Cairo. Anyway, can you handle the five o'clock newscast?

Use your gas station story and then read from the wire service copy."

"I'll do my best."

"I should be back before morning."

"I hope everything works out okay."

"Yeah," Horace said.

Vic went on the air at five and signed off at six, having stretched his gas station piece to an absurd three minutes and having read a lot of words written by wire service reporters, four commercials, and a public service announcement that urged listeners to be honest with their children. He waved to Danny, the engineer, and went back to the computer.

He Googled McFeeley Manufacturing and learned only that the company made plastics, was privately held by the McFeeley family of Hub City, had been started by a man named Eustis McFeeley, and seemed to be currently operated by McFeeley's daughter, one Emiline Grandyfan. He next consulted a local directory and learned that there was, indeed, a McFeeley residence in the area. He jotted down the address on a piece of paper and left the building.

In the VW, he punched the McFeeley address into the global positioning unit and saw that the place was at the edge of Hub City, near the manufacturing facility. He made the drive in forty minutes. The sun had set, but there was a bright moon, and in its glow Vic could see that the McFeeley home had, in its time, been splendid. It was a huge, white Colonial, complete with a portico and eight white columns. But the ground was barren and the few trees twisted. The windows and doors of the house itself gaped open; it was obviously deserted. Here, the stench from the plant was particularly unpleasant.

Vic turned around and went back to the main road. There, he found himself in dense traffic—a steady stream of cars and pickup trucks coming from the direction of the plant.

Must be a shift change . . .

The traffic thinned as he passed the turnoff that led to Hatch's tabernacle. Vic estimated that more than a third of his fellow drivers were going there, which meant that either the locals were unusually pious or Hatch was offering goodies of some kind.

Vic continued toward Tot's. He was passing a tavern—a roadhouse, really—that he had never noticed before. On impulse, he parked, went in, and looked around for someone who might be interested in beating him up. But the only patrons were an old couple at a corner table eating from bowls and a skinny kid drinking a cola behind the bar.

Not gonna get the shit kicked out of me here, dammit . . .

But as long as he was there, he might as well eat. He sat at a table near the old couple and, when the kid shambled over and asked what he'd have, Vic nodded to the couple and said, "Whatever they're having and coffee."

The kid brought him a bowl of chili and coffee in a cracked mug. The coffee was no better than Vic expected, but the chili was excellent. Vic ate it all and went to the bar to pay his bill. As the kid made change, Vic said, "I'm new around here. Looking around. Saw some kind of mansion."

"Oh, yeah," the kid said, counting out the change. "The McFeeley place."

"Looked deserted."

"Has been for, uh, five years. Old lady McFeeley went to live on a boat. She has a weird name . . . Emmy-something."

"Emiline?" Vic asked.

"Sounds right."

"You mentioned a boat. What, a yacht or something?"

"No, I hear it was more like one'a them old boats with the big wheel in the back. Like Mark Twain druv."

"You got any idea where this boat is?"

"Way up the Ohatchapee, I hear. Way up at the state line."

Where the water is probably not fouled . . .

"Okay, thanks," Vic said, putting a dollar bill on the bar.

"You come back now," the kid said, but he didn't sound like he meant it.

Vic considered checking out Mark Ten-Nineteen. But the moon was smaller and dimmer and he didn't have the night vision lenses with him, so he probably couldn't see much. And his adventure at Fermin's had taught him not to blunder in just anywhere. So he drove home and went to bed early.

The next day, Horace telephoned Vic at the station to say he was delayed and would not be back in time to do the five o'clock news. Vic assured him that he could handle it, culled a few stories from the papers and a few more from the wire services, and went on the air.

"You're getting to sound real professional," Danny told him.

Later, Vic followed the GPU directions and found Mark Ten-Nineteen. The grounds were vast, at least twenty acres, Vic estimated, and there was no doubt about the security. The fence was high and every forty feet or so bore red signs warning that it was electrified. The only other sign was on one of the stone pillars on either side of a high fence that led to a winding road. It read, simply: 10:19. The countryside was dark—it was almost seven on November 3—but Mark Ten-Nineteen was well lit, mostly by mercury vapor lamps perched atop dozens of poles. Vic could see buildings: a large one—the school?—and four others. One looked like a multivehicle garage, two others like dormitories, the last an old-fashioned Quonset hut. Four of the black Humvees were parked in a neat row near the Quonset. Vic saw no guards, nor humans of any kind, but he didn't have to wonder about dogs, not here: There were at least five Dobermans, and probably more, ranging around the area, dark and silent.

It's like a prison . . .

Vic turned the VW around and sped toward Rodor's.

"You've got to prioritize," Tot was telling Vic as they sat warming themselves in front of a fireplace full of burning logs. "You've given yourself several tasks. Rescue Myra Connelly, assuming she wants or needs to be rescued. Find out what's going on, exactly, with Reverend Hatch and his congregation. Find out what's going on with the mayor. Did I miss anything?"

"Yeah," Vic said. "Jackie. Myra's kid."

"Ah, yes, the prodigal daughter. You think she's being held at the school?"

"Makes sense. But there has to be more to the place than imprisoning one little girl. Jackie—hell, they could shove her into a coal bin someplace. They wouldn't need acres and buildings and watchdogs."

"They could have other children imprisoned?"

"That makes sense, too. Maybe people who *aren't* just children."

"What's your first move?"

"Sleep. Richard said that sometimes the subconscious solves problems better than the waking mind."

"Yes, yes . . . Einstein and his sailing . . ."

"I'll assume that what you just said makes sense and wish you good night."

Vic did sleep, for the next eight hours. Then he awoke, did his morning routine, ate breakfast sitting across the table from Tot, and went to the station.

Horace was waiting for him. "Bad car crash on Highway 4. Just heard about it on the scanner."

"I'm on it," Vic said, and twenty minutes later was looking at the shapeless wreck of a minivan that had been struck by a tanker truck. The minivan driver, who had apparently not used his seat belt, had been thrown from his seat into a tree. A state cop told Vic that the medics had taken off the man's coat and tried to revive him, to no avail. The body was already gone. Vic inspected the van and saw, in a cracked but unbroken portion of the windshield, a sticker that entitled the vehicle to a spot in the McFeeley parking lot. Vic walked over to the tree the driver had hit and found the driver's coat, abandoned on the shoulder of the road. Pinned to the coat's front was a plastic-encased badge identifying the bearer as an employee of the McFeeley Corporation.

Which gave Vic an idea. He unpinned the badge and put it in his pocket. He had no idea whether the badge would be missed, and a qualm about stealing something that might be valuable to the driver's family.

But I should be able to return it in a day or two . . .

One of the state cops spoke a few sentences into Vic's recorder. Vic drove into the city, to the morgue, and got a few more sentences from the medical examiner, a physician with a bushy white mustache who must have been at least eighty.

"Yep-sireee, deader'n a doornail. Prolly dead before he hit he tree. Gone to his reward."

Vic thanked the doctor and returned to KWLM. He told Horace he'd have something for the five o'clock broadcast and asked about Horace's son.

"Kid's a mess," Horace said. "More my fault than his mother's, though her hands aren't exactly clean, either. I got him into a rehab—not the best, but the best I can afford. Maybe it'll do some good."

Vic had no idea what to say. He mumbled something and went to read the papers.

"I heard your newscast," Tot said as he ignited logs in the fireplace. "Are you all right? That crash sounded horrible."

"I didn't actually see the body. Just a lot of twisted metal."

"Thank heaven for small favors."

Vic removed the badge from his pocket and gave it to Tot. "This belonged to the victim."

Tot looked at the badge lying on his palm and then, with raised brows, at Vic.

"I'm thinking that if my photo were on it instead of the driver's, it might get me into both Hatch's tabernacle and the plant."

"Not *your* photo," Tot said. "We're pretty sure they're on the lookout for you."

"Maybe a photo I could be made to resemble?"

"That has possibilities. Yes. How about consulting with those theatrical people you met in New York?"

"Sure, maybe."

"As for the badge itself . . . I have a friend in St. Louis who has a pretty good photo lab. I was planning to go to a Rams game—"

"You're a football fan?"

"Occasionally. Anyway, my friend could probably duplicate the badge and then you could pretend to have found the original and return it. That way, there won't be any missing badge and the curiosity that might arouse."

"I didn't consider that, the curiosity part."

"That's why I get the big bucks. Or used to, anyway."

The next morning, Vic posted a message on the computer bulletin board and waited to be contacted by his benefactor. And the morning after that, just after he'd come into the Rodor house after doing his morning routine outdoors, the phone rang and a familiar voice asked, without any preamble, what he needed.

"I need a disguise," Vic said.

"Why?"

"Because I need to get into somewhere I can't go as myself."

"As *either* of yourselves?"

"Yeah, as either of myselves."

"What is this place?"

"It's called the Tabernacle of the Highest Holiness. I have a hunch that whatever's going on is centered there."

"You can't sneak in? Break in?"

"I don't know. I don't think so, not without calling a lot of attention to myself. My*selves.*"

"Can you get to New York?"

"Not easily."

"Gotham City?"

"Same answer."

A pause. Then: "St. Louis, Sunday morning. I'll get back to you with time and address."

"Okay, can do."

"Are you making any progress?"

"Some. Have you ever heard the name Crate?"

"No."

"Watch for it."

Vic's benefactor hung up and Vic began to make breakfast.

Vic decided to leave for St. Louis on Saturday afternoon, which meant he had a day and a half before he had to be on his way. He went to work, covered a couple of local stories by phone, and completed the day by going on the air. His few minutes of airtime were becoming a regular part of his routine, and an enjoyable one. The reporter job had originally been a means to an end, but now he was liking it.

That was Thursday, and Friday was almost a duplicate of it.

Friday evening, Vic told Tot about his travel plans.

"Any reason we can't go together?" Tot asked.

"That's right, you're going to the Rams game."

"And to visit my photographer friend."

"Okay," Vic said. "Deal."

They left immediately after breakfast and drove through back roads lined with trees that were full of fall colors. As they were turning onto the interstate, Vic's cell phone rang.

Tot, at the wheel, asked, "Are you expecting a call?"

"Matter of fact, I am." Vic said hello into the phone and listened to his benefactor recite an address in a suburb called "Florissant."

"Ten o'clock tomorrow morning," the benefactor said, and before Vic could reply, broke the connection.

"Was that who you were expecting?" Tot asked.

"It was. You ever hear of *Florissant*?"

"No, but we'll find it," Tot assured him.

By seven, they had checked into a hotel that was within sight of the arch.

"Separate rooms," Tot insisted.

"Sure, but why?"

"You'll thank me. I have it on good authority that I snore. Like a foghorn."

They had dinner in the hotel dining room and then

walked around the area, through the parkland around the arch and down the riverfront, past a big, silver casino boat and other, smaller amusements. The parking lots were full, the sidewalks crowded with couples and families out for a good time. Tot and Vic people-watched for a couple of hours, and when the air grew too chilly for their light jackets, returned to the hotel. Before separating, they agreed that Tot would take a taxi to visit his photographer and Vic would use the VW.

In his room, Vic watched a TV movie until he realized that staring at the carpet would be more entertaining. He went to sleep.

And awoke early, as usual. He went to the window and watched the sun rise over the Mississippi, then meditated and did the yogic part of his morning routine.

In the hotel lobby, he studied a map of the area. Florissant was a suburb north and west of the city proper. He bought a cup of good coffee from a pretty young woman at a cart near the check-in desk and went out to the VW. He fed the address he'd been given into the GPU and followed the map on the screen to Florissant, and into a subdivision full of curving streets lined with manicured lawns, their grass now brown, brick ranch houses, and colorful trees. His destination was the smallest building on the block, with a small patch of yard in the front and a smaller one in the back.

He rang the bell and when the door opened, he was facing Olga Knauseley. She grinned, and hugged him, and ushered him into a pleasant room obviously furnished from a department store.

"Tell me the problem, Vicky," she said. Vic told her

what he needed. She nodded, put her forefinger on her cheek, and said, "Let's get busy."

Four hours later, Vic was staring at a man with full, chipmunkish cheeks, a head full of shaggy black hair streaked with gray, dark brown eyes, a thick, black mustache, and olive skin. The man was staring back at him from a mirror.

"It's pretty simple and almost foolproof," Olga said. "The skin darkener won't rub off unless you use a cream I'll give you and the contact lenses shouldn't be a problem either. You'll have to be careful with the wig—that *will* come off. Not easily, but it's not glued on."

"I look like Zorba the Greek," Vic said.

"You could do worse. Now, the tricky part." Olga opened a suitcase and took out a pair of orthotics. "Put these in your shoes. They'll throw you off-balance—not the way the back brace does, a different way."

"What *about* the brace?"

"Don't wear it. Zorba the Greek is a good idea. Think Zorba the Greek."

"How did you know my shoe size?"

"My dear Vicky, I spent *time* with you. And I *do* have eyes in my head."

Vic asked Olga how much he owed her and she told him that it was taken care of.

"By my mysterious benefactor?" Vic asked.

"As always," Olga replied.

"What's your relationship with him?"

"I don't exactly have a 'relationship.' Every so often, he sends me money and asks me to do something. I have no idea who he is. But he did once warn me that what he does is dangerous and that some of his enemies are smarter than he is, so conceivably I might someday be in danger. It's a risk I'm willing to take."

"For the money?"

"I won't lie and say money isn't a consideration, but more than that . . . I have a strong conviction that your benefactor is on the side of the angels. Call it an old woman's fancy."

Vic grinned. "Or feminine intuition?"

"Maybe."

Vic thanked Olga and received both a hug from her and a plastic container she called a "goody bag" and went to the VW. In the car, he checked his cell phone's voice mail. There was a call from Tot asking that Vic meet him at an address in South St. Louis. Vic programmed the address into his GPU and, forty minutes later, arrived at a large, old brownstone house on a gated street. He went up steep steps and across an expanse of lawn and up more steps to the porch and front door. It opened before he could knock and an elfin man with a white goatee and huge belly beckoned him in.

"Andy Holbein," the man said, shaking Vic's hand. "You're Aristotle's friend? Follow me."

Holbein led Vic to a room at the back of the house that was fitted as a photography studio. Tot was sitting on a stool, paging through a magazine. He nodded to Vic and said, "You don't look like yourself."

"Then how do you know I'm me?"

"It's a bit early in the day for metaphysics."

"Tot, it's nighttime."

"It's *always* too early in the day for metaphysics."

Holbein directed Vic to sit on another stool in between a blue sheet and a tripod-mounted camera.

"Should I say cheese?" Vic asked.

"No," Holbein said and began snapping pictures.

An hour later, Vic and Tot were driving toward downtown St. Louis. In Vic's pocket was a duplicate of the McFeeley employee badge he'd found at the car wreck, with a photograph of the person he now looked like in place of the crash victim's picture. The original badge was nestled next to it.

They ate dinner at the hotel restaurant. Vic's darkskinned, mustached, shaggy-haired appearance attracted no particular attention.

After the meal, they wandered around the riverfront for a while, then went to their separate rooms. Vic removed his wig and phony mustache and opened Olga's goody bag. He removed a jar of cream and, using the bathroom mirror, smeared the goop on his face. He felt foolish, and glad nobody was witnessing this. But the dark makeup came off on a piece of tissue and when Vic went to bed, he again looked like Vic.

CHAPTER **THIRTY-ONE**

They were up before the sun and on the road before six. Tot, driving, asked, "You plan to sneak into Hatch's little party—isn't that the reason for your masquerade?"

"Right."

"Then I think you'll need new transportation. This crate is pretty recognizable—there aren't many left in operation—and my own car might be recognized, too."

"What do you suggest?"

"Let's see what we can rent in the next town."

They asked for information at a gas station and went to a place called Harry's Heaps, an open area filled with vehicles at least twenty years old, with a tar-paper shack in the center. They put a deposit down on the rental of a battered old Gremlin, which Vic drove back to Hub City.

He switched cars at the Rodor property and went to work. He was an hour late and stood contritely while Horace chewed him out, then went to cull stories from the wire service copy and newspapers.

After his five o'clock newscast stint, he went back to Rodor's and, in the bathroom, covered his face, hands, and lower arms with the olive makeup Olga had given him. He pasted on the mustache, pulled the wig over his real hair, put the orthotics in his shoes, and presented himself to Tot.

Tot gasped, loudly and theatrically, and whispered, "Who are you?"

Vic went to the nearest mirror and reinspected himself. The disguise wouldn't fool anyone who was expecting Vic Sage, but what he saw did not exactly resemble his everyday self. He decided this new persona should have a name. Zorba? No. But Nikos? Yes, Nikos was perfect.

So it was *Nikos* who got the rented Gremlin from the barn and drove it to join the parade of vehicles going into the Tabernacle of the Highest Holiness parking lot. The lot was almost full. He noticed, for the first time, that most of the cars, SUVs, and pickup trucks were new and pricy, not the kind of wheels he might expect factory workers and farm folk to own. There were even a couple of sports cars, a Corvette and a Porsche.

He joined the shuffling throng inching toward the entrance. Five of the black Humvees were parked near the front walk, and next to them, an old-fashioned yellow school bus. There were four men in the black watch caps and jumpsuits flanking the door, as Vic expected. One of them stared hard at him and for a second he thought his disguise hadn't worked and considered his options. Run back to the Gremlin? Run into the Tabernacle? Try to take these guys out? But the man looked down at his clipboard, shrugged, and did nothing else except say, "Good evening and may the Lord bless you."

So far so good . . .

The inside of the Tabernacle hadn't changed since he had visited it with Myra. There were the upholstered pews, the stained-glass windows, the scarlet cloth covering the walls.

The place was absolutely full, and people had begun to stand at the rear.

The lights dimmed, organ music swelled, and Hatch, again illuminated by a single white spotlight, appeared at the silver pulpit.

"Good evening and may the Lord bless you," he said, a hidden microphone amplifying his voice.

"May the Lord bless you," the congregation echoed.

Hatch began his sermon, another bigoted diatribe in sanctimonious rhetoric. Vic allowed himself to scan the area, surreptitiously, because surely there were cameras trained on the congregation. He counted a dozen of the black-clad guards ranged at regular intervals around the hall. They seemed to be unarmed, but Vic was certain that their trusty metal batons were hidden somewhere near them.

Hatch concluded his speech, bowed, rolled his eyes upward, and said, "And now . . . the chill-der-in!"

The what . . . ?

The lights brightened, revealing, behind Hatch, a row of boy and girls, some almost infants, some preteens. Their heads were bowed, their hands clasped. They had identical short haircuts, they were all dressed alike, both males and females in black jackets and pants, and white shirts with black ties, and they were all sickly: pale, trembling, some barely able to stand.

Hatch raised his arms and said, "O Lord, have mercy on these little ones and help me confer your blessings upon them. Which one, O Lord? Which one is to receive your special grace?"

He passed in front of the children, placing a flat palm over each one's head until he stopped, abruptly, and stiffened, and screamed, "Yes yes *YES!*"

He turned to address the congregation. "The Lord has moved through me, has spoken to me in words of fire and lightning, has shown me His choice." He turned back to the children and tugged a small boy, no more than six years old, to the front of the pulpit area. He positioned the boy to face the congregation and stood behind him, hands over the boy's head.

"Almighty Lord, what is this child's name?" He paused, in an attitude of listening, and continued: "Alvin? Is that what you said? Alvin? Then hear me, O Lord. Thy servant Alvin is sore afflicted with the woes of the flesh. He is an innocent, O Lord, and his parents . . . what are their names, Lord? Betsy and Jake? Well, Betsy and Jake are thy good and faithful servants, so thy will be done and let this sorely afflicted child be free of his tribulations."

The lights went out and for almost a minute, the hall was dark. Then, the room brightened. Hatch and Alvin were still standing at the center of the podium area, in front of the other youngsters.

"How are you feeling?" Hatch asked Alvin.

"Better," Alvin mumbled.

"Have the afflictions of the flesh been lifted from you?"

"Yessir."

"Show us."

Alvin ran across to the podium, jumped in the air, and ran back to Hatch.

Hatch looked out at the auditorium. "Are Betsy and Jake present on this holy occasion?"

A middle-aged couple rose from one of the front pews and went to Alvin and hugged him and each other.

"Let us sing His praises as he has delivered Alvin, son of Betsy and Jake, from suffering. Betsy, Jake, sing hallelujah."

"Hallelujah!" Betsy cried.

"Hallelujah," Jake said tentatively.

The organ blared and Hatch shouted, "Go in peace."

The lights dimmed and people began leaving the pews. Vic stayed where he was, watching the line of children being led off by two of the guards. He stood, then, and joined the shuffling crowd. At the rear of the auditorium, there was a second, smaller line of men waiting to get into a bathroom.

The woes of the flesh . . . Maybe I can hide in the john . . .

Vic moved toward it, past one of the guards who was staring straight ahead. Then, a woman who was near the exit stumbled and fell and cried out, and the guard moved toward her. It was totally unexpected, and Vic instantly amended his plans. He ducked back into the auditorium and flattened himself under one of the pews. He heard someone say, "She'll be all right."

He waited. The area got quiet, the lights went out. Vic heard the *thunk* of a large door being closed and then it was quiet except for the distant hum of heating machinery. Vic rolled out from under the pew and raised himself to a crouch. Except for the red glow of *Exit* signs, the auditorium was dark. He knew that those cameras would still be operating, but he was hoping that either they wouldn't work in darkness or no one was monitoring them. If he were mistaken in either hope, he'd know soon, and probably painfully. He duck-walked to the front of the auditorium and went where the children had gone. Then he was in a waiting area. A large board full of electric switches and dimmers occupied most of one wall, and a bank of television screens, all dark, another wall. There was a door, partially ajar, at one side, and through it Vic could see steps going down.

He heard voices through the door:

". . . return to the school." That sounded like Hatch.

"Can't we just keep him overnight?" Jake.

"Please?" And that was Betsy.

"The Lord's will," Hatch said, and evidently that closed the subject.

There were scufflings on the steps, a lot of them. Vic looked for a place to hide and, finding nothing, flattened himself against a wall in deep shadow. Betsy and Jake emerged from the stairwell. Jake's arm was around his wife, and she was sobbing into his shoulder.

One of the guards, holding a six-cell flashlight, came up the stairs next, followed by the children who had stood with Hatch. Another guard, also shining a light, came at the rear of the group. The first guard opened a door, which, Vic realized, led to the parking lot. Through it, Vic could see the yellow school bus.

As the children passed near him, Vic saw their faces in the glow of the guard's flashes. All looked pale and sickly, including Alvin, who had presumaby been *cured* only minutes ago. Then Vic suppressed a gasp: The last child in the line had chestnut hair and a mole on her left cheek. She was Jackie Connelly, Myra's daughter. Like the others, she looked wan and ill.

The guards herded the children onto the bus and closed the door. A few seconds later, Vic heard the coughing of an engine and knew the bus was leaving.

Should he make his escape now? Or was there more to be learned?

He decided that he'd seen enough, and that the risk of remaining in the Tabernacle was not worth anything he might find out. He could run into one or more of the guards at any time and he wasn't ready for a confrontation, not yet.

He crept to the door through which the children had gone, opened it a crack, and peered out. What he could see of the parking lot was empty except for three of the Humvees. He slipped out, closed the door softly, and rounded the corner of the building. His rented Gremlin was standing by itself under one of the lights. Except for the Humvees, parked near the building, all the other vehicles had left.

Something's not right . . .

But he could see no danger. So he sprinted. And halfway to the car, he realized what was wrong. A car, unaccounted for, remaining after nobody should be there. The guards would *have* to notice . . .

Headlights were suddenly, blindingly, shining from the darkness. Vic increased his speed. The headlights were being pushed by the remaining two Humvees, speeding from the darkness.

I can't outrun them . . .

What'll I do . . . ?

And he remembered Richard's words: *Don't stop to think. Just be. React.*

The lead Humvee skidded to a halt in front of Vic and a guard, holding a baton, exploded from the driver's side. The *presence* that Vic had just become observed that the guard was wearing a bulletproof vest, but nothing to protect his head. Vic kicked his leg out from under him, and as the man fell Vic punched the side of his head, and in the same motion whirled to face the driver of the second Humvee, who was firing a taser. Vic dropped to the ground and the two electrified darts passed over him, and as the guard started to retrieve them Vic leaped to his feet and struck the guard under the chin with the flat of his palm.

Vic was aware of none of this until he remembered it later.

But his thinking mind returned and he realized that the Gremlin would never be able to outrace the Humvees. He looked at the closest guard, who was beginning to moan; there was a military K Bar knife in a sheath at his side. Vic removed the knife and jabbed in into two of the closest Humvee's tires. Then he moved to the second Humvee and jabbed two more tires.

The guard who had moaned was trying to sit up.

"Stay there!" Vic commanded, and went to the Gremlin.

Vic sipped the hot cider Tot had just given him and turned to the crackling fire.

"Are you too tired to tell me about it?" Tot asked.

"No, not at all. In fact, I'm on an adrenaline high."

"Is that good?"

"I used to think so. I don't anymore. But I'm not accomplished enough to avoid it."

"Is anyone?"

"Yeah, I'm pretty sure Richard is, and Shiva. And it wouldn't surprise me if my benefactor is, too."

"If you say so."

Vic described the visit to the Tabernacle and his escape. When he was finished, both he and Tot sipped cider and stared into the flames.

"A few things are beginning to make sense," Tot said finally.

"Yeah. Such as Myra's situation. Obviously, Fermin and company are holding her kid hostage."

"Since before the wedding, I should think."

"Exactly. Which is *why* there was a wedding. Another thing . . . I'm beginning to think that the kid was taken the day Shiva beat me silly."

"Explain," Tot said.

"Remember that I went to meet Myra and met Shiva instead. Myra set me up. Why? Because her daughter was in danger and my life was the price of her safety."

"And Hatch is part of this . . . whatever it is," Tot said.

"And the McFeeley plant is in on it."

"Yes," Tot said. "And don't forget the school. All you have to do is figure out how all these disparate elements are connected."

"I'm not sure I want to figure it out. I'm not on a crusade. I just want to get Myra away from Fermin, and to do that, I've got to rescue Jackie."

"Aren't you forgetting something?"

"I don't know. Am I?"

"I'd certainly say so. The reason you came back here. Your identity."

"I haven't forgotten it. Well, not exactly. It's just that . . . it's taken a backseat. I'll get back to it after I've taken care of this other stuff."

" 'Other stuff' being the rescue of Ms. Connelly and her child?"

"And maybe the other kids, too, if it turns out that they need rescuing. And maybe finding out what's really going on at the plant. But that's it. Once those things are handled, I'll move mountains to learn who dumped me on those church steps."

Tot raised his eyebrows. "Mountains?"

"Well, okay. Foothills. Knolls. *Ant*hills, then." Vic rose, stretched, and said, "See you in the morning."

A cold wind blew across the school grounds to where Colonel Crate stood in front of his men, who were at rigid attention, their eyes staring straight ahead. The light of the propane lanterns around the group threw wavering shadows.

"Harcourt! Smith!" Crate barked.

Two men stepped forward.

"You know what you did?"

"Yessir!" Harcourt and Smith answered in unison.

"You allowed an intruder to escape."

"Yessir."

"That can't be ignored. That can't go unpunished."

"Yessir."

Crate handed the men metal batons and said, "Redeem yourselves."

For the next ten minutes, Harcourt and Smith fought, circling, weaving, swinging and occasionally striking with the batons, doing little damage. Finally, Harcourt feinted to the left with his baton and kicked Smith in the groin. As Smith involuntarily doubled over, Harcourt hit him twice in the head with the baton and Smith dropped and lay still.

"Very good," Crate said to Harcourt. "Now you fight me."

Crate held up his open palms, to show that he had no weapon.

Harcourt charged. Crate kicked him in the side of the head and rammed his fist into Harcourt's belly. Harcourt dropped his baton and fell. Crate picked up the baton, leaned over Harcourt's body, and struck.

Crate turned to the other men. "He's dead."

"Yesssir!" the guards cried.

"Now listen up," Crate said. "We're under assault here. The other night, someone broke into the City Hall. Tonight, someone penetrated the tabernacle. We don't know who he is, we don't know if he's one man or fifty or a hundred. But this we do know. He is the enemy. We will find him and we will destroy him and until we do we will be constantly alert. Understood?"

"Yessir!"

"Jameson, Haregeiff, you're the burial detail. Dispose of the casualties. The rest of you—*dismissed!*"

The next morning, after Vic had done his routine, over breakfast he and Tot made plans. They agreed that Tot should return the Gremlin to Harry's Heaps in Springfield. Tot agreed and could probably keep himself amused until six, when Vic would pick him up.

Vic, in the VW, followed Tot as far as the interstate, in case any of the black-clad guards happened to spot the Gremlin. None did, and Vic went to work.

It was an extremely routine day: bad coffee, newspapers, phone calls, a few minutes reading wire service copy into a microphone at five-fifteen. He removed his headphones, nodded to Horace, and left the building.

There was construction on the interstate that narrowed the road to one lane and backed up traffic for miles, so Vic was an hour late meeting Tot.

"Sorry," Vic said.

"No problem. But you could have called."

"Well, you could have called *me.*"

"For all I knew, I would have been interrupting your radio broadcast."

The truth was, Vic was not yet used to having a cell phone. He apologized again and treated Tot to dinner at a family diner.

The next evening, Vic didn't go to Tot's when he left the radio station. Instead, he drove to the school and kept driving, following the GPU map to the entrance to

Hatch's tabernacle. Then he retraced his route. The night was dark and there were no street lamps on the county's back roads, but the VW's high beams gave Vic all the light he needed. He drove the route again and again, and finally went home.

He told Tot what he'd been doing.

"Apparently, you have a plan," Tot said.

"Yeah, I do. I woke up with it this morning."

"Your subconscious must have been busy last night."

"Must have been, all right. For this thing to work, I need more info. I have to know how often the kids are taken to Hatch's services, and the exact route of the bus. If it's the *shortest* route, I'm good, I've got that covered. If not . . . more reconnaissance."

"You couldn't just break into the school?"

"Too risky. Those creeps in black are probably all over the place and one of these days, they might get lucky and beat me."

"Or shoot you."

"Or shoot me. And I don't know how the place is laid out, exactly where the kids are kept, in one room or many . . . too many *ifs*. What I have in mind is dangerous, but at least there are fewer variables."

"You sound like a military man."

"Bite your tongue."

"You've never been in the army?"

"No. I'm too young for the draft, and I just didn't give it much thought. I've always been able to find work . . . and I don't like being bossed much."

"You don't seem to mind being bossed by your friend Richard."

"When he does it, it doesn't seem like bossing. More like reasonable suggestions. He doesn't lord it over me. He doesn't seem *better* than me. He's just a friendly guy who knows more than I do."

"I think you've just described an excellent teacher."

After he was done at the station the next day, Vic cashed his paycheck at a bank that had evening hours, then went shopping at the interstate mall. At a sporting goods store, he blew about half of what he had earned on a pair of binoculars with night lenses and a sportsman's watch with a stopwatch built in. At a bookstore he bought five paperbacks and had a sandwich and a cup of really good coffee at the bookstore's café. As he was turning from the sprawling parking lot, he noticed, for the first time, a state police substation adjacent to the mall.

Wonder if the state cops are in Fermin's pocket . . .

He drove home. Tot had already retired. Vic thought he'd make an early night of it. He read one of his new paperbacks in bed for a while, and by eleven was asleep.

The next day was Tuesday, election day. Horace told Vic to go to some polling places and see how the voting was going.

"Who's running for what?" Vic asked.

"I think there's a city council seat open—"

"Hub City *has* a city council?"

"Of course."

"What does it do?"

"Beyond exist? I dunno . . . issue checks to its members, I guess. The mayor's office is also up for election."

"Who's running for *that* august position?"

"The honorable Benedict Fermin."

"Anyone else?"

"I doubt it. Maybe that's something you should find out."

Vic looked in the phone book for a Board of Elections listing and called the number listed. He let the phone ring fifty times before he gave up and drove to City Hall. He was not surprised to find a black Humvee parked in front of the building, nor that two men in black jumpsuits flanked the door. He recognized neither. When he tried to enter, they stepped in front of him and asked what his business was.

"I guess I want to vote."

"Are you registered, sir?"

"I don't know . . . I guess not."

"You'll have to move along. Sir."

"I'm a reporter. I want to do a story."

"The press is not allowed in the polling place."

"Did either of you guys ever hear of the First Amendment?"

"You'll have to move along. Sir."

Vic felt the sweet rush of adrenaline . . . and suddenly, he was aware of his weak posture, caused by the back brace Olga had given him, and the fact that he had been speaking in a voice a half-octave higher than normal. And anyway, obeying the adrenaline could only get him into trouble.

"Okay, sure," he said.

A woman, stooped, wearing a long gingham dress and

carrying a parasol, at least eighty years old, brushed past the guards and started down the walk.

"Pardon me, ma'am," Vic said. "Did you vote?"

"What the heck kinda question is that?" the woman screeched. "Askin' me that . . . s'a'matter with you? It's your fault, you and your kind. I oughtta teach you some manners."

She began to hit Vic with her parasol. His first reaction was to take it away from her, but he realized that here was the opportunity he'd been seeking.

"Ouch, ouch," he cried, stumbling backward. "Don't hit me, please don't hit me." He scurried down the walk and got into his car.

That *should convince them that I'm a wimp* . . .

At six, the polls closed: early, but this was Hub City. Vic called the Board of Elections number again and, again, got no answer. On a hunch, he phoned the Tabernacle of the Highest Holiness. A woman answered and Vic asked her if she happened to know who won the election.

"Why, Mayor Fermin," she said.

"The city council seat?"

"Whoever was on the ballot, I suppose."

Vic thanked her and called City Hall. He identified himself to an answering machine and told it that he would like a statement from the winner and still mayor, Benedict Fermin. He was slipping into his coat when the phone rang. He picked it up and heard Fermin say, "Hello. Sage, is it?"

"It is. Nice of you to return my call, Mr. Mayor."

"You want a statement, is that it?"

"Yessir. If you'll give me a moment..." Vic got a small tape recorder from a desk drawer and held it near the phone. "I wonder if you have anything to say to the people who have re-elected you."

"Well, sure, 'course I do. I just wanna say how it is my honor and privilege to serve the wonderful folks of our wonderful town that's been a shining example of freedom and democracy since the Civil War, and how we're gonna keep on protecting everyone from the commies and terrorists who... want to hurt us real bad."

"Thank you, Mister Mayor."

"Why, thank you, too. 'Night now. You have a good one."

He's flattered ... maybe nobody ever asked him for his opinion before ...

Vic left the station. It was mid November, a week past the end of Daylight Savings Time, and the countryside was dark except for a dim moonglow. Vic went to a spot in the woods above Ten-Nineteen, the school that was, he knew, a prison, and for several hours watched through his new, night vision binoculars. There were a few lights on in the main building, but otherwise, no sign of life.

The next day, Wednesday, he handed Danny the engineer the cassette on which he had recorded Fermin's statement and asked if it would be possible to use the mayor's words on the air.

"Sure," the kid said. "Just nod when you want me to play it."

During the five o'clock newscast, Vic said, "As expected, Hub City mayor Benedict Fermin was re-elected yesterday. He had this to say to KWLM."

Vic nodded to the kid and heard Fermin's voice in his earphones.

He left the studio and as he entered his cubicle, the phone rang. The caller was Fermin. "I just want to thank you for giving me time on your radio," the mayor said.

"All part of the job."

"Well, I wanna thank you anyways. 'Night."

Vic repeated his vigil that night, and on Thursday, Friday, Saturday, and Sunday as well. On Saturday, he saw the SUV he now knew belonged to Fermin stop at the main building and Myra, wearing a fur stole, got out and entered the school. An hour later, she got back into the SUV and it drove toward the interstate.

Other than that, Vic saw nothing.

But on Monday, a week after he began watching, one of the guards drove the yellow school bus from an outbuilding to the school, and the children Vic had seen at the tabernacle climbed into it. Even from a mile away, Vic could hear the bus engine cough and sputter as the old vehicle rolled off in the direction of the tabernacle.

So Monday's when the kids are displayed . . .

Vic ran to the VW and pursued the bus. He wasn't surprised when it turned into the tabernacle property. He parked a bit beyond the shoulder of the road and waited. About ninety minutes later, the bus lumbered out of the tabernacle lot and headed for the school. Vic followed in the VW until he saw the bus pass through the school gate and then continued to Rodor's.

Tot had headphones on and was listening to a CD next to the fire. When Vic entered, he removed the headphones, looked up, and asked, "Well?"

"A week from tonight," Vic said.

"That's when you'll raise your ruckus?"

"Oh, yeah. Big ruckus. Assault, kidnapping, grand theft auto, and that's just for openers."

"Your reconnaissance was a success, I take it."

"I don't know everything, and I'm aware that a lot could go wrong with what I'm planning, but yes . . . I'd call it a success."

"Care to share details?"

"I'm afraid *talking* might get in the way of *doing*."

"I'm too old-fashioned to understand that. Or perhaps I'm too much of a rationalist. In any case . . . if there's anything you need me to do, I'll do it. I probably won't be happy, but I'll do it."

"Thanks, Tot."

The following day, using the radio station's computer, Vic posted a message on the website's bulletin board and wondered how long it would take his benefactor to call. He culled stories from the papers and wire services and, as usual, went on the air fifteen minutes into the five o'clock newscast. He read an item about gasoline prices and another about a livestock exhibit in a neighboring county, nodded to Horace and the kid engineer, and left the studio.

He expected to hear from his benefactor the next day, but he didn't, nor did the man call on Thursday or Friday.

Maybe I'm on my own . . .

But on Saturday morning, the phone rang and when Vic picked it up, he recognized the voice of his benefactor—a voice that was abrupt, with none of the charm of the voice that had told him the joke about the moths.

"You're going to move."

"Yes," Vic said. "This is my plan—"

"Save it. I can't possibly advise you unless I'm there and anything I might say could confuse you. And I don't want to be a part of your failure."

"I'm going to fail?"

"I don't think so. But you might. And if you do, I want none of it."

"Well, I'll do myself the favor of thinking that you wish me luck and let you go . . ."

"Not yet. I have information for you about the man you'll be going against. You should know that he won't be easy to defeat."

"Okay, shoot."

"Look in the mailbox."

The line went dead.

Vic walked out to the Rodor mailbox, a cylinder on a post at the gate to the property, and found a thick manila envelope in it. No stamp, no postmark.

How did he get it in there . . . ?

He went to his room, sat on the bed, and opened the envelope. Inside, he found a sheaf of photocopied documents, including some with FBI and CIA headings that were stamped *Secret.* Taken together, they told him a story, the story of Colonel Thaddeus Crate, once an officer in the United States Marine Corps, now a gun for hire. No, actually, *twenty* guns for hire.

Thad Crate had been born Thaddeus Grandyfan, and until he made a serious mistake, he had been a golden boy. Orphaned at age four, he was raised by an aunt and a grandmother. Straight A student, varsity athlete in base-ball, basketball, and football, prom king, then more athletic glory at Annapolis. Upon graduation from the naval academy, he asked for and got a transfer to the Marine Corps. He was sent to various combat training centers, and excelled in everything, but especially in tactics, marksmanship, and unarmed combat. He was on track to become the youngest general officer in the history of the Corps.

Then, his career stopped. The documents did not say exactly how or why. He was posted to a peacekeeping force in the Middle East, put in charge of a brig where convicted Marines did jail time and . . . What? The next document was a discharge paper. Grandyfan had been discharged "for the good of the service," whatever that meant. Shortly thereafter, he had changed his name to "Crate."

The next documents were copies of CIA reports about Crate, nee Grandyfan, who had reinvented himself as a mercenary. He had killed for money in Africa, the Middle East, South America, and in the process, had recruited, if not an army, then at least a company of men with military skills and bad records, men whose crimes ranged from smuggling to wholesale slaughter.

Vic paused and mulled. So Crate was Grandyfan and Grandyfan, Tot had informed Vic, was the name of Eustis McFeeley's daughter. Which meant that Crate had a connection to the factory. And why the name change? Maybe because he had brought disgrace to the family? Or maybe just because "crate" sounds macho?

Vic turned to the final document. This was not a photocopy, but a letter obviously intended for him, composed on a PC and rendered by some kind of ink jet printer:

> *There is reason to believe Crate's current group is the worst of the worst, culled largely from psycho wards around the world. Do not underestimate them.*

That was it. Vic's benefactor had, in effect, given him a warning. Vic was grateful, but he couldn't help wishing that the warning had been accompanied by some practical advice on how to deal with a herd of armed psychotics. And he was beginning to wonder just what his benefactor's interest was in the Hub City situation. A simple desire to be helpful? No: The voice Vic had heard on the phone an hour ago did not belong to any garden variety do-gooder. Vic was sure the man had another motive and would have given everything he had, which admittedly wasn't much, to know just what it was.

For Batman, the case had begun two months before Charles Victor Szasz had returned to Hub City. Bruce Wayne, known to the world at large as a somewhat ditzy rich guy—good-hearted enough, but totally unfocused and maybe a bit light in the upper story—had been operating as Batman for several years. Only one other individual knew that handsome, affable, clutzy Bruce had a second identity—that Bruce was, in fact, the disguise and Batman the genuine person. That individual was Alfred Pennyworth, who had been part of Bruce's life since before his parents were killed in a random street crime and his psyche had twisted into that of a dedicated avenger.

Bruce and Alfred were in the cave below the huge Wayne Manor. Alfred, a tall, gaunt Englishman dressed in traditional butler garb, was pouring tea from a bone china pot as Bruce slipped into the elaborate armor, mask, and cape of his alter ego.

"And what frolic do we have planned for tonight?" Alfred asked. "Another costumed maniac on the loose?"

"We haven't seen any of those since I finally managed to land the Joker in Arkham Asylum," Bruce replied. "No, tonight I'm after something more prosaic, but potentially far deadlier."

"And that is?"

"A gang that's smuggling arms to the Middle East, but not just any arms. These guys have guns and ammunition made entirely of *plastic*. They do the job of the metal ones, but they're lighter, easier to carry, and most important, they don't set off alarms."

"Such as those at airports and the like?"

"Exactly. Given the world situation, you can see why I'm anxious to put these creeps out of business."

"Two questions, if I may. First, are these 'creeps,' as you call them, terrorists?"

"No, they're worse. Terrorists, at least some of them, believe in their causes. These guys are in it for profit."

"Second question: You generally confine your activities to Gotham City and its vicinity. You once remarked that you can't protect the whole world, but you *might* be able to protect your home town."

"None of that has changed, Alfred. The arms dealers

have been filtering their shipments through Gotham."

"Filtering them from where?"

"I'm not sure. It looks like the shipments originate in Hub City."

"The place the comedians are forever making fun of?"

"Right. 'The armpit of the Midwest,' and so forth."

"Does this mean that we'll be vacationing in the armpit?"

"No, all I plan to do is stop the Gotham traffic. Though I wish I knew someone I could trust to send to Hub City."

"How about the fellow who advised you? The one with the laugh."

"Alfred, he's *ninety-five*. And besides, he's a bit too bloodthirsty for me."

"Point taken, Master Bruce. What is your immediate agenda?"

"Gordon learned that a tractor-trailer is going to bring the guns into a small airfield near Blüdhaven, where they'll be transferred to a helicopter, one of those big Sikorskys, and from there they'll be flown to a freighter anchored off Gotham. I plan to stop them in Blüdhaven."

"May I inquire as to why Commissioner Gordon does not employ the resources of the police department to perform this mission?"

"He has no jurisdiction in Blüdhaven, and the freighter is beyond the three-mile limit, in international waters."

"Why doesn't he enlist the aid of the Blüdhaven police?"

"You'd have to ask him, Alfred. If I had to guess, I'd guess that he doesn't trust them."

"Something to do with the politicians?"

"Probably. If I ever get done cleaning out the gutters, I'm going to start on the statehouses."

The oddly shaped vehicle with the dead-black paint job and balloon tires glided to a halt behind a hangar located in a tiny airstrip that bore no identification of any kind. Batman left the car and melted into the shadows of the building. He didn't need to glance at his watch to know the time; his mental clock told him it was quarter to midnight. If Gordon's information was correct, the truck should be arriving within the next half-hour.

A few minutes later, he heard a laboring engine and saw approaching headlights. A cab hauling an eight-wheel trailer pulled onto the tarmac in front of the hangar and stopped, its motor idling. Batman moved to the rear of the cab, yanked open the driver's side door, and pulled the startled driver from his seat. The driver started to reach for something under his jacket. Batman hit him once. The man lay still. Batman found what the driver had been reaching for—as expected, it was an automatic pistol—and pulled a ring of keys from the driver's belt.

On the second try, Batman found the key that opened a padlock on the rear gate of the trailer. He lifted the gate, took a small flashlight from under his cloak, and shone it on the stacks of crates the trailer was carrying. He lifted one down onto the tarmac and, with a tool he pulled from his own belt, pried it open. Inside, he found a dozen weapons of a type new to him. The guns were molded from plastic, extremely light, and collapsible; they could be compressed into handguns or extended to become shoulder weapons. Rectangular slots behind their triggers indicated that they were meant to hold clips of ammunition, which meant they were probably capable of automatic fire.

Batman stopped his inspection, cocked his head, then went to the cab and carried the still-unconscious driver to the trailer. Batman put him inside, closed the gate, ran to the cab, and hopped up behind the wheel. He saw a helicopter's landing lights descending from the inky sky, and waited. The chopper landed, its twin rotors slowing, and three men emerged from it and ran toward the truck, their heads bowed, although the rotors were well above them. When they were beside the cab, Batman kicked open the door, hitting the first man and knocking him backward. Before the remaining two could react, Batman was on the tarmac kicking and punching.

He fastened the three unconscious men's hands behind them with disposable plastic handcuffs and reopened the trailer gate. He heaved the men inside, next to the driver, and resumed his inspection. After opening two more boxes of guns and three filled with ammunition clips molded of the same plastic used for the guns, he went to his vehicle and got a large toolbox. For the next hour, he processed both the truck and the chopper: developing fingerprints, checking for traces of explosives, photographing every inch of cabin space and the serial numbers of every piece of machinery. Then he went to the trailer and photographed both the men themselves and everything they carried. Finally, he loaded one of the guns and fired into the tires of the truck and helicopter, shredding them. The weapon vibrated in his hands, but did not recoil, and there were tiny explosions where the projectiles struck.

Whatever these things were shooting were not conventional bullets.

In his vehicle, heading for the road back to Gotham City, with one of the plastic guns on the seat beside him, he said aloud, "Gordon." There was a momentary hum and then the voice of James Gordon came from a speaker in the dashboard.

"It's me," Batman said. "There were four of them. Three dozen guns. No known make, of extremely high quality. I estimate ten thousand rounds of unknown ammunition. Explosive pellets, I think. I'll be certain later. Everything you need is waiting at the airstrip."

"Everybody in one piece?" Gordon asked.

"Slightly damaged, but intact. I'll call you in the morning."

Batman said "out" and the speaker hummed. Then he said "Oracle," and the speaker hummed and a female voice asked, "That you, boss?"

"In about forty minutes, I'll be sending you a lot of raw data, including serial numbers. I want everything it's possible to get."

"And you want it yesterday."

"Out," Batman said, and the speaker hummed.

In the cave, Batman sent his ninety-three photographs by computer transmission to a loft in downtown Gotham where, apparently, the young woman who called herself "Oracle" never slept.

He shed the upper half of his costume and, working in tights and T-shirt, took the plastic gun to a work area fitted as a chem lab and analyzed the components of the plastic.

He had no need to make notes; he remembered everything.

Next, he went to a large communications console and looked at a screen, on which were a list of names and addresses. He said "Oracle," and the young woman's voice issued from a speaker.

"Yo, boss. You want chapter and verse or should I cut to the chase?"

"For now, the chase," Batman said. "Later, if we have to help Gordon get a case ready for prosecution, we'll have to include the rest."

"Okay, here goes. The chopper and the semi were both hired from independent contractors with ties to the old Zeus mob, and one of those contractors does a lot of business with rogue nations. And he's tied, by a banking connection, to something called the McFeeley Works, in Hub City."

"What do you know about McFeeley?"

"Company's eighty years old. Started by Eustis McFeeley, a hardware salesman. He went to his reward about five years ago. He had a daughter who was married at eighteen and widowed at twenty-one. Her born name is Emiline McFeeley, but she's an old-fashioned kinda gal who adopted her husband's name, Grandyfan. *Emiline Grandyfan*—sounds like something out of a Victorian novel. I don't find any mention of McFeeley's widow, so she might still be with us. Mrs. Grandyfan had a son, Thaddeus. Apparently, he managed to go to some fancy schools and did time in the military. He seems to have dropped off the Earth, which may mean that he changed his name for some reason."

"Okay."

"Anything else, boss?"

"Yes. I'll read you a list of components of a plastic material. I want to know if they point in any particular direction."

"You can't be more specific than that?"

"Not right now."

Batman said "out" and returned to his laboratory. He turned his attention to the ammunition the guns used and soon learned that his first guess had been correct: The guns shot pellets, each about a third the size of a small pea, and when the pellets struck something, they exploded with surprising force; each was the equivalent of about half a stick of dynamite.

"And each ammunition clip holds five hundred of the pellets, which makes them the nastiest firearms on the planet," Bruce Wayne was saying to Alfred Pennyworth an hour later. They were in the library of Wayne Manor. Alfred was, as always, dressed in his "butler's uniform," a morning coat, cravat, striped trousers, and, his one extravagance, shoes made to order in London. Bruce had on a T-shirt and jeans, his feet bare. They were drinking tea from Alfred's cups.

"Do you expect more shipments to pass through Gotham?" Alfred asked.

"No, nor through Blüdhaven, either. Gordon got enough information from my prisoners to stop this end of the pipeline. So our job's done. But I hate the thought of those weapons being bought and sold on the international market. And I'm beginning to get an idea of how we can stop it."

"You'll move your operation out of this area?"

"No, but maybe I can enlist help. See if you can track down where Shiva is, will you?"

"The martial artist?"

"The same. I'll be in the cave."

Bruce went to a tall old grandfather clock and set the hands at ten-ten. A section of a nearby bookcase pivoted open, revealing a steep flight of steps. Bruce descended the steps and moved through the cave until he came to a gym area, with rings, parallel bars, a swinging trapeze, a couple of horses, and a large mat. For the next hour he did gymnastics. Then, mopping his face with a towel, he moved to his communications console and said, "Oracle."

"Yo, boss," Oracle said.

"What have you got?" Bruce said, speaking in the growl he used as Batman.

"Well, I can say two things about the chemicals you asked about—tetrachloroethene, chlorobenzene, poly-chlorinated biphenyls and the rest. One, they're used in making plastics, and two, they're pollutants. Remember the Love Canal scandal in upstate New York? This stuff was in the toxic soup that the canal became. So that gave me an idea. I ran the data and found that the river most poisoned by these particular toxins is called the Ohatch-apee, which runs through Hub City. That info any use to you?"

"It confirms something I've begun to suspect. In this case, all roads lead to Hub City. Nice work. Out."

Alfred came down the steps. "Tea, Master Bruce?"

"I've already had enough to float an aircraft carrier. Any luck with Shiva?"

"She is currently in Mexico. Near Tijuana, I believe."

"You know what, Alfred? I suddenly have an urge to attend the manufacturers' convention in San Diego. Can you get me a flight?"

As it turned out, all flights from Gotham to San Diego were booked and not even the name Wayne could buy one, so Bruce chartered a Lear Jet. He appeared at the huge San Diego convention center long enough to get the number of a model who was decorating a booth devoted to a new cell phone technology and, apparently accidentally, knock over a table laden with snack food at a reception later that same day, and still later, run his rented Ferrari into a potted plant in front of his hotel.

Yes sir, Bruce Wayne was in town!

Early the following morning, dressed in a loud Hawaiian shirt, straw hat, shorts, and large sunglasses, he rode the streetcar across the border to Tijuana. He met Shiva in front of a drugstore that sold largely to American tourists and followed her on a long walk out of town to a deserted bull ring.

"I have seen to it that we will not be disturbed," she said.

"What do you have in mind, Shiva? The usual?"

"Yes. We will fight for exactly one hour. I will try to kill you. You should try to kill me."

"You know I won't."

"That is your choice. It is stupid."

They fought, brilliantly, relentlessly, with incredible skill and agility, for exactly one hour. Then both stopped at once. Neither looked at a timepiece.

"A draw," Bruce said.

"You are not surprised."

"Not after all these years."

"You are entitled to a favor. I do not suppose that a kiss will repay my debt."

"I can honestly say that there's almost nobody on Earth that I'd rather kiss—"

Shiva grinned. "*Almost?*"

"Almost. But I have something I'd like you to do, and if I kissed you, you'd have no reason to do it."

"Tell me."

"Visit a place called Hub City."

"The one they make the jokes about."

"Yes. Take a look around. Find out if there's any honest men there. Then give me a holler."

"I have made plans to visit Richard next week."

"Visit him. I'm in no hurry."

They walked back to Tijuana and had an early dinner at a cantina. Then Bruce got back on the trolley and rode to San Diego, where he made a spectacular fool of himself at an awards ceremony, went to the airport, boarded his chartered plane, and flew to Gotham City. It had been a busy thirty-six hours.

The next thirty-six months were also busy. More than once, Alfred Pennyworth had to assist Batman in the field, which is something Batman hated to ask of him, and Alfred's skill as an amateur physician was sometimes demanded when Batman returned at dawn, exhausted and bleeding.

In late summer, life in Gotham City quieted. Batman had managed, with help from James Gordon and his ward, Dick Grayson, to put three homicidal maniacs into the padded cells of Arkham Asylum, and to send a chemist who made counterfeit drugs to prison.

"I'm going to visit Richard," he announced after lunch one afternoon.

"Time to hone our martial arts skills, Master Bruce?"

"There is that. But mostly, I want to meet Vic Sage."

"That gentleman being the person Lady Shiva located?"

"The same. He's been with Richard almost a year. I want to see if he's learned anything."

"Such as the latest methods of averting lethal attacks with medieval weaponry?"

"Oh, I'm sure he's picked up fighting techniques. But the important stuff Richard teaches has nothing to do with them."

"And that is?"

"I'd call it 'character building,' but that wouldn't exactly be accurate. And it wouldn't exactly be *in*accurate, either."

"Ah, the mysterious East . . ."

"Richard is no more Asian than you are."

"In that case . . . ah, the mysterious West . . ."

"Those weapons have been showing up around the world—"

"The weapons you suspect are being manufactured in Hub City?"

"Yes. And they're doing a lot of harm. If Richard's new student can stop them, he can save a lot of lives."

Bruce was gone a week. When he returned, he immediately answered a summons from Gordon and, as Batman, worked the next three days without sleep or food. He awoke at noon the fourth day and gratefully accepted the large breakfast Alfred offered.

"I trust the latest crisis is averted," Alfred said.

"It is."

"And how did the sojourn in the Midwest go?"

"Pretty good. This Vic Sage has a lot of rough edges, but he might do all right."

"As a 'mystery man'?"

"I hate that term, as you well know, but yes, as one of us. He's ignorant, though he's managed to teach himself a fair amount as an autodidact—"

"As did you yourself."

"Yes, but my autodidactism was financed by my family's money. Sage has neither family *nor* money, and little formal schooling, so his learning comes from paperbacks read after hours of manual labor. Makes him pretty admirable."

"Do you think he'll put the kibosh on the Hub City villains?"

"I'm not sure he wants to, but if he does . . . he'll probably get killed. That's how we know if we should be doing this work. If we get killed, we shouldn't."

"Admirably pragmatic, and a bit callous."

"It's a callous world, Alfred."

"Does he have any allies?"

"He seems to have befriended one Aristotle Rodor, who's something of an American original. He dropped out of MIT just five hours short of a doctorate in physics, started a company with a partner, made millions, and was on his way to making billions when the partner pulled some legal maneuvers and got control of both the company and most of its patents. Rodor managed to hang on to enough to give himself a comfortable, though not lavish, living. He could be useful to Sage the same way Lucius Fox and you are useful to me."

"I will not press my luck and ask exactly how that is."

"I don't really have any idea how things are going to go with Sage, but I think I'll put him in touch with Olga."

"The New York theatrical Olga."

"The one and only."

That Monday, months after Bruce Wayne's conversation about Vic Sage with Alfred Pennyworth, Vic awoke before dawn as usual and found Tot already up, which had never happened before.

"Tonight's the big night," Tot said.

"I guess you could put it like that," Vic said, and went outside and performed his morning routine. Halfway through his yoga, he stopped and sat still, watching the sun rise over the distant mountain peaks. He remembered Tot's words: "Tonight's the big night."

Indeed it was.

If he did, tonight, what he planned to do, he would be crossing a threshold that he could never *un*cross; his life, his very being, would change forever. It was not too late to change his mind. He could be satisfied with what he had, a pleasant living situation, a job he liked—the best place he'd ever been in. And sooner or later, because the world operated as it did, he would probably meet a pleas-

ant woman and enter into a relationship with her and . . .
he guessed that marriage and children were possibilities.
He could be a normal man, maybe even a happy man. He
would never have his questions answered, never know
who his parents were. But how important was that?
Maybe it *seemed* important only because he had nothing
else to care about.

He stood and stretched and walked slowly to the
house.

"You've been thinking," Tot said.

"I've got until tonight to make up my mind," Vic said.

"I'm sure you'll make the right decision."

"I'm not."

If he did do what he was contemplating, rescue the
children, it was vital that his actions during the day seem
as normal as possible. So he arrived at the station at nine,
drank bad coffee, conferred with Horace, went out to interview a truck driver who'd won a million dollars in the
state lottery and a farmer with a hen who had laid an egg
with what looked like the president's picture on it. At
least, maybe it looked that way to the farmer. To Vic, it
looked like a blotch.

"It is a sign from on high that our president is holy," the
farmer said.

"Yeah," Vic said.

"You think maybe he'd come to see it if somebody told
him about it, the president?"

"Well, you know, he might."

*And then he'd put it on an altar in front of the Washing-
ton Monument so people could file by and genuflect . . .*

"That'd be something, that would," the farmer said.

"Sure would," Vic said, and thanked the farmer for his time and drove back to the station.

At five-fifteen, as usual, he took over the newscast and informed the world that the millionaire truck driver planned to pay off his mother's mortgage and buy a new gas grill, and that a farmer had a blotched egg that might resemble the president. He nodded a farewell to Horace and the engineer, left the studio and the building, and went to the Rodor property. Tot was waiting on the porch. Without a word, Tot got into the VW. He remained silent until they were approaching a crossroad. Then he said, "You know, sonny, we don't have to turn right up there. We could keep going straight on to the interstate. Go to the mall. Have dinner at the Outback. Catch a movie at the multiplex, get home in time to get eight hours."

"That's a possibility."

"But you don't think so, huh?"

Vic slowed the VW and said, "If I don't do it tonight, I'll wonder if I should do it next week. If I never do it, I'll wonder if I should've."

And I'm nothing, and after tonight I'll be something—something bad, maybe, but something . . .

He turned right and realized that he had always been intending to turn right, even if he hadn't known it.

He parked the car on the shoulder of the road, next to a slope covered with brush and trees. He removed his mask from an inner pocket, smoothed it into place, and pressed the stud on his belt buckle. Mist puffed out, momentarily enveloping him, changing the color of his garments, smelling faintly of talcum powder.

"If I'm not back in fifteen minutes, go home."

"That's what we agreed on," Tot said.

Vic climbed out and began to run up the slope. The night was dark, with the moon hidden by clouds, but Vic's night vision lenses enabled him to avoid running into tree trunks. He reached the top of the slope and ran along a ridge for a quarter of a mile until he reached a place where the road below was only one lane wide. He climbed out onto a tree limb that overhung the road and waited, his head turned to the north.

He heard the bus before he saw it, the rumble and roar of an ill-used engine echoing through the night. Then he saw the twin headlights and tensed as the bus passed under where he crouched.

Last chance . . . I can still go back . . .

He stepped from the branch onto the roof of the bus and immediately flattened himself. A gust of wind caught the brim of his hat and he pulled the hat down until the crown of his head filled it. The bus swayed and Vic could barely maintain his grip on the ridged edge of the roof. He pulled off his right glove with his teeth, then his left. His bare fingers could maintain a hold, but barely. The bus turned and dipped sharply to the left, and Vic's gloves slid off.

A few minutes later, the bus slowed and tilted, slightly this time, as it turned into the tabernacle parking lot. Anyone looking at exactly the right angle would see a man in a black trench coat and hat stealing a ride. It was unavoidable, a risk Vic had to take.

The bus moved slowly between rows of parked cars until it reached the area beside the main building. With a screech of brakes, it stopped, and Vic scooted forward and to the right until he lay directly above the bus's front door.

He heard it creak open and looked down to see two of the jumpsuited guards step onto the pavement, one on either side of the door. In the ambient light from the lot, he could see that they had the usual metal batons thrust into their belts, but there was something new, something he hadn't seen the guards carry before: holstered pistols.

If I'm on my game, they'll stay holstered . . .

Vic stood, and jumped.

He landed between the guards but slightly ahead of them, and thrust both his elbows backward, jabbing them into the guards' chests. Both men wheezed and fell against the bus. Vic swung the backs of his fists into their chins and they sank to the ground.

Two down . . .

Vic leaped up two steps and was standing beside the empty driver's seat, looking at a busful of wide-eyed children.

"Okay, kids, little change of plans. You're gonna go see some nice policemen."

He got into the driver's seat and used a lever to close the door. As he put the bus into gear, he looked over his shoulder and said, "If you wanna sing or anything, go ahead."

Three rows back, a little girl stared at him, her lips parted. He recognized her: Jackie, Myra's kid.

It had been over two years since Vic had last driven anything larger than a car, not since his brief stint as part of a construction crew in Galveston, and the bus was a lot crankier than the Galveston truck had been. It lurched forward and momentarily stalled as Vic turned it toward the exit to the access road. The clutch felt as though it were packed in thick molasses, and the brakes had to be pumped several times before they did any slowing. But Vic got the thing onto the road and pushed down the gas pedal. He glanced into the rearview mirror: Nobody was chasing him, not yet.

Just twenty miles to go . . .

The gas pedal was against the floor, and the speedometer needle pointed to forty. The bus was moving as fast as it could.

"Where are the kiddies?" the Reverend Hatch asked. "We're already late getting the service started."

Colonel Crate looked through the one-way glass out at an auditorium full of parishioners, some with their heads bowed in prayer, some staring ahead as though expecting something wonderful to appear in the front of the tabernacle. "You think they won't wait for you?"

"I just don't like to be tardy," Hatch said.

"I heard the bus stop a while ago." Crate said. "I'll go see what's keeping 'em."

He went through a rear door and saw the men lying on the ground. He scanned the parking lot: no bus.

He ran toward a nearby Humvee.

Inside, he barked orders into a microphone, and started the vehicle.

Vic steered the bus up a ramp and onto the interstate. Again, he glanced into a mirror and saw no one behind him.

Fifteen miles to go.

Crate's Humvee passed a side road where two others were

. . .

waiting. They moved into place behind him and the mini-convoy sped toward the interstate.

Vic had hoped for a traffic jam of some kind, to provide plenty of witnesses to whatever happened and to assure that any pursuers could go no faster than he could. But the rush hour was past and Monday evening was a time when the locals tended to lock their doors behind them and plant themselves in front of their televisions, so there was only a scattering of cars and trucks on the interstate.

Three miles to go.

"Almost there, kids," he yelled over his shoulder.

Once more, he looked into his rearview mirror—and saw headlights behind him, moving fast. The vehicle—he was pretty sure it was a Humvee—had to be doing ninety.

I knew it was too good to last . . .

The vehicle—it *was* a Humvee—roared past the bus. Vic saw a flash from the rear window and heard a *clang* from the bus's fender.

The bastards are shooting . . .

Ahead, the sky glowed from the mall's lights. To his left, Vic saw Humvees, *three* of them now, and to his right, a gentle, grass-covered slope.

Vic twisted the steering wheel and the bus left the highway and bumped up the slope. In the mirror, he saw the Humvees pass the place where he had turned and skid to a halt.

At the top of the slope was an old, cinder-covered road ending in a fence that ran around the mall's parking lot.

The Humvees were speeding up the slope. But they

weren't quite fast enough. Vic crashed the bus through the fence, hit a station wagon parked near the hardware store he had recently patronized, and went between the rows of cars to the far end of the lot, through another fence and onto the state police grounds. The bus hit a police car and stopped.

Vic stood and faced his white-faced, trembling passengers. "Wasn't that fun, kids? Now just wait a minute until the nice policemen come and they'll . . . give you cookies, maybe."

Vic opened the door and jumped from the bus. Something tugged at his sleeve and in the same instant he heard the flat *krak* of a pistol shot. A Humvee was a few yards away and a jumpsuited man was leaning from the opened rear door and shooting an automatic pistol at Vic.

There were more shots. Suddenly, Vic was aware that stray bullets might go through the bus's windows and strike kids. He ducked and scurried behind the police car he had hit. He moved around it, staying low, and was suddenly facing one of the state cops, gun drawn. Vic slapped away the weapon and hit the cop, not hard.

Sorry . . .

Vic ran.

"He's heading for the mall," someone shouted behind him.

Vic dashed into a crowd of shoppers, managing not to knock anyone down, through doors, into a long, wide corridor lined with stores. Heads swiveled to watch his progress. There was a huge Christmas tree at the end, its lights twinkling.

A shout: "In there!"

Vic circled the tree and saw an unmarked door. He ran through it and found himself in a big room filled with cardboard boxes—obviously a storage area. There was no exit.

Trapped . . .

But not caught, not yet. Vic touched the stud on his belt buckle and, for a moment, he was enveloped in mist, and smelled talcum powder. He peeled off the mask and had just thrust it into his pocket when he heard voices on the other side of the door. He tossed his hat behind a box and fell to the floor.

The door burst open and three cops, guns out, came through it.

"Where the hell you guys been?" Vic moaned, rubbing his cheek with the back of his hand. "Guy punched me so hard, I thought he'd take my head off."

"Is that him?" one of the cops asked, gesturing to Vic.

"No," another said, one whom Vic recognized as the cop he'd hit a minute ago. "The skel was wearin' black. This guy's wearin' white."

"Yeah, he is," the third cop agreed.

"He didn't have a face, either," the cop Vic had hit said. "This guy's got a face."

"Yeah, he has," the third cop said.

The cop Vic had hit asked, "Where'd he go, this mook who hit you? And by the way, did he have a face?"

"No, no face," Vic said. "And I don't know where he went. I was too busy kissing the floor to notice."

"Fan out!" the cop ordered, and he and his companions began prowling the storeroom.

Vic retrieved his hat, went out the door, and walked

quickly to an exit. He crossed the parking lot to the police property and looked it over. There was a cluster of patrol cars, the bus, its engine still smoking, and the three Humvees. He saw a man in a parka leaning against one of the patrol cars and a jumpsuited guard at the wheel of the nearest Humvee.

Vic sauntered, hands in his coat pockets, whistling tunelessly—just a fella out for a walk around the police station on a brisk November night. When he reached the Humvee, he yanked open the driver's door and grabbed a handful of jumpsuit collar. He pulled the guard out and jabbed his stiffened fingers into the man's chest. Before the man had finished falling, Vic was behind the Humvee's wheel, putting it into gear. The door beside Vic slammed shut as he sped from the police station grounds and onto the interstate. He knew that within seconds the other guards, and maybe some cops, would be chasing him. Where would they expect him to go? Squinting through his night vision lenses, he spotted a country road running parallel to the interstate. Only an uneven strip of earth separated them. Vic twisted the wheel to the right, jolted, swerved, and got onto the small road. Then he remembered to switch off the Humvee's lights.

CHAPTER THIRTY-TWO

Thad Crate had several decisions to make, and he had to make them in a hurry. Four state troopers were approaching his vehicle, guns drawn. He could simply speed away, of course: The vehicle had bulletproof tires and windows, and it could probably outrun any cop car. But the officers *would* chase him, and he couldn't run all night; it was essential that he return to the tabernacle and, later, to the school. The operation was falling apart and he had to resume command as soon as possible.

The cop who was leading the others barked, "Outta the car, sir."

Crate obeyed, his hands open, palms up, at his waist. "I'd like to show you some identification, officer."

"Okay," the cop said.

Crate looked at the insignia on the cop's shirt collar and asked, "Should I call you captain?"

"That'll do," the captain said.

Crate got out his wallet, removed his driver's license, and handed it to the captain.

"Whaddaya do, Mister Crate?" the captain asked.

"I'm in charge of security at the Tabernacle of the Highest Holiness."

"Over in Hub City?"

Crate nodded.

"I'm Catholic myself," the captain said. "Can you tell me what's going on?"

Crate said that a busful of children had been kidnapped by a person in a trench coat and hat and he had pursued, and that the perpetrator had escaped in a stolen vehicle.

"Your men was shooting," the captain observed.

"We have permits for our weapons and we all carry deputy sheriff's badges," Crate said.

"Which in the real world are worth about as much as Crackerjack prizes," the captain said.

"I'll tell Mayor Fermin you said that. Now, I'd like to return the young ones to their parents. The poor people are probably worried."

"No doubt. But the way it's gonnna work is, the parents are gonna come here and after I talk to them, I'll give them the kids."

"That seems hardly necessary—"

"To you. To me, it seems real necessary. Why don't you just come along with me into the station and we can get busy contacting them parents."

"Captain . . . what is your last name?"

"You can call me Captain Seven-Ten. Seven-Ten's my badge number. My name ain't none'a your business."

"Captain, detaining me hardly seems necessary . . ."

"To you. To me, it seems real necessary. Ain't we already had this conversation?"

"I'd like to make a call on my cell phone."

"That's your right."

The Reverend Jeremiah Hatch had just come from the main auditorium of the tabernacle as his cell phone began to buzz. He grabbed it and Crate quickly told him what had happened.

"What should we do?" Hatch asked.

"Get my men. Have four of them guard you. Deploy half of the rest around the tabernacle and send the rest to the school."

"What about Mayor Fermin? Shouldn't he be protected?"

"If something bad, something permanent, happened to Fermin, it might just save us trouble down the line."

"He's one of the Lord's creatures."

"So he won't mind going to heaven."

Vic braked the Humvee and twisted in the seat to look out the rear window. He saw nothing except road and trees and, through the barren branches, the moon. Nobody was following him.

He got out his cell phone and dialed a number.

"You okay?" Tot asked after a single ring.

"I'm fine. I'm approximately five miles from the Fermin place."

"That's your next stop? Planning to rescue the fair princess from the evil ogre?"

"Something like that."

"What about the young'uns?"

"Last I saw, they were in the state police lot. I'm assuming they'll stay there for a while."

"What do you need from me?"

"I'm not sure. Why don't you park outside the north fence of the Fermin place. That's the one closest to the house."

"Easy to reach if you got to run?"

"Exactly."

"Okay. How long should I wait?"

Vic tugged back his sleeve and looked at the luminous face of his watch. "It's ten now. Give it till midnight. If you think you're in any kind of danger, get out."

"Nobody ever mistook me for a hero, sonny. See you later."

Vic broke the connection and dialed another number, the one he had noted in Myra's bedroom telephone.

Ten rings. Then, Myra: "Hello?"

"This is . . ."

"Vic?"

"Yeah. Myra, it's about your daughter . . ."

"The state police just called. She's all right. What do you know about it?"

"Long story."

"My husband's gone to pick Jackie up."

"Why didn't you go with him."

"He . . . wouldn't let me."

"Listen, Myra, I'm coming to see you. I'll be there in a few minutes. Are you alone?"

"I think so. My husband's gone and I don't see any of the others."

"Okay, see you soon."

This is going to be way easier than I thought . . .

Vic put the Humvee in gear.

CHAPTER **THIRTY-THREE**

He circled the Fermin grounds twice. There were no vehicles in the driveway, nobody moving on the lawn. There was a light on in the house, behind a narrow balcony, the same one he'd seen on the night Myra had shot him.

All he had to worry about was the dog, assuming that he hadn't killed it or that, if he had, it hadn't been replaced.

Shouldn't be a problem this time . . .

He crashed the Humvee through the front gate and drove it to a place directly below the lit window. Though he wasn't wearing his night vision mask, he could see the area around him by light from lamps on the walls of the house and garage. No dog. But it wasn't a good idea to take any more chances than necessary. He opened a door and hoisted himself onto the Humvee's roof and from there to the balcony. Then he kicked the window and stepped through the curtains into the room.

Myra, wearing a robe, was reaching for the gun in the bedtable drawer.

"It's me," Vic said.

Myra close the drawer and faced him. She took a half-step forward, raised her arms, lowered them, and asked, "What's going on?"

"I'm rescuing a fair maiden. Two fair maidens. You and Jackie."

"You think we need rescuing?"

"Yes, I do."

"Well, you're right. Do you have a plan?"

"Sort of. What I'm thinking is, we'll wait until Fermin gets back with your kid. We'll take the kid and go somewhere safe. Not in Hub City. Maybe not in the state."

"What if Benedict resists?"

"I'm prepared to deal with that."

"You don't sound worried."

"About Fermin? Should I be?"

Myra shrugged. "I guess not."

"While we wait, let me get a few facts straight. I'm guessing that Fermin forced you to marry him by threatening Jackie."

"Yes. He took her to that school and said I'd never see her again unless I . . . agreed."

"He's tight with Hatch and the jumpsuits. Exactly what are they up to?"

"I'm not sure. It has something to do with the McFeeley works."

"Where exactly does Fermin fit into the picture?"

"He doesn't seem very important to the others. They need a figurehead and he's it."

"Nothing more than a figurehead?"

"Vic, they don't exactly confide in me."

"Right. Sorry."

Vic moved to the window, tugged aside the curtains, and scanned the yard and lawn. No cars, no people. He glanced at his watch: eleven-twenty-five. How long would it take Fermin to claim Jackie? Would the cops even let him have her?

When Vic looked back, Myra was extending her gun to him, butt first. "You might need this."

"For Fermin? Come *on*!"

Myra put the gun back in the drawer and sat on the edge of the bed.

Benedict Fermin didn't like these state police bozos, not one bit. They treated him as though he weren't a *mayor*. But after an hour of stupid questions, they escorted his stepdaughter from a back room and turned her over.

"The governor's gonna hear 'bout how you treated me," Fermin promised.

"Geez, you think he'll make me stay after school?" the head cop, a captain, asked.

In Fermin's SUV, Jackie huddled against the passenger door, her eyes squeezed shut.

"When we get home, you can have some milk," Fermin said. "Maybe some cookies, too. The chocolate ones with the white stuff in the middle. You'd like that, huh, wouldn't you?"

Ashely did not reply.

"I really love your mama, you know that?" Fermin asked her. "Loved her from the first minnit I seen her.

Never thought I'd git a chance to make her my wife, though. Funny how that worked out. Ain't you got anything to say, girl?"

Ashly shook her head.

"Well, all right. We're almost home anyways."

Fermin saw his front gate, torn and mangled. He stopped his SUV, peered at his property, and saw the Humvee below Myra's window.

"Mama's got a visitor. Looks like one'a Crate's men or maybe Crate himself. No, wait a minnit . . . The police said the fella raised all the ruckus stole one'a them Hummers. Well, if it's him, he's gonna git the surprise of his life. You wait here, girl."

Fermin got out of the car and trotted to the garage. He was gasping for breath by the time he arrived and went through a side door. He lifted a twenty-gauge shotgun from a rack above a toolbench and loaded it from a box of shells he took from a shelf. Then he left the garage and moved toward the house.

CHAPTER THIRTY-FOUR

"Myra, you'd better dress for outdoors," Vic said. "Once things start to happen, they'll happen quick."

"All right," Myra said. She opened a closet and began removing garments.

Vic turned his back on her and said, "I'm thinking I'll stash you and Jackie in a motel. In Springfield, or maybe even St. Louis."

"It'll have to be on your dime," Myra said. "Benedict doesn't let me have credit cards or money."

"No problem. Your husband sounds like he has old-fashioned ideas."

"If you consider Genghis Khan old-fashioned . . . You can turn around now."

Vic did, and saw that Myra had changed to jeans and a red-and-white-striped blouse. The robe lay on the bed.

"The only decent clothes I have left," Myra said. "Everything else makes me look like a hooker."

"I've noticed."

Vic saw that the bedtable drawer was slightly open and was about to comment when there was a soft tapping at the door.

Myra crossed the room and opened it. Fermin looked past her, at Vic, shoved her aside and, as Vic leaped at him, fired his shotgun. Vic stopped, gasping, and Fermin chambered another shell and, as Vic twisted to the left, fired again. Vic stumbled back against a dressing table and slid to the floor.

Fermin turned to Myra, tears spilling from his eyes. "What was you gonna do, run away with him?"

"Where's Jackie?" Myra asked.

"Outside, in the car. Answer me, woman. Don't'cha know I love you?"

"Is that empty?" Myra asked, pointing to Fermin's shotgun.

"I don't know . . . How many times'd I shoot? Twice? Then it's empty."

"Good." Myra pulled her small revolver from under her blouse and pointed it at Fermin. "Drop the gun."

"What the hell you *doin'*?" Fermin muttered.

"Drop the gun," Myra repeated.

Fermin let the shotgun slip from his grasp.

"Now stand against the wall," Myra ordered, and Fermin stepped backward.

Still aiming her revolver at Fermin, Myra knelt next to Vic. He was clutching his chest and gasping.

"I've got to leave you," Myra said. "I've got to get Jackie to safety. But I'll send someone, a doctor."

"Call Rodor," Vic whispered.

Myra stood and said to Fermin, "Car keys."

"I left 'em."

"If you're lying or if I don't find Jackie, I'll come back and shoot you. Give me your wallet."

"Wait a minnit, woman . . . Let's talk this over. We can work things out."

"The wallet. Drop it on the floor and kick it over to me"

Fermin did as Myra said. She picked up the wallet and ran from the room.

CHAPTER THIRTY-FIVE

Myra got into Fermin's SUV, reached across the seat, and hugged Jackie. "Everything's fine now, sweetie," she said.

The engine was still running. Myra put the car in gear and drove toward the interstate.

It was almost one in the morning and Tot had heard nothing from Vic in hours. He used the VW's scanner to monitor the police bands and heard nothing new: no talk of the incident at the mall, and only occasional traffic calls. KWLM had gone off the air at midnight, as had most of the local radio stations in the area, and listening to newscasts from St. Louis, Cairo, or Springfield would do him no good, so he didn't even bother switching to the AM or FM bands.

He went home, and was taking his first sip of hot chocolate when his kitchen telephone rang.

"H'lo, Vic?"

But the caller was Myra Connelly. She quickly described what had happened at the Fermin house.

"I don't know who to trust," Myra concluded. "I don't know how far Fermin's influence extends."

"Vic figured the state police're okay, but he wasn't sure. Me neither. You go on till you get at least across the state line and then look for help. I'll see what I can do for Vic."

"I feel terrible leaving him, but I was afraid Crate would show up . . ."

"You did fine. Vic might not be as bad hurt as it looked. Some of what he was wearing was bulletproof. Anyway, you get going and call me tomorrow."

Vic watched Fermin make a call from Myra's bedside phone, heard him talking to Crate. Vic still couldn't breathe normally, but a lot of the pain was gone and he was getting a decent amount of air into his lungs. If he hadn't benn wearing the bulletproof trench coat, or if either of Fermin's shots had hit him directly, or if Fermin had been using a larger gun, he'd be dead. But he wasn't, and in another minute or two, he'd be able to act.

Fermin hung up the phone, lifted his shotgun and aimed it at Vic.

"You know she don't love you," he said. "She truly loves me, underneath it all."

"Is that why you think I came here, to steal your woman?"

"Ain't it?"

Now that you mention it . . .

Vic raised himself to a sitting position. "If you love her so damn much, how come you treat her like you do?"

"I treat her fine."

"Making her dress like a two-dollar whore?"

"Man's got a right to be proud of his woman, show her off."

"Not letting her have money or credit cards?"

"A woman don't need them things, she's got a man to take care of her."

"Okay, answer this. Why can't Jackie live with her mother?"

"The little girl is sick. The school is the best place for her."

"Says who?"

"Says the reverend, and he oughtta know. He's the Lord's representative on Earth."

"You really believe that, don't you?" Vic rolled onto his knees and started to rise.

Fermin jabbed the gun at him. "I didn't say you could get up."

"Well, can I?"

"I don't know . . . No!"

"You keep threatening me with that thing. It's empty, remember?"

Fermin worked the shotgun's bolt action and pulled the trigger. There was a roar, deafening in the small room, and buckshot shredded the rug next to Vic. Startled, Fermin dropped the shotgun. Vic was already grabbing Fermin's legs and pulling. Fermin toppled onto his back as Vic launched himself forward. Vic chopped to the side of Fermin's head and Fermin lay still.

Vic stood and moved toward the broken window. He hesitated, got out his cell phone and speed-dialed numeral 1. Tot answered on the first ring and Vic told him what had happened. Then Tot told Vic about Myra's call.

"So she's safe now, she and the kid?" Vic asked.

"Don't know any reason they wouldn't be."

"Mission accomplished, I guess. I'll ditch the Humvee near the tabernacle and hoof it from there. It's"—Vic glanced at his watch—"one-forty-five now. I should be home no later than three. No reason for you to wait up."

"I will, though. Don't think I could sleep anyway. Haven't had this much excitement in years . . . Years, hell! Ever!"

"Okay, I'll see you later."

Vic heard a moan and turned to look at Fermin, eyes open, still lying on his back.

"I'd stay there, if I were you," Vic said.

"Don't take her from me." Fermin was pleading. "'Cause she's my wife and I love her. You can understand that, can't you?"

"Not exactly. Don't try to follow me."

Vic shoved the phone into his hip pocket, went through the window onto the balcony, vaulted the railing, bounced from the top of the Humvee onto the ground. He got into the driver's seat, started the engine, and steered toward the broken gate. No sign of Fermin's car: Of course not—Myra would have taken it.

Suddenly, headlights were shining into his eyes, partially blinding him. He blinked and looked to the side. In his peripheral vision, he could see the shapes of three vehicles like the one he was driving, blocking access to the road. Vic yanked at the gearshift and the Humvee went into reverse. The other three sped forward and two of them slammed into the front of Vic's Hummer. The engine died. Vic remembered to gain control of his breathing and his adrenaline, and got slowly out and stood waiting as three of the black jumpsuits approached him, hands on holstered pistols. When they were standing in front of him, a foot away, he punched to his left and right, his fists catching two men on the chin, and kicked the third man in the belly.

Spurts of dust rose from the ground at his feet, and the dirt was pocked with a line of tiny craters.

Vic turned. Colonel Crate, silhouetted against headlights, was holding a weapon.

"I almost wish I had more troops for you to beat up," Crate said. "You're very good at unarmed combat."

"How about yourself? You and me, hand-to-hand, what do you say?"

"You tempt me. But that would be taking an unnecessary chance. So I'll pass. By the way, in case you're wearing armor, this weapon can make cheesecloth of Kevlar."

Vic knew that was true. He stood still, waiting for the moment to act.

Crate approached, keeping the muzzle of his weapon aimed at Vic's throat.

Now . . .

But Crate moved first, jamming his weapon against Vic's forehead. Vic was falling when something hit him a second time.

CHAPTER THIRTY-SIX

Someone was tugging at him, pulling him from . . . what? A vehicle. His head hurt. Now he was sitting. The ground beneath him was cold. Where was he?

He opened his eyes and looked up. Crate, holding his weapon in one hand and a shovel in the other, stood above him.

"On your feet," Crate ordered.

"I need a doctor," Vic said. It was true: He thought it likely that his skull was fractured.

"No, you don't."

Vic stood slowly, and glanced around. There was Crate and six of the jumpsuits, all carrying holstered pistols.

Crate handed him the shovel. "You are, I judge, a bit over six feet tall. Therefore, you will dig a vertical hole of five feet, two inches."

Vic dug. He found that once he had gone below four feet, he couldn't move the shovel and had to widen as well as deepen the hole. Despite the chill, he was sweating.

"Can I take off my coat?" he asked.

"Go ahead," Crate said.

Vic shed the trench coat and tossed it beside the growing pile of dirt. Crate picked it up and rubbed the material between thumb and forefinger. "Very nice. Bulletproof fabric. As light as ordinary cloth and just a bit stiffer. Tiny wires woven throughout . . . to spread the impact of a bullet? Yes, has to be."

"I'm glad you approve," Vic said. "I assume this will end with my obituary."

"Am I going to kill you? In all probability, yes. But not right away. You interest me. I've never seen a man your size fight as you do. I wonder how tough you really are."

"I eat Buicks for breakfast."

"Don't try to be funny with me. I have no sense of humor."

"No kidding."

Vic dug in silence. The sky in the east was just beginning to lighten.

"I'm curious," Vic said after a few minutes. "What are you? Some kind of rent-a-cop?"

"Are you trying to infuriate me? Insult me?"

"Not at the moment. Maybe later. Right now, I just want to know your story."

"I am a member of the oldest and proudest of professions. I walked with Alexander, Caesar, Hannibal, Napoleon, MacArthur. I am a warrior."

"And who do you do your warrioring for?"

"I am what I am because it is my destiny, as war is the destiny of all mankind."

"Yeah, but somebody must be paying the bills. That wouldn't be a McFeeley, would it?"

"For whatever it may be worth, the answer is yes. Working with McFeeley, I am developing new and better tools."

"Tools for warfare?"

"The only kind of tool there is. When has mankind not employed his ingenuity and skill to kill more efficiently? What inventions have not been used to further the warrior's task in one fashion or another?"

"You certainly sound convinced."

"I pity those who are not."

"Pity them enough to spare their lives?"

Crate made a sound that might have been a laugh. "To kill most men is to do them a favor."

"What about when you die? You figure on going to some kind of bad-ass heaven?"

"I have ruled out the existence of Valhalla. But a glorious death would be its own reward."

"I don't guess you'd care to define 'glorious.'"

"A death without cowardice, preferably facing an enemy."

"Sounds like a ton of laughs."

"Stop digging." Crate motioned to the men who were still standing at attention. Vic waited in the hole he had dug. Two of them, holding shovels, stepped forward and began filling the hole, dirt bouncing off Vic.

Vic looked up at Crate. "The ol' buried-alive gag, huh? Always a hit at parties."

"Not completely buried. Your head will remain above ground. Consider this a test of your will to survive. At any time, you may ask to be released. One of my men will then shoot you in the head and you will die quickly and painlessly. I doubt that you will exercise that option."

"Why?"

"Because I detect in you spirit. So the question becomes, how long will you will yourself to withstand the severe cold? How long can you delay death by hypothermia?"

Vic's hands were in his hip pockets. The dirt was above his wrists.

"Aren't you going to a lot of trouble just to off one lousy reporter?" he asked.

"I do not know what you are, but it is more than a lousy reporter. This is a learning opportunity for me."

"I kind of wish you'd just taken a correspondence course."

"As I said, I have no sense of humor."

"That might not be the only thing you lack."

"You flatter me with the truth. I also lack cowardice, sentimentality, and stupidity."

"Two outta three ain't bad . . ."

The dirt was up to Vic's neck. The two guards tamped it down with the flats of their shovels and then rejoined their companions.

"We will leave you now," Crate said.

"What if I want to exercise my shot-in-the-head option?"

"I am leaving one of my men. He will accommodate you."

Crate led his men around the corner of a nearby building, leaving Vic alone with his keeper, buried up to his chin.

CHAPTER THIRTY-SEVEN

As soon as Crate had ordered him to stop digging, Vic thrust his hands into his pockets. He had an idea, one lonely idea, and he had no idea if it would work. But it was all he had. His fingers found his cell phone and his thumb pressed the "on" button.

He spoke loudly, to cover any sound the phone might make. "The ol' buried-alive gag, huh?"

He ran his fingertips over the phone's buttons and located "1." He pressed it. Now, if all was going as advertised, the phone would speed-dial Tot. He wouldn't know if Tot answered—his hearing wasn't nearly that good—and he couldn't speak to his friend directly. But maybe he could communicate another way. He began to tap his thumbnail on the bottom of the phone, where the transmitter grid was.

Tot was sleeping in his easy chair in front of a fireplace full of ashes when the phone rang. He twitched, opened his eyes, looked around and, as the phone rang a second time, picked up the reciever.

"Vic?"

There was no voice, only the hum of the transmission and something else, a tapping sound.

"Vic?" he said again.

Only the tapping.

"Vic, is that you?"

The tapping.

He listened: *tap tap tap tap tap tap tap tap tap tap.*

Silence. Then: *tap tap tap tap tap tap tap tap tap tap tap tap tap tap tap tap tap tap.*

Silence. Tot started to put down the receiver when he heard: *tap tap tap tap tap tap tap tap tap tap.*

Silence. And: *tap tap tap tap tap tap tap tap tap tap tap tap tap tap tap tap tap tap.*

"To hell with you," Tot said, and slammed down the reciever. "I got no time for this."

He took two steps, halted, spun, and picked up the reciever again. "Wait a minute . . ."

Vic had a lot of questions: Had Tot heard the phone ring? Did the phone even work, buried under several feet of dirt? Would Tot understand Vic's message? If he did, would he know what to do? How long could Vic continue tapping? And how long would he last in this bitter cold? How long before hypothermia killed him?

A lot of questions. No answers.

The sun was higher in the sky. What time was it? Six, maybe seven. How long had he been here? A half-hour? That was about right.

Vic began to shiver. That was good, wasn't it? His body's way of keeping warm. But what happened when he *stopped* shivering?

Questions.

He looked up at his keeper, silhouetted against a wispy cloud.

"Don't suppose you'd be up for a game of twenty questions?" Vic asked.

The man in the black jumpsuit neither replied, moved, nor gave any indication that he had heard Vic.

The sky had darkened, and bloated gray clouds hung low in it. Then a few flakes of snow wafted down and landed on Vic's upturned face.

Inside his hip pocket, he switched the phone to idle. He hadn't recharged the battery since Horace had given it to him, and he might need the device later.

Tot tried to sleep. After two hours, he climbed out of bed and went into the kitchen. Dammit, he couldn't get the tapping sound out of his mind. He made coffee and sat staring out the window, sipping and remembering. The tapping had been divided into sections . . . the second one considerably longer than the first. He wished he'd recorded the call, or at least counted the taps. He emptied and refilled his coffee cup and sat again.

Snow had begun to fall.

The damn tapping.

It meant something. What?

.   .   .

Vic could see snow collecting on the shoulders of the jumpsuit, and on the watch cap above them. The guard did not move.

They make 'em tough, where he comes from . . .

He could see the blur of flakes clinging to his eyelashes and feel moisture on his scalp. His shivering had become violent. He began to use some of the techniques for warming himself that Richard had taught him, and they seemed to help.

Tot had an idea. He went to the phone and pushed *66, the code that automatically redialed the last number received.

Vic felt something vibrate against his thigh. It took him a moment to realize that it was the cell phone. He thumbed the "on" button and began to tap.

This time Tot counted. After a minute, he had what he wanted. There were ten taps in the first group, and nineteen in the second. Ten-nineteen? That sure as hell meant *some* damn thing . . .

How long had he been buried? More than four hours, fewer than six. How long could he last? Why hadn't he taken more first-aid courses? Or paid attention to the ones he *had* taken? But maybe it was better not to know. Maybe knowing would discourage him, make him try less to survive . . . or maybe not. He had seen Richard laboring in fierce blizzards wearing only jeans and a T-shirt and had asked Richard how he kept warm, and Richard had said it was a matter of getting some control of the autonomic nervous system and focusing available heat in the body's core. But Richard hadn't taught him how to do that. In fact, Richard had said something strange: "When you free yourself of the need for violence, you can access other possibilities." Vic had not known what that meant at the time, and he didn't know now, and what good was not knowing doing him . . .

A guard approached from the school building, nodded to the one who stood near Vic—no salute—and took his place as the first man walked stiffly away.

Vic said, "Hi, my name is Vic Sage and I'll be your helpless victim today."

"Ask to die," the man said, not looking at Vic.

Tot had given up and was tinkering with an idea for a heat converter when suddenly the ten-nineteen made sense to him. It was the school. Sure, the damn school! The school was *called* Ten-Nineteen! And it didn't take a genius to figure out that the school was where Vic was, probably being held prisoner. For some reason, he couldn't talk into the phone, but he could tap it, send a message that way.

Call the cops? Not the locals. Even if there were any left, they'd be in Fermin's pocket. But maybe the state cops.

Twenty minutes later, after speaking to two sergeants and a lieutenant, Tot slammed down the receiver. He'd been told that the school was in Hub City's jurisdiction, and unless Hub City authorities asked for help, they, the Hub City authorities, would handle any matter connected with the school without outside assistance, and have a nice day, sir.

So okay. The badges were useless as teeth on a rainbow, as usual, and what else was new.

"Maybe I can do this job myself," Tot muttered.

Yeah, sure, Aristotle Rodor, with his seventy-one-year-old knees and elbows, who hadn't fired a gun in forty years and hadn't had a fistfight in fifty, he was going to charge into a nest of trained killers, kick their collective ass, and rescue his friend. Right after he was elected pope, that would be.

What else?

The Internet bulletin board Vic had told him about? Well, yeah, using the bulletin board and a code, Vic had said that he could get in touch with this Richard bad-ass, and maybe the other guy, the mysterious one, and maybe even the good-looking female ass-kicker.

Tot went to his computer and began typing.

One of the jumpsuited men, one Vic had not seen before, led ten children from the main building of the school to where Vic was buried. The children stood in a straight line in front of him and looked at him solemnly. After maybe ten minutes, the jumpsuit clapped his hands and the children filed past him. As each stood directly over him, they spat. Gobs of saliva soon mingled with the snow on Vic's hair and dribbled down his face.

CHAPTER THIRTY-EIGHT

The Batmobile burst through the hidden entrance and came to an abrupt halt on the floor of the cave. Batman sprang out and walked two hundred yards to the communications console, where Alfred waited for him.

"The test went well?" Alfred asked.

"Yeah, the new stuff works," Bruce said, pulling off his mask.

"I trust you were careful not to be seen."

"You trust right. What brings you down to the nether regions?"

"The computer alarm. It buzzed. Someone has left a coded alert for you on the bulletin board."

"Which one?"

"Cincinnati."

"Then it's probably Richard."

Bruce went to a keyboard and busied himself for a minute. Then he punched a number into the system and waited while, a thousand miles away, a phone rang.

Tot answered. Bruce, speaking in Batman's growl, asked what he wanted and Tot described the events of the previous twenty-four hours, beginning with Vic's decision to rescue Myra Connelly and her daughter.

"Why is this any of my business?" Bruce asked.

"'Cause Vic needs help and you're his friend," Tot said.

"I'm not his friend. If he got himself in trouble, he'll have to get himself out of it."

Bruce broke the connection.

"Do they still call you Mr. Congeniality?" Alfred asked sweetly.

"Little early for sarcasm, isn't it?"

"I understood you to be this Vic Sage's mentor."

"Boy, Alfred, did you get *that* wrong. I'm *nobody's* mentor."

"Master Dick?"

"Okay, *maybe* I'm Dick Grayson's mentor. But nobody else."

"Perhaps you would care to explain to a dimwitted old family retainer exactly what your relationship to Vic Sage is."

"To put it in a way you won't like . . . I saw him as a potential tool. I can't spare the time or resources to deal with what's happening in Hub City. He was there and he was interested and looked pretty competent. Richard said he probably didn't have the genetic equipment to be as good as I am, but he could still be pretty good—better than most who choose to be 'mystery men.' At least, for him, it wasn't about parading around in a costume and ego gratification. So I nudged him in the direction he wanted to go anyway. But I didn't take responsibility for him. I *don't* take responsibility for him. Anyone who chooses this path has to walk it alone."

"Including you."

"Including me."

"Master Bruce, Master Bruce . . ." Alfred sounded like an exasperated schoolteacher. "May I remind you that you—and Batman—benefited greatly from your family's fortune and name? That Mr. Fox supplied you with all the technology you could have hoped for? That at least twice during Batman's first year you survived because I was available to assist you? That Commissioner Gordon has often been invaluable to your efforts? That you learned your combat skills from a man who, however villainous he may have been, treated you like a son?"

Bruce turned away and went to where clothes were hanging on a bar. He removed the Batman garb and put on exercise clothes and sneakers.

Alfred waited.

Bruce strode over to a set of parallel bars and began to do gymnastics.

Alfred waited.

Bruce finished at the bars and began to execute a complicated series of martial arts moves.

Alfred waited.

Bruce finished the martial arts series and wiped his face on a hand towel. He asked, "Alfred, have you been in the philosophy section of the library again?"

"Only to dust it, Master Bruce."

"Then you must be taking your wise old man pills . . . well, wise *middle-aged* man pills."

"I find the chocolate ones particularly delightful."

In a different tone of voice, Bruce said, "Thank you."

Bruce returned to the communications console. "I have no idea what I can do for Sage. But maybe I'll think of something."

CHAPTER THIRTY-NINE

If the winter's first serious, no-holds-barred blizzard had not hit the Pennsylvania mountains a day earlier, Richard would not have gotten Bruce's message in time. But snow and sleet had blown down from the sky, covering the peaks and obliterating the roads. Richard decided to make his bimonthly visit to the post office anyway, and, wearing a parka and high boots, began to trek through snow that dampened the knees of his jeans. It was slow going, but Richard did not mind; he was enjoying the exercise.

About a mile from the town boundary, he saw a van canted into a ditch, smoke billowing from its exhaust pipe. A man was at the wheel, not moving. Richard managed to wrench a door open and pull the man out. The man's forehead was bruised and bloody. Richard lay him on the shoulder of the road and covered him with his parka. Then he waved down a passing pickup truck.

Twenty minutes later, Richard helped a paramedic load the van driver onto a gurney and watched as the man, still unconscious, was wheeled into the emergency room of the local clinic. Next, Richard talked, first to a doctor and then to a local deputy. Finally, everyone seemed to be satisfied that Richard was only a Good Samaritan who knew absolutely nothing about the injured party. Richard reclaimed his parka from a receptionist and continued to the post office. The slow walking through deep snow and his Good Samaritanism had delayed him considerably. It was noon when he reached the post office, two hours later than he usually arrived.

The postmaster, who was also the local hardware store owner, looked up at Richard through the bars of his cage and said, "Fella just called for you. Said I was to give you a message if I seen you. Strange name, the fella had. I wrote it down here somewheres . . ." The postmaster thumbed through several scraps of paper. "Here it is. Name's Vespertillo."

"What was the message?"

The postmaster read from the paper: "Can you find the Kali gal? Urgent."

"Thanks. Anything else?"

"You mean mail? No, nothin' this week. Snow might be slowing down the delivery from Chicago and anyway, this time of year, everything's slow, what with the Christmas cards and packages and all."

"Okay, thanks."

Richard went to a sidewalk pay phone outside the combination post office/hardware store and, using a credit card number he had memorized, made a long-distance call to an answering machine in Argentina. He hung up and sauntered around town, enjoying the cold and the white mountains, and fifteen minutes later returned to the pay phone, which had begun to ring. Richard lifted the receiver and heard a familiar voice describing the Hub City situation.

"Sounds bad," Richard said. "But I'm not much closer to Hub City than you are, and I don't have a plane or car."

"What about Kali?"

"Well . . . I think she may be in a hospital in Kansas City."

"She's ill?"

"No, nothing like that. She's involved in some kind of test."

"Which hospital?"

Richard told him and the conversation ended.

Shiva had been at the medical facility, one attached to a small university, for almost ten weeks. She had heard of the experiment from a chiropodist she met at a martial arts exhibit in Newark. The experiment was pretty complicated, involving a lot of drugs and medical procedures, but what it amounted to was that the subject—Shiva— would be put through about eighty-three kinds of hell and then examined to learn what permanent damage had been done. It sounded pretty interesting, so Shiva volunteered. And it *was* pretty interesting. At the end, the chief doctor said that they would have to rethink their theories and design some more rigorous experiments because, as far as they could tell, Shiva had sustained virtually no harm.

She was sitting on a table in an examination room,

wearing only a paper gown and talking to the doctor. The doctor wanted to know if Shiva would be willing to return after all the data had been processed.

"I think I would be bored, doing it again," Shiva said.

A nurse stuck her head in the door and said, "Miss, there's a call. I *think* it's for you."

Only Richard knew where she was. She had told him because, if she did not survive the experiments, she wanted him to be sure her body was left to some good medical school—that, or be cremated and the ashes sent to whoever happened to be governor of Texas, she didn't care which.

She spoke into a phone at the nurses' station. "Richard?"

"No. Me."

"What do you want?"

Bruce told her.

In the cave, Bruce broke the connection and rose from the communications console. "It's up to her now. She's only a couple of hundred miles from Hub City. She can get there by nightfall."

"Does this terminate your involvement?" Alfred asked.

"Before we had our talk this morning, it would have. Now . . . I think maybe Bruce Wayne needs to see a certain heiress in the Midwest. How about arranging transportation while I deal with a potential problem."

"Which is?"

"It occurred to me that having Richard contact us through the Argentina connection is not a good idea. Too easy to trace. With Oracle's help, I should have something else in place in an hour. Then, it's off to the heartland. By the way, when you were mentioning all the people who have helped me, you forgot Oracle."

"I did not forget, Master Bruce. My point had been made and I did not wish to beat you about the head with the obvious."

"I should have known."

"I'm sure you'll have a lovely time with the heiress," Alfred said, and moved to the steps.

Vic had been observing his guard. The man was standing with his feet apart, hands behind his back, staring straight ahead. He seemed oblivious to Vic. Vic began to wriggle, trying to loosen the dirt around him, maybe free one of his arms. The guard turned, strode to Vic, leaned down and punched him in the face.

"No moving around," the guard said. He returned to his post. "You can ask to die."

Vic nodded, though he did not know why.

Shiva stepped from the university building into a cold, snowy afternoon. She was wearing the clothes she had brought with her weeks earlier, when the temperature was almost thirty degrees warmer, but she gave no sign of being cold. She scanned the street and fastened her gaze on a messenger, bundled into a bomber jacket, twill trousers, leather mittens, a Cossack hat with ear flaps, and boots. He was striding toward a red Harley motorcycle. Shiva smiled and hurried down a short flight of steps.

She confronted the messenger and said, "Give me your keys."

The messenger fumbled off his mittens, reached into a pocket, and produced a ring of keys. He handed them to Shiva. She nodded, mounted the motorcycle, put the proper key into the ignition, and kicked the starter.

She smiled at the messenger and roared down the street.

Vic raised his eyes. The sky was darker: Judging by the position of the smudge of light that was the sun, it was midafternoon. His shivering had lessened, but snow was clogging his nostrils and hanging from his eyelashes. He exhaled violently and was able to breathe a bit easier.

His shivering lessened. Was that good or bad?

Tot was dozing in front of his fireplace when he heard the roar of a two-cylinder engine coming from his driveway. By the time he opened his front door, a woman was standing on the porch.

"I am Shiva," she said.

"Vic's friend," Tot said, stepping aside.

Shiva entered the house. "Not his friend."

"Okay, his savior then."

"Not his savior."

"Dammit, I don't care what you call yourself. Sit down by the fire. Those clothes you're wearing wouldn't keep a snail warm. You want something to eat or drink?"

"Yes, my body requires food."

·　　·　　·

Vic was vaguely aware that his guard had been replaced, but only vaguely. He was becoming sleepy. Didn't seem to be as cold. Wasn't shivering as much. Felt good.

The private jet Bruce had chartered couldn't land at its first destination because the tiny airport was snowed in.

"We'll have to divert to Midway," the pilot told him apologetically.

"That will suit me just fine," Bruce said. "I haven't been to Chicago in ages. Isn't that where they have something called an 'art institute.' I like art. Sometimes."

Bruce leaned back and watched the clouds outside his window.

Shiva wiped her lips with surprising daintiness on a paper napkin and said, "The food was good."

"Damn right."

"Tell me of Charles Victor Szasz."

"Who . . . Oh, Vic. How'd you know his real name?" Shiva smiled.

"Okay," Tot said, "*keep* your damn secrets. Listen good."

Tot described the past twenty-four hours to Shiva and concluded, "I keep calling Vic's cell phone, but no answer. Not even the tapping."

"That is not good," Shiva said. "These enemies of his, they have had ample time to kill him."

"Or move him somewhere else."

"But you are convinced that he was first taken to the school?"

"That's what the tapping *had* to mean."

Shiva stood. "I will investigate."

"I'll come with you."

"No."

"Don't want to be slowed down by an old man, huh?"

"You are not old." Shiva leaned over and kissed Tot on the lips. "I have known far older than you."

Tot had not yet moved from where he was sitting when he heard the motorcycle engine roar.

CHAPTER FORTY

Vic was aware of the sound of motors. He could have maybe twisted his head around to see where it was coming from, but that would have taken a *lot* of effort, and for what? To look at some motors? He had already *seen* motors.

As he drove his Humvee past where Vic Sage was buried, Crate said to the man next to him, "He still hasn't asked for mercy. I don't expect him to. He'll probably die of cold first. He would have made a good soldier."

Crate's vehicle was followed by two others, all an identical matte black, all containing six armed men. They passed the turnoff that led to the tabernacle, went onto Hub City's Main Street, continued through the business area, and out the far end. Approaching the McFeeley plant, they slowed. A gate in the fence surrounding the buildings swung open and the Humvees went through it, leaving deep tracks in the snow.

•   •   •

Vic had stopped shivering, stopped completely, and *that* was nothing to complain about. Much nicer not to shiver. Much more comfortable. Of course, it *might* mean that his body was succumbing to the cold—that he was, in fact, freezing to death. But he could worry about that later. Or not worry about it at all.

An image of a boy with red hair and big ears flashed into his mind, Alfred E. Neuman . . . *What, me worry?* Alfred had the right attitude.

Vic felt himself drifting into a peaceful sleep and this was welcome, sleep was always good but it was especially good now, what with him worrying so much and all . . . And who had we here? Our old friend, the Dream. No . . . not the Dream. *A* dream. Quite a well-populated dream. There are a row of children, all with blank ovals for faces, and behind them, a row of adults, also with blank ovals for faces. The children step forward and, one by one, drop rose petals onto Vic and then the adults step forward and, one by one, peel away the blank ovals to reveal . . . Well, this is Sister Hectora and next to her, shy, sweet Sister Francesca, and then Father Damien Szasz. And three old girlfriends—how did *they* get here? And Horace, and good old Tot and Richard and the mysterious benefactor and Olga Knauseley and Andy Holbein and the pretty girl from the park in St. Louis and the old man at the crossroads . . . Old bosses. Men he'd met on jobs. Women he'd dated. All peeling away the white ovals to reveal faces beneath. And more: Fermin, Crate, Hatch and . . . Shiva? Was that Shiva? She

had no white oval and she seemed less substantial than
the rest . . .

"I don't understand."

Whose voice?

Someone else speaking: "You do not have to understand."

The dream ended. Vic opened his eyes and was looking
at Shiva.

CHAPTER FORTY-ONE

Later, more to satisfy his curiosity than for any better reason, Bruce Wayne tried to make sense of what had happened that day on the outskirts of Hub City. He interviewed survivors, including Vic and Tot and some of Crate's guards, and drew a time line and did a bit of the combination of deduction and imagination that occasionally served his purposes and . . . at the end, he still wasn't certain of much.

This he knew: Shiva had parked the motorcycle and scaled the fence. (The driver of a propane delivery truck remembered seeing her.) Once inside the school grounds, she somehow entered the locked building and rendered the three guards who had not accompanied Crate unconscious. She did not kill them; Bruce never ascertained why. Then she went out a rear door and found Vic and his keeper. She somehow took away the keeper's weapon and broke a number of his bones but, again, she did not kill. Then, she unburied Vic. How? Crate had apparently taken the shovels with him and there were no other tools Shiva could have used. But somehow, she got it done.

"He was suffering from hypothermia," Tot eventually told Bruce. "Can't blame him. That woman, that Shiva, figured that keeping his hands in his pocket and having his feet below ground kept frostbite from doing any permanent damage. Anyway, I hadn't done what she asked. I followed her out to the school and saw her toting Vic toward the gate. I got it open with a pair of metal snips I keep in my toolbox and together Shiva and me got him loaded into the car. I was all for taking him to the hospital but Shiva said no. We went back to my house and Shiva raided my medicine chest and my kitchen pantry and got busy with Vic. She must be a hell of a doctor because a few hours later, he was up and around."

Vic swung his legs out of the bed and realized that he was wearing only undershorts. Shiva, standing a few feet away, obviously did not care.

"This is the second time you've saved my ass," Vic said.

"Yes, it is," Shiva said.

"I'm grateful, but I'm curious, too."

"You always seem to be curious."

"Guilty. Anyway, why bother with me?"

"If I knew why I do what I do, my life would be unbearably boring."

"You're not kidding, are you?" Vic began pulling on his clothes.

"No."

"What's next for you? You off to somewhere exotic?"

"There is an interesting situation in a place called 'Peoria,' but Hub City might offer more amusement."

"Does that mean you're sticking around?"

"It might. What are you offering?"

"I assume you're not referring to money."

Shiva made a sound that might have been a snort.

"I thought not. Okay, I need information."

Vic followed Shiva downstairs. They found Tot in his favorite chair in front of the fireplace reading a very thick book. He looked at Vic and said, "Spry and snappy again."

"Within limits, yes. We should talk."

Vic told the others what had happened to him and when he finished describing being spat on by the schoolchildren, he said, "I'm guessing that Myra and Jackie are safe."

"They are," Tot said. "Stashed in a motel. I spoke with Myra."

"But the rest of the kids are back under the control of Crate and Fermin and whoever else is involved. That can only mean that their parents collected them from the state cops and sent them back to the school. Why?"

"Blackmail?" Tot suggested.

"It's a stretch to think that ten or fifteen sets of parents would be guilty of something so serious they'd sacrifice their children to keep it quiet."

"War crimes, maybe," Tot said.

"Maybe. But not likely. I think it has something to do with the kids themselves. Maybe we should begin by learning just who those parents are."

"Seems like a good place to start," Tot said. "But let me

ask you something, Vic. Why are you bothering? You set out to rescue Myra Connelly and her daughter and you've done that. Why not call it quits?"

Vic rubbed the back of his neck. "I don't know. It just seems like something I have to see through. A job I have to finish."

"Perhaps you are becoming like me," Shiva said.

"How so?"

"If you knew why you act as you do, you would be bored."

"Interesting suggestion, but this is the first time I've ever not known the reason for my actions."

"Welcome to my life," Shiva said.

"If you two are done staring at your navels," Tot said, "maybe we could get back to the subject. That sound reasonable to anyone around here?"

"Right," Vic said. "So we begin our next phase by finding out the parents' names. Anyone have a quick and easy way to do that?"

Shiva said nothing. Tot shook his head.

"Maybe my boss can help," Vic said. "Assuming that he *is* still my boss and hasn't fired me."

Someone spoke from a corner of the room that was in deep shadow: "There might be a quicker way. I can help with that."

Tot and Vic jerked their heads around. Shiva only smiled. The newcomer stepped into the light. "Remember me?" he asked Vic.

"*Buenas tardes,*" Shiva said.

"Hello," Vic said. "I didn't see you come in. To what do we owe the pleasure?"

In an apologetic voice, Bruce said, "Well, I was on my way to Chicago to visit with my dear friend . . . what's-her-name, and I seem to have taken a wrong turn. Perhaps more than one."

"Is somebody going to introduce me?" Tot asked.

"As the estimable Mr. Dylan said, my name ain't nothing, and shame on him for the grammar, but never mind . . . What's important is we're all here together having fun and discussing those parents and that most peculiar school. You need their names and if you allow me a few moments to make a call, I might be able to provide them. Perhaps our gracious host would prepare hot drinks?"

"Coffee or cocoa?" Tot asked.

"I'm afraid coffee would jangle my nerves, but a nice, hot cup of cocoa would be a real treat. May I use the other room?"

"Go ahead," Tot said, moving toward the kitchen.

Bruce went into the empty dining room and a minute later was talking to Oracle in Gotham City.

"Shouldn't be hard," Oracle said into her telephone headset's mike. "Can you hang on?"

"Yes," Bruce said into his phone, his voice low and hoarse. He heard the tapping of Oracle's computer keyboard.

Then she said, "Looks like the school doesn't exist. At least there's no record of it at either the state or federal local. I checked the teachers' union, too. Zilch."

"I'm not surprised. Now look at the employees and management of a company called the McFeeley Works in

Hub City. I'm particularly interested in scientific and technical personnel with children."

"That'll take a while," Oracle said. "I'll get back to you."

"Sooner is better than later."

Bruce found Vic, Shiva, and Aristotle Rodor gathered around the fireplace holding cups.

"Your chocolate's getting cold," Tot said.

Bruce accepted a cup from him, sipped, and said, "Ah-hhhh. Better than I expected. Nothing like a cup of steaming cocoa on a cold December day. Now, if you'll indulge me, I'm not quite clear on a few points."

For the next thirty minutes, Bruce asked, and Vic and Tot answered. Shiva drank her cocoa in silence until Bruce turned to her. "Am I right in thinking that there were only four men at the school when you rescued Vic, here?" he asked.

"Yes," Shiva said.

"You're sure you didn't miss any? Didn't see them, I mean."

Shiva frowned.

"I apologize," Bruce said hastily.

"So where are they—Crate and the rest of his pals?" Vic asked. "Did they just go somewhere for the day? Will they return to the school?"

"All good questions," Bruce said. A buzzing sound came from the pocket of his blazer. "Excuse me," he said and went into the dining room.

He spoke into his phone. "Yes."

Oracle said, "Boss, you don't give me the easy ones. The McFeeley operation has done a great job of not leaving any kind of paper or administrative trail. But the company changed hands about five years ago, so I hacked into a few professional association databases to see if any of the kind of people you're interested in changed jobs in the last five years. I got five hits, five scientists and one engineer with a background in munitions whose forwarding addresses are in the Hub City area. All of them have children."

"Good. Now check possible foreign sources—I'd think India might be a possibility . . ."

"And England, Australia, New Zealand, maybe Pakistan, Japan . . ."

"You've got the idea."

Bruce broke the connection and returned to the living room.

"I've had a thought," Vic said.

"Shoot," Bruce said.

"Those kids at the school . . . they all looked sickly. Every one of them. I'm wondering—could Crate, or Hatch, or Fermin, or the whole bunch of them . . . could they be poisoning the kids?"

"Go on," Bruce said.

"Maybe that'd explain why the parents cooperate."

"Hell," Tot said. "It'd explain why the parents gave 'em back after the fracas at the state cops."

"Yeah," Vic said. "If the bad guys convinced the parents that only they could keep the kids alive. Might explain Hatch's 'miracles,' too."

"Sure," Tot said enthusiastically. "It'd do that. Every once in a while, he gives one of the little ones an antidote and claims to be a healer. Gives the parents hope."

"Helps build his ministry, make him rich," Vic said.

"That all sounds just preposterous enough to be true," Bruce said. "There may be a way to verify it. Didn't you say Myra Connelly and her daughter escaped? We can have the little girl tested."

"I'll get in touch with Myra," Vic said.

"Perhaps you would be better employed in visiting the Reverend Hatch's tabernacle," Bruce said. "You or your blank-faced friend. Mr. Rodor might find time to call Ms. Connelly."

"Gotcha," Vic said.

"Be my pleasure," Tot said.

"And I?" Shiva asked. "Should I take up knitting to pass the time?"

Bruce grinned at her. "If you can be patient for a few hours . . . well, how does combat with a score of highly trained and well-armed soldiers sound to you?"

"Delicious."

Alfred was driving through mid-Illinois, going exactly sixty-five miles per hour, his back straight and his hands at the three- and nine-o'clock positions on the wheel, when he got the call. He used a voice command to activate the car phone, knowing Bruce Wayne was calling because only Bruce had this number.

"Yes, Master Bruce?"

"Got an ETA, Alfred?"

"Perhaps six more hours."

"And the stuff I need is packed?" Bruce was referring to Batman's costume and tools; taking them on aircraft, even private aircraft, was risky in these days of Homeland Security, so Alfred was bringing them by ground transport.

"I do not believe I am accustomed to erring in such matters."

"You know . . . now that I think of it, you aren't. My apologies. I want you to meet me at Aristotle Rodor's house. I'll use my laptop to feed the directions into your GPU."

"I shall await them with eager and tremulous anticipation."

"Okay, I deserve the sarcasm. See you soon."

Alfred returned his full attention to the highway.

Vic parked the VW in a wooded area near the tabernacle. He peeled off his coat and shirt and unbuckled the brace that made him move awkwardly. He tossed it into the backseat and briefly wondered if he'd ever have to wear it again. He redressed in shirt and coat, smoothed the white mask over his face, and pressed the stud on his belt buckle. Mist rose, there was the smell of talcum powder, white clothing became black. Vic left the car and sprinted toward the sprawling building, visible mostly because of the snow on its roof. This was not a night when services were held; the parking lot lights were unlit and the tabernacle itself was dark except for a glow in one rear window. Vic saw no Humvees, no black SUVs. He was hoping he wouldn't meet any of Crate's goons; this was not an attack, but rather a reconnaissance. He had in his coat pockets a roll of duct tape, a small flashlight, a screwdriver with a changeable blade, and a can of black spray paint. There was a small pry bar shoved into his waistband. He was better equipped than he had been when he'd broken into Fermin's office, but just barely. As before, he was counting on his ability to improvise. And luck.

He had his spray can out and, peering through his night lenses, was scanning for security cameras when he heard the sound of an engine and saw the splash of headlights on the snowy pavement. He ducked around the corner of the building, squatted, and took a quick look.

A gray Lincoln towncar stopped near the tabernacle's rear exit and Hatch got out, went to the door, and unlocked it. He went inside and let the door swing closed behind him. Vic strode from his hiding place and got his fingertips against the door before it locked, leaving it open a crack.

Now, if Hatch doesn't notice . . .

Vic waited and listened. After a minute, he gently pushed open the door and slipped past it. Even with his night lenses, Vic could barely see where he was, the area behind the main altar where he had watched the children being herded onto the bus. Then the edges of the door that led to the auditorium glowed, dimly, and Vic knew that Hatch had turned on some kind of small light.

I just hope whatever he's doing keeps him busy for a while . . .

Vic moved to the stairway and went down the steps. At the bottom landing, he saw two doors. He opened the nearest. In the greenish glow of night vision, he could see three sofas, two easy chairs, a refrigerator, a long, buffet-type table, and, on a counter along the rear wall, a large coffee urn. Obviously, this was a waiting room, where guests bided their time before being summoned into Hatch's presence. Vic closed the door and opened the one next to it.

This is more like it . . .

An office. Hatch's, no doubt. A desk, several filing cabinets, a computer and printer on separate tables. Vic quickly went through the desk's drawers. No help: only small-office supplies. Next, he checked the files: again, no help, only folders full of paper. But there was another door, behind the overstuffed desk chair. Vic passed through it and found himself in a bathroom: toilet, shower, and an oversize medicine chest. In the mirror, he saw himself—a green-tinted phantom in hat and coat. He opened the chest and saw a row of glass vials with rubber stoppers, the kind that accommodate hypodermic needles. Vic grabbed three of them and crammed them into his pocket, next to the duct tape.

He left Hatch's domain and went back up the steps. There was still a glow around the door to the auditorium. Vic could hear a drone—a human voice? It was coming from the auditorium.

Curiosity's going to get me killed . . .

Vic flattened his ear against the door: definitely a human voice and . . . yes, definitely Hatch's. Vic opened the door a crack and looked into the auditorium. Hatch was kneeling at the foot of the altar, his eyes raised, his hands folded, his eyes closed, his brow furrowed. Vic tried to discern what he was saying in his droning voice, but the syllables did not form words. Suddenly, Hatch moaned, coughed, bent over his knees. He straightened and said, "You know I'm doing my best to serve you. To bring about your Armageddon. To cleanse the Earth of iniquity. This person they've told me about, this person who has been tormenting us . . . is he a devil? Or is he one of your angels come to tell us that our efforts are not worthy?"

He's talking about me.

Vic stepped into the auditorium and said, "Boo."

Hatch swiveled his whole body around and stared. "You have no face."

"Shaving accident."

"What *are* you?"

"Ninety miles of bad road for you unless I get some answers."

"Are you from Satan?"

"Well, maybe, according to some nuns . . . But I'm asking the questions, and the first one is, what did you mean when you mentioned Armageddon?"

Hatch rose to his feet and used the tone and cadence Vic had heard when he first saw the reverend, when he'd visited the tabernacle. "It is coming, oh, yes, it is nearly upon us, the day of judgment when the heavens will open and rain brimstone down upon the just and the unjust alike . . ."

"And exactly how does this involve you?"

"I am the instrument of the Lord. It is His will that I hasten the day when mankind destroys itself to make way for the new millennium."

"Let me get this straight. You're helping these mercenaries and arms dealers to hurry up the end of the world, or at least the end of civilization?"

"Amen."

"I can't believe you said that. Anyway, that was question one. Question two is . . ." Vic pulled one of the glass medicine vials from his pocket. "This stuff. What is it?"

"If you were from Heaven, you would know."

"You make a good point, but the question stands—what is it?"

Hatch clasped his hands together, raised his eyes, and cried, "Lord, deliver me."

"When I walked in here," Vic said, "I was thinking maybe I'd punch you. But no. Consider yourself delivered."

An hour later, Vic was seated in front of Tot's fireplace, cradling a cup of hot chocolate and saying, "He believes it. He believes every word of what he preaches. That's why I couldn't beat him up."

"Maybe you're not the beating-up kind," Tot said.

"I've got plenty of scars that contradict you."

"They're old scars."

"We can debate this later. For now, what did you find out? You talked to Myra?"

"I did," Tot said. "She and the youngster were watching cable TV in a motel. I told her to stay put."

"Good. Where are Shiva and . . . the other guy?"

"They took off in his car 'bout the same time you left. Said they wouldn't be gone long."

Vic sipped his cocoa and began to wait.

It was as though the river were a funnel delivering cold wind to the loading dock behind the smaller of the two McFeeley plants. The men who were loading crates onto a barge were white-faced and some of them shivered, but they worked steadily. For an hour, Crate had been standing in the doorway of a shack on the riverbank, watching and supervising. Now, he turned and went inside, where a man in a black jumpsuit and Benedict Fermin were waiting.

"You gonna help me get my wife back?" Fermin asked.

"When the barge is loaded. That should be in less than thirty minutes. Your . . . wife obviously doesn't realize that the vehicle she stole is equipped with a LoJack. We know exactly where she is. You and my men will enter her room and bring her back in Hub City."

"Where she belongs. Why ain't we done it yet, again?"

"I will explain it one more time. It was imperative that we get the merchandise loaded and on its way tonight. That required all my personnel. As soon as that task is complete, personnel will be free to undertake other missions, including yours."

One of the jumpsuits entered and said, "The job is finished, Colonel."

"Excellent. The tugboat will arrive shortly. Meanwhile—" He turned to Fermin. "Why don't you wait in the vehicle?"

"If you think that's best . . ."

"I do. Someone will join you directly."

Fermin shuffled from the shack. Crate looked at the third man and said, "Let me go over your mission one more time. You will enter the motel room and render the woman and child helpless. The woman should have a small revolver somewhere among her possessions. You will use that to kill Fermin and then you will use the weapon I provided you with earlier to kill the woman and child. Be careful to shoot Fermin and the woman in the front of their heads. It must appear as though they killed each other. If you cannot locate the woman's revolver, you will arrange for all parties to die in a car crash. You will ascertain that you are not being followed and then you will report to me at the school."

The jumpsuit saluted. "Yessir."

The jumpsuit did an about-face and marched outside. Crate went to a wall phone, punched eleven numbers, waited, and said, "Everything is on schedule. I've arranged for the cleanup operation we discussed. Fermin, his wife, and her daughter will be eliminated before morning. I suggest we deal similarly with the pupils at the school, and their parents . . . I'm not sure about the parents. But the pupils—I rigged what will look like a gas leak some months ago, as a contingency device. The building can be made to explode and burn, with a hundred percent casualties. As I said, the parents will remain a problem, but I am confident we will be able to deal with it."

Crate hung up the receiver and strode from the shack.

At midnight, just as the snow began to fall again, Vic and Tot heard the sound of a car engine. They went to the front door and met Vic's benefactor, who carried a suitcase, and Shiva, and a tall, thin man with wisps of white hair and the kindest smile Vic had ever seen.

"I'm not going to make introductions," Bruce said. "The chances of your connecting any name I might pronounce to what would endanger you to know is a thousand to one, but thousand-to-one events *do* occur."

"And a happy how-de-doo to *you*, too," Tot said. "Well, come on in anyhow."

When they were all in the living room, Alfred looked around and said, "Rustic and utterly charming."

"Okay," Bruce said, dropping his suitcase and looking at each of the others in turn. "Time to make plans. Before we begin, I confess that this is somewhat unusual to me. I'm used to working alone."

"I'm not used to working at all . . . at least not *this* kind of work," Vic said.

Bruce stared directly at him. "Tell me everything that's happened within the last twenty-four hours."

Vic put himself in reporter mode and, tersely and accurately, described his freeing of Myra and Jackie, his capture, his rescue by Shiva, his search of the tabernacle, and his encounter with Hatch.

"You have those vials you swiped?" Bruce asked.

"Right here." Vic dug one of the small glass containers from his pocket and displayed it.

Bruce turned to Tot. "We need to know exactly what that stuff is. Can you analyze it?

"Don't have the equipment," Tot said. "Not sure I have the skill, either. I know chemistry, but not a lot of pharmacology."

"You know anyone in the neighborhood who could do it?"

"Nope."

"We could get it to Goth . . . er—our home base by tomorrow evening," Alfred said.

"I know someone in St. Louis who's up to it," Bruce said. "Be faster. If you start now, you could be there by dawn."

"I'm on my way,"Alfred said.

"Roads around here are trickier'n hell in optimum conditions, and that snowstorm out there doesn't equal optimum conditions," Tot said. "I better ride shotgun."

"Good idea,"Bruce said.

While Alfred and Tot were putting on their coats and leaving, Bruce continued: "It's obvious that we have three locales to worry about. The school. This *tabernacle.* And the McFeeley plant."

"I don't think the tabernacle is a problem," Vic said. "I had a pretty good look around it and I'm sure it's exactly what it seems to be—a meeting place and a cash cow."

"I'm inclined to agree," Bruce said.

"You're sure about the McFeeley end of it?"

"Absolutely. That's what this is all about—the manufacture and export of illegal arms, and McFeeley's is where it happens."

"Something else is bothering me," Vic said.

"Spit it out."

"Myra and Jackie are alone and defenseless. And Myra is driving Fermin's car. I'm wondering if Crate has some kind of locating device on his vehicles and if that means Myra isn't safe."

"You may make a detective yet," Bruce said. "All right, we prioritize. Shiva and I will reconnoiter McFeeley's and deal with anything immediate there. You get the Connelly woman and the child and put them someplace out of harm's way. If none of us is stopped for any reason, we'll reassemble here at six. Then we'll deal with the school."

"How will we stay in touch?" Vic asked.

"I've never *had* to stay in touch before," Bruce said. "One of the many advantages of operating solo."

"Cell phone?"

"I hate to use anything that isn't secure, but . . . okay. Simple code: You're Number One. I'm Two. Shiva's Three. Rodor and my friend are Four. The school is Five and the plant Six. Can you remember that?"

"Yes. What about right here, this house. Seven?"

Vic ran to where Tot had left the VW. The snowfall was moderate, but steady, and Vic wondered about how the small car would fare on slickened back roads. He got in and started the engine.

Bruce took his suitcase into the kitchen and a minute later Batman emerged.

"You do not deceive me with your foolish masquerade," Shiva said.

"I know. But this outfit has tools we may need. I'd rather wear it than have to improvise."

"Is that the *only* reason you dress up as a bat? You do not enjoy it just a little?"

"Fortunately, I don't have to answer that."

"Not to me. But one day, to yourself."

"Shiva, I've got to ask you to promise something."

"Oh?"

"Don't kill anyone. I'd like to say, don't kill anyone

ever. But I'll settle for tonight. Don't kill anyone while you're with me."

"Or?"

"I'll have to take you down."

"You believe that a possibility? You have never defeated me before."

"In our previous encounters, all I was doing was preserving my own life. This would be different. I'd be preserving who I am."

"You are a little girl. But you are also a warrior, who may be my equal or, like Richard and no other, my better. For the warrior, I will do as you ask. The warrior I respect. The little girl I despise."

"I can accept that."

"You have no choice."

Vic needn't have worried about the car. It handled the snowy roads well and it took him only a few minutes to reach the interstate.

Tot was driving his Toyota, with Alfred tense beside him.

"Relax," Tot said. "I've been piloting this countryside for the past sixty-one years."

"I do not mean to impugn your skills," Alfred said, forcing himself to lean back into the seat. "But I am not accustomed to being a passenger."

"Never too old to learn."

"So they say."

"Sounds like you don't believe it."

"My . . . employer has taught me to disregard hearsay and believe only empirical evidence."

Tot accelerated, and snowflakes rushed past the station wagon's windows. "Your 'employer,' heh? That'd be the guy you came with?"

"I am not at liberty to say."

"And you think I'm dumb as a post. Answer me this . . . you an actor?"

"Not since I was twenty-one. Why do you ask?"

"You sound like an actor, is why. Your boss an actor?"

"Again, if I may . . . why do you ask?"

"'Cause I don't know what he is, but he isn't what he seems to be. I was staring at him in the living room for what . . . a half-hour? And I'm not sure what he looks like."

"You are a very astute man."

"And you're a slippery one, at least when it comes to giving a straight answer."

"I will take that as a compliment."

"Okay by me," Tot said. "Can you tell me what you do for this fella who doesn't look like anybody?"

"I am his . . . butler. That is the word that best describes my position, I suppose."

"Never met a butler before. You go to school for that?"

"One can. There are institutions that teach the requisite skills. But I am self-taught."

"Me, too, mostly."

"You're an inventor, Mr. Rodor?"

"Yep."

"And did *you* go to school to learn how to invent?"

"No. I do have a degree or two, but I got 'em almost by accident. I'd get to tinkering with something, a piece of machinery or an idea, and pretty soon I'd need to know more about it, and I'd either find a way to learn it myself or find somebody who'd teach me. Every once in a while, I'd turn around and some fella'd be handing me a sheepskin."

"You are an American original, Mr. Rodor."

"Yeah. Damned if I know what *you* are."

Alfred smiled, leaned back in his seat, and relaxed.

Vic turned onto the interstate and the going became easier. Obviously, a snowplow had been through the stretch he was on and, despite the weather, driving was no problem. The highway was empty except for one vehicle about a half-mile in front of Vic, blurred by the snow blowing into the VW's windshield. Whatever it was, it was speeding: Vic was doing eighty and the other vehicle was pulling away from him. That made him curious and he accelerated. A minute later he was close enough to be almost certain that what he was following was a black Humvee.

"There it is," Fermin said, pointing to a sign: *EZ Rest Motel—Vacancy.* The jumpsuited driver beside him glanced down at a small, round screen on the Humvee's dashboard and said, "Yeah."

"Gonna see my baby," Fermin said.

"Yeah," the driver said.

Jackie had been getting sicker by the hour. It began with complaints about not feeling well and escalated into tears and moans. Myra held the child and tried to comfort her, and eventually Jackie fell asleep. But it was not an easy rest; she continued to moan and twitch. Finally, Myra decided that her daughter needed help. Was there an emergency room nearby? An all-night clinic? Maybe the clerk would know. She put her coat over her nightgown, and her boots, and left the tiny, one-room motel unit. She walked toward the office and was knocking on the door when she heard the familiar rumble of an engine. She turned and saw a black Humvee turning off the interstate. She reached for a side pocket and even as her hand was moving realized that she was wearing nightclothes; her dress, and her gun, were in the room. She turned and ran. Her slippered foot slid on the icy sidewalk and she fell. She scrambled to her feet and again ran, hearing a door slam somewhere behind her.

Then, a familiar voice: "Myra. Myra, honey, it's me, come to take you home."

She looked over her shoulder. Benny Fermin was scurrying toward her and behind him was one of Crate's thugs, the one she knew as Wilson. She reached her room, dashed inside, and slammed the door. The gun was in her dress pocket, just across the room . . .

Her fingers were curling around the grip of the revolver when the door slammed against the wall and Wilson, followed by Fermin, entered. On the bed, Jackie whimpered.

Myra aimed her gun at Wilson. Wilson pointed his own weapon at the bed, at Jackie.

"You shoot me, I shoot her."

"Not if my shot severs your spine," Myra said.

"You that good? With a little .32 popgun?"

Fermin inserted himself between Myra and Wilson.

"Now hold on," he said. "There ain't no need for this. We're all friends here."

Wilson slapped him with the gun barrel and Fermin collapsed to the floor.

Vic swerved into the motel parking lot. Smoke was curling from the Humvee's exhaust and the driver's side door was open. Yellowish light was coming from the open doorway of one of the rooms. Vic left the VW.

Wilson reaimed his gun at Jackie and asked Myra, "Her next?"

Myra dropped her revolver.

"Kick it to me," Wilson said.

Myra obeyed. Wilson picked up the revolver, aimed it down at Fermin, and pulled the trigger. Then he pointed his own gun, a semiautomatic, at Myra. "Your turn," he said.

Vic came through the door low and fast. There was nothing graceful about him, nothing of what he had learned from Richard. He merely bulled his way in and hit Wilson with his head and shoulders. Wilson went down and twisted and swung up at Vic. Vic took the punch on his left forearm and hit Wilson twice with his gloved right fist. Wilson lay still.

Myra was on the bed, cradling Jackie. "See about Benedict," she said.

Vic went to Fermin, removed a glove, and put two fingers on the side of Fermin's neck. He looked at Myra. "Dead."

"He was a bastard, but he didn't deserve to die like that," Myra said.

"We'd better get out of here. Somebody probably heard the shot and we don't want to answer a lot of questions."

"Jackie's sick," Myra said.

"Okay, we'll get her to a doctor."

Myra bundled Jackie in a blanket and lifted her from the bed.

"We'll take my car," Vic said. "It doesn't come equipped with tracking devices."

A minute later, they were on the interstate. The snowfall was thicker now, and the wind more fierce.

CHAPTER FORTY-TWO

Batman and Shiva had no difficulty in getting past the McFeeley plant's security; it had not even been necessary to knock anyone unconscious. If Shiva was disappointed, she did not show it.

The two of them stood in the shadow of the larger of the two buildings, looking down at the pier and the river beyond. A tugboat, water churning at its stern, was backing up to the front of a barge laden with crates. Four men in jumpsuits, carrying submachine guns, were on the bank, watching.

When the boat was in place, three of the crew emerged from the cabin and hooked it to the barge. The crewmen, their task finished, returned to the cabin. Batman and Shiva moved.

The submachine gunners literally never knew what hit them.

The tugboat crew sat in the tiny galley, drinking hot coffee. Suddenly, the door to the deck opened and for a moment they saw only darkness. Then the darkness seemed to congeal into a human shape and a hoarse voice said, "Everyone but the captain will go ashore. The captain will follow my orders."

"Like hell," a burly crewman said, and rose, lumbering toward Batman. And somehow there was a woman in green in front of Batman who did something that caused the crewman to fall unconscious.

"Please, someone else challenge my friend," Shiva said, smiling.

The remaining crewmen shook their heads and left the boat.

"You do not need me any longer," Shiva told Batman. "If I remained, I would be bored. The fun tonight is at the school."

"Okay, but I need one more favor. Be sure a vehicle is waiting for me five miles downriver."

"Perhaps."

Batman nodded and, as Shiva glided onto the outer deck, turned to the captain. "You will proceed downriver five miles. You will then unhook the barge. In the meantime, you will show me how to operate your radio equipment. If you cooperate, you will come to no harm."

"Mister," the captain said, "I think you're crazy and crazies're dangerous."

"I'm glad you realize that," Batman said.

He and the captain climbed up to the pilothouse.

Vic and Myra sat in the hospital waiting room. An intern had been examining Jackie for about fifteen minutes. "This is where I did my first reporting job," Vic said.

"Something about a car crash," Myra said.

"Right. A fifty-something couple. The man was a chemist who worked for McFeeley's. They were both scared—didn't want to talk to me. I did a little more digging and found out that they'd recently lost a son, a ten-year-old."

"You think he was a pupil at Ten-Nineteen."

"Yeah. And he either died accidentally or Crate and company killed him. There was nothing else the bad guys had to hold the Stabelhausens here. They ran and Crate's men caught up to them."

"That sounds about exactly right."

A young man in a lab coat with a stethoscope draped around his neck came from the examining room. To Vic, he looked like a teenager, but apparently he was old enough to put an MD after his name.

"Your daughter doesn't seem to be in any immediate danger," the young doctor told Myra. "I frankly don't know what the problem is. In a few hours, the lab will be open and we can get some blood work. Meanwhile, we'd like to keep her for observation. We have some empty rooms if you'd like to stay."

"I would," Myra said.

Vic arose. "You don't need me. I'll check back in a few hours. Between now and then, I'll try to learn what was in those vials I swiped. Info might help the kid."

"You're going to . . . wrap things up?" Myra asked.

"I'm going to try. If I don't, more people will get hurt. And there's another reason . . ."

"Which is?"

"I'm curious to see how it all turns out."

CHAPTER FORTY-THREE

Batman and the captain stood on the stern of the tugboat, watching the barge float away and vanish into the darkness.

"Do you know what's in those crates?" Batman asked.

"Don't know, don't care," the captain said. "I just haul 'em and deliver 'em."

Batman's tone deepened. "If that cargo had reached its destination, hundreds, *thousands* of people all over the world would have died. Their blood would have been on your hands. You should pay attention to your life. You should admit responsibility."

"I . . . I will. In the future."

Batman moved to the side of the boat and stepped down into a dinghy.

"You're leaving?"

Batman untied the dinghy and tossed the rope onto the tugboat's deck. "Yes."

"What should I do?"

"Take responsibility for your life," Batman said, and began rowing toward the shore.

Wilson had a purple bruise on his left cheek, and his right eye was blackened and closed. A thread of blood trickled from his nose. He stood at attention in front of Colonel Crate, in the colonel's office at the school. He had just finished describing what had happened at the motel.

"You allowed him to overcome you?" Crate asked.

"Yessir."

"You allowed him to defeat you in hand-to-hand combat?"

"Yessir."

"There is one way you can redeem yourself. Do you know what that is?"

"Yessir."

"Tell me."

"Kill the enemy, sir."

"Do you know what will happen if you fail?"

"Yessir."

"Tell me."

"You will kill me, sir."

"Eventually, yes, you will die. Eventually. Dismissed."

Wilson executed a brisk about-face and marched from the office.

Crate rested his elbows on the desk and put his face in his hands. A phone rang. He lifted the receiver and barked his name, and listened.

"The entire shipment?" he finally said quietly. "All right. I'll speak to you later." He hung up the phone and rested his face in his hands again. Then he lifted the receiver and dialed an eleven-digit number.

"Reporting," he said. "The news is all bad, ma'am. The enemy has gotten the entire arms shipment . . ." He paused, listening, and continued: "Fermin is dead, but the Connelly woman and her child were taken from us. My recon is bad. I don't know exactly where the enemy is. I don't know exactly *who* the enemy is." Again, he listened. "Yes. By morning. I'm sorry. I'm very, very sorry."

He stood and strode into the corridor outside, where seven jumpsuited men were waiting at parade rest. "Get the parents. Get everyone here within the hour. Hatch might be able to help."

Batman found the car parked on the shoulder of the road nearest to the riverbank. Snow was already covering its top surfaces and Batman wondered how long ago Shiva had left it and how she would get back to Hub City. But he knew she would, if she wanted to. She was Shiva.

Vic was sure that in an hour, or maybe less, the back roads would be impassable. Already, his small car was plowing through snow that was hubcap deep and made his headlights all but useless.

His experience with back roads was that snowplows got to them last. And given the general anarchy of Hub City, there might not even *be* snowplows.

He saw the school, a dark shape against a slightly less dark sky, and a procession of lights inching toward it. Cars and trucks, a lot of them, creeping through the storm. He glanced at his watch: two-forty-three. Surely, there were no school functions at this hour. Had Crate summoned reinforcements? Vic accelerated, his tires slipping and skidding, until he reached the rear of the procession. He was behind a big red pickup. He decided to stay there. That would at least get him onto the school grounds.

He drove through the gate, which had still not been repaired, and followed the pickup to the parking area behind the school where, a few hours ago, he had been buried and freezing to death. He put the car at the far end of the lot, away from the ambient light coming from the building. He pulled the mask from his pocket, smoothed it into place, and released the gas in his belt buckle.

As he was getting out of the car, someone murmured his name. He whirled, preparing to fight. Shiva was standing a few feet away, and through his greenish lenses Vic could see that she was smiling.

"I have been waiting for you," Shiva said.

"You have any idea what's going on there?" Vic asked, nodding in the direction of the building.

Shiva was already moving toward the school, her feet making only the tiniest of craters in the snow. Vic's feet made much bigger ones.

There were seventeen adults in the school cafeteria, not counting Crate, six of his men, and Hatch. Some had heavy coats pulled on over nightclothes, and most had the bleary-eyed look of people roused from sleep.

"Bring 'em in," Hatch commanded. Two of his men left the hall and, a minute later, returned leading nine children, who were all fully dressed and awake. The adults stirred and murmured.

"Go to your mothers and fathers," Hatch told the children. Each child looked at the adults, seated on folding chairs, and shuffled to a recognized face. The parents embraced the children and cooed to them. The children stood stiffly, not returning the hugs.

"That's everyone," Crate said to Hatch. "We might as well get to it."

"No, no, I must first deliver a brief homily," Hatch replied.

"Make it *damn* brief."

Hatch went to the front of the hall and clapped his hands loudly. "May I have your attention for just a moment," he shouted, and the murmuring quieted. "Tonight, you are truly blessed, truly blessed on this holiest of nights," Hatch said, adopting his sing-song delivery. "For tonight you are going to stand in the presence of the Lord Himself. His Face will shine upon you and you will commence your eternity of heavenly bliss. Oh, my friends and dear young ones, I do envy you, I do indeed envy you. Your travails are ended, your suffering is no more! Tonight, you will garner your reward unless you are a sinner. Tonight, unless you are a sinner, you will pass through the gates of glory and tread upon streets of pearl and gold . . ."

Shiva and Vic were flattened against a wall near one of the cafeteria doors that was ajar. Two of the jumpsuits were lying at their feet.

"He's going to kill them all," Vic whispered.

.   .   .

Batman felt a vibration against his skull and knew that
Oracle had activated the satellite communications device
built into his mask and cowl.

"Go," he growled.

"Patching Gordon through," Oracle said.

There was a brief burst of static and then the voice of
Gotham City's police commissioner, James Gordon: "Just
got a call from the Feds. Seems someone tipped the St.
Louis office that an arms shipment would be found floating on a river somewhere and guess what? An arms shipment was found floating on a river someplace. You have
anything to say?"

"Merry Christmas."

Vic followed Shiva outside and along the east wall of the
school. "What are we doing?" Vic whispered.

"You are familiar with the word 'tactics'?"

"Yeah . . ."

"We are about to employ tactics. Ah, here we are."
Shiva was grasping a handful of wires that led from a pole
to a portal on the school wall. She yanked them and—

The cafeteria lights flickered and darkened.

"Nobody move," Crate yelled. He groped his way to a
door and went into the corridor outside. He stumbled and
almost fell. He knelt, groped, felt the bodies of the men he
had placed here, to guard this exit. They were alive, but
they wouldn't be useful anytime soon.

"There are lights in the vehicles," he yelled. "Maintain
your positions while I get them."

.   .   .

"We're lucky they don't have a backup generator," Vic said, following Shiva back into the school.

"Luck has no part in it. I did not waste the time I spent waiting for you."

In the corridor, Vic saw, through his lenses, that Shiva was gliding silently toward two of the guards who stood alertly, their guns raised. How could she see them? Obviously, she couldn't. Then how did she know where they were—or that they were anyplace at all?

Her arms moved and the two jumpsuits fell on top of their weapons.

Crate got electric lanterns and road flares from three of the Humvees and trudged through the snow, back toward the building. He put his burdens down by the east entrance to the school and returned to one of the vehicles, where he pulled something wrapped in oilcloth from a storage compartment and carried it back to where he had left the other things. He opened the door and, holding it open with his foot, he took everything inside.

He stopped, listened: sounds coming from around the corner, by the rear of the cafeteria. He lifted one of the lanterns, switched it on, and aimed the beam down the corridor. Two of his troops were sprawled on the floor. Crate grunted, picked up a road flare, and, following his lantern light, moved cautiously toward where the sounds were coming from.

It was almost too easy. With his night vision lenses, Vic could attack the gun-toting jumpsuits in almost perfect safety. By his count, he and Shiva had downed nine of them. How many more could there be?

He saw three more jumpsuits emerge from the cafeteria. He recognized the man in the lead: Wilson.

Crate snapped off the top of the flare and the corridor was filled with scarlet light. He threw the flare around the corner and—

—suddenly, there was too much light. Vic was blinded.

The damn night vision lenses . . .

He heard someone moving near him and swung his fist and hit air.

None of them knew where Shiva had come from, but there she was, between Vic, Wilson, and the others. Her left leg snapped out and the weapons left the jumpsuits' hands and clattered into the darkness. Then she stepped aside and with a sweep of her right hand gestured toward Vic.

"You gonna let us at him?" Wilson asked.

"Be my guest," Shiva replied.

Vic's vision was a pulsing cloud of pinkish glare, but through it he could see, dimly and intermittently, the shapes of the three men moving toward him. But not clearly or steadily enough to fight them.

Got to get rid of this mask . . .

He touched the stud on his belt buckle and . . . nothing. How many times had he used the gas? He'd lost count.

Too many, though. The buckle was empty. The mask had to stay on—had almost become a part of him.

Something struck his belly—a foot, it had to be—and he doubled over, and was hit on the side of the head, twice, and on the temple, and the jaw. His chin struck the floor and he knew he had fallen.

Is Shiva going to let them beat me to death . . . ?

A boot struck his chest.

He felt adrenaline surging within him, but there was nothing sweet about it because it carried with it a huge load of panic.

He willed himself calm.

Another boot, this one to his collarbone. He grabbed and yanked and felt the leg he was holding jerk and heard a body strike the floor. He rolled to a standing position and sensed movement. He blocked a fist with his forearm and jabbed with stiffened fingers and heard a grunt. He jabbed again and as his opponent was dropping, pivoted to face where, somehow, he knew the last man stood.

"Bastard . . ."

Wilson's voice. A fist hurtling toward him. He moved his head slightly to the left, and as the fist passed it he twisted his hips to the right and punched with his left fist. His gloved knuckles struck Wilson on the point of the chin, a perfect knockout blow.

He heard clapping, made by someone in the darkness. He thought the applauder must be Shiva, but he could not see her.

Crate saw the fight end. He considered getting a weapon, trying to kill the faceless man himself. But there was a more important task. He ran to the heap of material he had placed next to the exit and unwrapped the item in the oil-cloth. He hefted one of the new submachine guns—plastic, explosive pellets, a thousand rounds a minute. The perfect terrorist weapon. This one he had kept for himself and tonight he would use it.

He went outside and saw headlights moving through the gate, glaring in the falling snow. Others were coming, other enemies, no doubt. He had to hurry. He trotted a few feet along the wall and down a short flight of concrete steps to a basement door. It was locked, and he had no time to figure out where the key might be. No matter. He went to the top of the steps, aimed, fired. The door disintegrated.

Crate ran into the basement and used his torch to light his way to a place behind the boiler. He twisted a valve and pressed the switch on a digital timer taped to a pipe.

Then he ran.

Vic picked up the road flare, which was still spreading its scarlet glow, and, shielding his eyes with his hand, entered the cafeteria. Through the pink glare that still clouded his vision, he could see the parents and children sitting on the folding chairs, expressions of bewilderment and fear on their faces.

"Get out of here," he shouted. "Get out now. Go!"

"Go where?" someone asked.

"Home. Go home. Stay there. Never come back. Go!"

Slowly, the parents and children began to file out of the cafeteria.

•   •   •

Batman saw one of the black Humvees speed down the driveway, skidding on the slickened asphalt, and turn onto the road. Probably someone who should be caught and incarcerated, but he couldn't be sure and he had other worries. What was happening in the school?

He stopped his car near an entrance. People—adults and children—were coming out, shivering, making their way gingerly through the snow.

Vic looked around the cafeteria.

"Anyone still here?" he shouted.

No answer. Good.

Something filled the doorway and congealed into Batman.

"Do I know you?" Vic asked.

"Nobody does. What's going on?"

"A certain sky pilot invited a lot of people here to kill them. But they're all safe now."

"You sure?"

"I can't be. But I think so."

The floor jumped beneath their feet and Batman said, "The window." But Vic was already running toward it, aware that a deafening explosion had just shaken the school, and of fire and smoke somewhere behind him. He crossed his arms in front of his face, jumped, and, in midair, straightened his body, diving through the window and rolling on the snow outside. Batman was rolling beside him. Almost as one, they rose and ran.

When he judged that he was safe, Vic turned. Most of the windows on the ground floor of the school were broken, and through their openings he could see licks of flame. Batman, beside him, was muttering, his words too low to be understood; Vic realized that his companion was speaking into a concealed transmitter.

"I've called for help," Batman said to Vic.

"There's a fire company in Hub City," Vic said, "but I doubt anyone's on duty. The next nearest is fifty miles away. By the time anyone from there can get here . . ."

"Yes. No more school."

"I wonder if everyone got out."

They heard a shriek. Vic spun and saw Hatch on his knees in the snow, hands folded, arms and eyes upraised.

"I'm in Hell," Hatch moaned. "O Lord, deliver me, for I am in Hell."

"Yeah, I guess you are," Vic murmured.

CHAPTER **FORTY-FOUR**

Within minutes, the parking lot was empty except for the car Batman had arrived in and Vic's VW.

"What's next?" Vic asked Batman.

"As far as I'm concerned, nothing. My job is done. The arms shipment has been intercepted, the Feds will raid the McFeeley plant tomorrow and confiscate anything useful to weapons manufacture . . ."

"Colonel Crate?"

"I've put him out of business. That's all I set out to do."

"The kids? The parents?"

"Not my concern."

"Pardon me."

"Look, years ago I learned, the hard way, that there's only so much I can do. I have to remember where my commitments lie. I have to pick my battles. If I didn't, I'd never accomplish anything."

"Understood—I think. But what goes for you doesn't necessarily go for me."

"True."

"Because, for me, this *isn't* over."

"You want to nail Crate."

"Because if I don't, he'll be free to start over some-place. But that's not all. I want to nail whoever's *behind* Crate."

"Richard would not like your undertaking a mission of vengeance."

"It's not vengeance I'm after, it's . . . well, for one thing, answers. For another, I don't want other kids to go through what the kids here have gone through."

"I can identify with that," Batman said, his voice low. "Do you have any idea where Crate's gone?"

"I'm pretty sure I know," Vic said. "His family has a boat."

"By the way, are you aware that you're bleeding?"

"No, and since I'm not, I'm guessing it isn't serious."

Batman spun and strode away.

He's not big on good-byes . . . Me either . . .

Batman stopped, turned, and said, "Shiva."

"I haven't seen her for about an hour," Vic said.

"Any chance she's still inside the building?"

"A chance, I guess."

They both looked at the school, engulfed in flame that reddened the snow around it. Gouting smoke into the graying sky.

"No point in trying to save her now," Vic said. "Is there?"

"She's a survivor," Batman said, and continued on his way.

Vic got into the VW.

．．．

Tot and Alfred were standing in a high-school chemistry lab, somewhere in Florissant, Missouri. A third man, wearing rumpled corduroy trousers and jacket, held up a strip of litmus paper and said, "This confirms the other tests."

"What are your findings, Mr. Matthew?" Alfred asked.

"Mild stimulant," Matthew said. "Not much stiffer than a cup of coffee. Might harm somebody with a pre-existing condition, but for a healthy body, no problem."

Alfred thanked Matthew, gave him a wad of currency, and said good-bye. He and Tot left the school building. While they had been watching Matthew do his proce-dures, the sun had risen, but snow was still falling and the light was dim.

"Back to Hub," Tot said, climbing behind the wheel of his station wagon. "If we can make it, that is. Roads'll be dogs. You up for some breakfast?"

"I could eat," Alfred said.

"Then let's see if we can find us an open counter some-where. First, though, we better let Vic know what's what."

Tot took a cell phone from his coat pocket and began dialing.

Vic was inching the VW along the road to the interstate when his phone buzzed. His progress had been slow, and would have been slower if another vehicle hadn't partially cleared a path. Vic guessed that one of the parents had been driving something equipped with a snowplow.

He braked the VW in the middle of the road—there was no traffic—and answered his phone. Tot told him that the drug Hatch had used on the kids he purportedly cured was not dangerous. Vic asked him to pass the information on to Myra at the hospital and broke the connection.

Vic caught a glimpse of himself in the rearview mirror. His hat was gone, left in the burning school, he guessed, and the white mask he wore was stained with red on the forehead and upper lip. He was, as Batman had said, bleeding. But there was nothing he could do about it; the mask would not come off.

He put the car into gear and continued on to the interstate. The four lanes were devoid of vehicles, but they had been recently plowed and Vic had no trouble negotiating them. The snow was thicker, fat white flakes dancing in the wind, disintegrating on Vic's windshield. He switched on the radio, hoping for a weather report, and heard a familiar voice: " . . . a white Christmas," Horace was saying. "A little too white, if the weather folks can be believed. They're predicting the heaviest snowfall in forty years—over two feet by this time tomorrow. And, for the first time since 1937, the Ohatchapee is frozen over, to the Mississippi in the south and . . . well, we don't know how far north. Anyway, we'll keep you posted. Now, let's get back to our Christmas morning music."

And Vic realized that it *was* Christmas morning. That, really, wasn't surprising. Christmas didn't mean much to him. He'd spent most of his Christmases in decidedly unfestive situations. Where had he been last year? Oh, yeah, he'd gone alone to a movie on Market Street in San Francisco and had dinner afterward at a fast food joint. The year before? Graveyard shift in a shipping terminal. And before that . . . who knew? Who cared?

He drove between the two halves of the McFeeley plant. There were clouds of roiling black smoke and licks of flame rising from the smaller of the two buildings, the one nearest to the river. He was pretty sure that the arms-manufacturing facility had been housed there. So what had happened? The same thing that had happened to the school. Crate was getting rid of evidence and running.

Vic turned north, onto a road that had been plowed, and accelerated. He might be completely wrong about where Crate was going, but he had no better idea. And it was good to be doing something.

He stopped for gas on the other side of the state boundary. He used his credit card and was filling the tank when a man stuck his head out of the gas station's office and asked, "What happened to your face?"

"Practicing my blank stare," Vic said.

He inspected himself in the car's side mirror. The blood had darkened to a brownish color and there wasn't any more of it than when he had last looked, which was fine. It meant he wasn't bleeding any longer. He *was* hurting, but he'd lived with worse.

The snow stopped for an hour, then began again. Vic checked his GPU. He should reach his destination any minute now . . .

And suddenly he did. He was at the top of a steep embankment. Tire tracks in the deep snow ended at the rear end of a black Humvee, which was parked beside an old-fashioned—a *very* old-fashioned—steamboat, complete with ornate woodwork, a fresh coat of white paint, and a huge, red paddle wheel at the stern. There was a large Christmas wreath hung on the side of the pilothouse.

Vic got out of the car and moved down the embankment in snow up to his knees and went up a short gangplank to the boat's lowest deck. What now? Yell "ahoy"?

A door opened and a white-haired woman stuck her head out and said, "Come to share some Christmas cheer? Well, come on in, young man."

Why not . . . ?

Vic followed her into what could have been a stage set for an old-style melodrama, the kind that featured mustache-twirling villains and simpering heroines. There was a lot of flowery upholstery, flowery wallpaper, a flowery rug, and a sofa with flowery upholstery. Against one bulkhead, below a round porthole, there was a long sideboard bearing an assortment of roasted meat, bowls of fruit, and a huge bowl of eggnog. The woman who had invited Vic in was ancient, her face a maze of wrinkles, her blue eyes magnified by thick glasses that had a velvet ribbon dangling from one temple piece. She wore a pink-and-blue-checked dress that hung to her ankles. There was a mixture of musk and incense scenting the air.

"Would you like some eggnog?" the woman asked.

Vic started to accept and then didn't, realizing that this person might be an enemy, so the eggnog might be an enemy, too, and anyway, he couldn't drink anything through the mask.

"I'll pass," he said. "I'm looking for a man named Crate."

The door opened behind Vic and Crate, wearing a khaki duster, stood framed in it. He saw Vic and was reaching into the duster for a weapon when Vic grabbed his collar and yanked him into the room.

The woman stepped forward and said, "Now you boys just stop that this minute, you hear me?"

"Yes, ma'am," Crate said.

Vic reached under Crate's duster and found one of the plastic submachine guns hanging by a cord from Crate's shoulder—an improvised holster. Vic pulled the gun loose, crossed to the door, opened it, and flung the gun over the railing. He heard it clatter on the frozen river.

He went back inside the room and closed the door behind him. The woman and Crate sat on the sofa, holding crystal cups filled with eggnog.

"Sit *down,* young man," the woman said.

Vic perched on the front edge of a straight-backed chair with a cane seat that was placed in front of the eggnog bowl, his legs solidly beneath his hips, ready to move.

"This is my nana," Crate said, nodding toward the woman.

"Nana . . . as in *grandmother*?" Vic asked.

"Emiline Costas Dierdorfer McFeeley," the woman said. "Emmy to my friends. Married Eustis McFeeley in nineteen eighteen and never regretted it for a second. Taught me what's what, Eustis did. Been dead these five years, Eustis has. Five years on Christmas Eve."

"You own the factory in Hub City?" Vic asked.

"Started that business the year after we were married, Eustis did. I took it over when he passed. You sure you won't have some eggnog?"

"It's good," Crate said. "Nana makes great eggnog."

"No thanks," Vic said. He looked directly at Crate's nana and asked, "Are you aware that the factory was used to make illegal arms?"

Nana met Vic's gaze. "Well, I signed right off on it, didn't I?"

"And you know those guns are used against innocent people?"

Nana waved a hand. "Oh, heck. Innocent-schminnocent. Negroes and A-rabs and foreigners."

"That's why you agreed? You want to kill foreigners?"

"Well, no, silly! If I hadn't, the business my husband started would have gone straight down the drain, what with the unions and all, and I couldn't let *that* happen, could I?" She patted Crate on the shoulder. "So when Junior here came with his idea I talked it over with my spiritual adviser—"

"That would be Hatch?"

"The *Reverend* Hatch, if you don't mind. We all agreed that making those guns would be a fine solution for everyone, so I told Junior to go ahead with it. And that is the end of the story."

"Not exactly. There are those parents and kids and the school . . ."

"What about them?" Crate asked.

"I'm guessing that they're the scientists and technicians you need—the parents are. You conned them into putting their children into your school and then held the kids as hostages."

"Why, the Reverend Hatch *cured* those rug rats," Nana protested.

"No, the Reverend Hatch kept them drugged and every once in a while staged a phony cure, maybe to give the parents hope."

"Got it all figured out," Crate said.

"Just about," Vic agreed. "You know it's all over, don't you? The Feds have your arms shipment and by now the parents and kids are beyond your reach."

"Of course I know it's over," Crate said irritably. "That's why I destroyed all the evidence."

"I guess that just leaves you and me," Vic said. "You know, if you hadn't involved the kids, I'd probably let you walk. I'm not a cop . . . hell, I'm not even much of a vigilante. But you did involve kids, so you've got to go down. How do you want to do this—take off our coats and start punching?"

"You'd win," Crate said. "I've seen you in combat. A good tactician knows when to quit."

"Well, *I'm* not ready to quit," Nana said, reaching behind the sofa. She brought out two objects, one of the plastic submachine guns in her right hand and an ammunition clip in her left. "How the heck do you make this thing work?"

Crate took the gun and shoved the clip into its housing as Vic grabbed the punch bowl and flung it across the cabin. The bowl struck Crate on his left forearm, knocking it and the weapon it held to the side, and splashed onto Crate, Nana, and the wall behind them. There was a *popping* sound and Vic, his body flat, dove into Crate. Crate slammed into the wall and held up his hands, palms out.

"I give up," he said.

There was a bubbly moan and both men looked at Nana. Blood was spreading from a hole across the front of her dress, mingling with the eggnog already staining it. Crate dropped to his knees and cradled her head. She sighed, and stopped breathing.

Crate looked up at Vic, his eyes wet. "You killed her. You killed her with eggnog."

"No, you did." Vic picked up the weapon. "With a gun. I'll let you figure out how to surrender."

He left the cabin, tossed the gun onto the river, and went to the Humvee. The door was unlocked. Vic released the emergency brake, put the vehicle in neutral, turned the wheel, than got out and pushed. The vehicle bumped over the snow, nosed into the river, and began to sink.

In his VW, Vic used his cell phone to call nine-one-one and report a disturbance at the McFeeley boat.

"Who are you, sir?" the operator asked.

"Damned if I know," Vic told her.

He was utterly exhausted. He sat staring out at the falling snow for a long time. Then he heard a muffled explosion, and a crackling. He saw the stern wheel of the boat churning water and throwing chunks of ice into the air.

The damn thing works . . .

As the boat inched away from the riverbank, Vic got out of his car and began running. But there was a layer of ice beneath the snow crust. Vic's shoe soles slipped on it and he fell.

The boat, now about twenty yards out, suddenly listed to the starboard side and began to sink. Vic heard the wail of sirens, coming closer. He was not ready to answer questions. He started the VW. Its tires did a lot of slipping and sliding, but Vic managed to steer it onto the road. He turned and looked back at the river. Where the boat had been there was now only ice, water, and bubbles.

CHAPTER FORTY-FIVE

"Way I'm figuring it," Tot was saying, "you got nothing to worry about. What I think Hatch's goons did was keep the youngsters lightly sedated and used the stuff we had analyzed when Hatch wanted to put on his dog-and-pony show. I guess we'll be seeing you soon."

"Thank you, thank you so much," Myra said, handed the telephone to the smiling woman behind the counter at the nurses' station. She went down a corridor that smelled of antiseptic and into the room where Jackie sat propped up by pillows in a big bed, watching a jolly polar bear on a television that was hung by a brace from the ceiling.

"Good news, sweetheart," Myra said. "You're going to be fine."

Jackie stared at the polar bear for a few moments, then turned to her mother. "Mommy, when can I go back to school?"

. . .

Snow had been dropping steadily onto the ground for more than two hours and, finally, the roads became impassable. Vic estimated that he was about two miles from Tot's house when he decided to abandon the VW and walk the rest of the way. He knew the going would be slow and arduous, but, somehow, he didn't care.

He began to trudge.

The next day, a lot of questions would be answered, by police, by federal investigators, and even by reporters from station KWLM in Hub City. Most interesting to Vic would be that the bodies of Colonel Thaddeus Crate, late of the United States Marine Corps, and Mrs. Emiline Costas Dierdorfer McFeeley, widow of Eustis McFeeley and sole owner of the McFeeley Works, Inc., were found aboard Mrs. McFeeley's steamboat, which had sunk in twenty feet of water. There was a hole in the hull near the main boiler, which had apparently exploded when someone had put it into operation. Mrs. McFeeley had died of multiple wounds inflicted by some sort of unidentifiable projectile that had detonated inside her body. But, apart from minor scrapes and bruises, Colonel Crate's body was unharmed. He had died of drowning, and authorities were puzzled because he should have had enough time while the boat was sinking to leave it and walk on the frozen river to safety.

Another explosion, this one apparently caused by a military device, had destroyed half of the McFeeley Works. The company's few remaining employees were seeking jobs elsewhere.

The Reverend Jeremiah Hatch had taken an indefinite

leave of absence from his duties as chief minister of the Tabernacle of the Highest Holiness.

And still another explosion had caused substantial damage to Mark Ten-Nineteen, a private school near Hub City. Although fire had gutted the building's lower floor and a meeting of the parents' association was known to have been in session shortly before the conflagration, no bodies were found, no fatalities reported.

Questions, questions . . . asked and answered on Monday, the day after Christmas. But on Christmas Day itself, under a bleak, gray sky, Charles Victor Szasz plodded through a white countryside, snow dampening his pants to well above the knees.

He stopped, and suddenly realized how absurd he was, a man who had set out to learn his parents' names, and failed, and now was alone in the middle of a blizzard, wearing a disguise no one could see.

As he approached the Rodor acreage, the mask began to peel from his skin. He pulled it off and stuffed it into a pocket and went into the house. In the mirror above the fireplace, he did not recognize the face that stared back at him.

ACKNOWLEDGMENTS

When you accompanied Charles Victor Szasz on the road between those two factory buildings, you left our world and entered what has become known as the DC Universe. It's where super heroes can live, and a lively and entertaining place it is, but it doesn't exist outside the imaginations of thousands of writers and artists and millions of readers. So don't look for Hub City, or Gotham City, or Blüdhaven, or the mighty Ohatchapee River in your atlas, or seek them on MapQuest, and don't think they have exact analogues on our Earth. They don't. I have, with malice aforethought, fuzzed the geography of the novel in your hands until it is, at best, a caricatured amalgam of regions I once called home.

Some thanks are in order. First, my gratitude to one of comics' greats, Steve Ditko. He created The Question and though the character has evolved into something quite different from Steve's original concept, without his work later incarnations could not exist.

Bill Finger and Bob Kane gave the world another character who has done his share of evolving. But the first Batman was theirs. I am one of many who has benefited from their efforts, and so owe them recognition.

Large chunks of the first version of this story appeared as issues of a comic book edited by Mike Gold, who gave me more freedom than a commercial writer has any right to expect. Denys Cowan provided most of the art for the series, and did a nifty job of giving faces to imaginary people. From across the years, a bow to both gentlemen.

For the better part of a decade, Charles Kochman urged me to write "the Question novel," which we assumed Charlie would edit. By the time circumstances permitted me to do the book, Charlie's life and career had taken him elsewhere, but before he went, he hired a most able successor named Chris Cerasi. They are both exemplary editors, and it is always a pleasure to do business with them.

Dennis O'Neil
Nyack, NY
February 2006

ABOUT THE AUTHOR

Dennis "Denny" O'Neil is a comic book writer and editor, principally for DC Comics.

His best works include *Green Lantern/Green Arrow* and *Batman* with Neal Adams, *The Shadow* with Mike Kaluta, and *The Question* with Denys Cowan, all of which were hailed for sophisticated stories that expanded the artistic potential of the mainstream portion of the medium. As an editor, he is principally known for editing Batman.

His 1970s run on Batman is perhaps his most well-known endeavor, turning Batman from the campiness of the 1960s TV show to "The Batman," getting back to the character's darker roots and emphasizing his detective skills. This grimmer and more sophisticated Dark Knight, as well as new villains such as Rā's al Ghūl, brought back Batman from the verge of pop culture oblivion. His work would influence later incarnations of Batman, from the seminal comic *Batman: The Dark Knight Returns,* by Frank Miller, to the movie *Batman Begins* in 2005.

LAST SONS

ISBN: 0-446-61656-7

By Alan Grant

SUPERMAN. MARTIAN MANHUNTER. LOBO.

Interplanetary bounty hunter Lobo is a notorious maverick. Happily wreaking havoc as he brings in his prey, he cares little who his clients or targets are—even when his latest quarry is J'onn J'onnzz, Martian Manhunter of the Justice League of America. Suddenly Lobo finds himself confronting . . . Superman. Cogs in the machinations of a powerful artificial life-form, these three aliens, the sole survivors of the planets Krypton, Mars, and Czarnia, have only one thing in common—they are the last of their kind. . . .

LAST SONS

Available wherever books are sold.

INHERITANCE

ISBN: 0-446-61657-5

By Devin Grayson

BATMAN. AQUAMAN. GREEN ARROW. NIGHTWING. ARSENAL. TEMPEST.

A gunshot shatters the Gotham night as Slade Wilson, the superhuman killer-for-hire Deathstroke, fails to assassinate the young son of a visiting Quarac dignitary. Now three legendary crime fighters, Batman, Green Arrow, and Aquaman—and the three young heroes who had once been their loyal sidekicks—join forces to stop Slade and those who hired him. But as the hunt stretches across continents, opening lost memories and old wounds, it turns into a desperate race against time: for Deathstroke is but one player in a plot to destroy all of Gotham . . .

Available wherever books are sold.